THE VICAR

BOOKS BY A. J. CHAMBERS

STANDALONE NOVELS
The Vicar

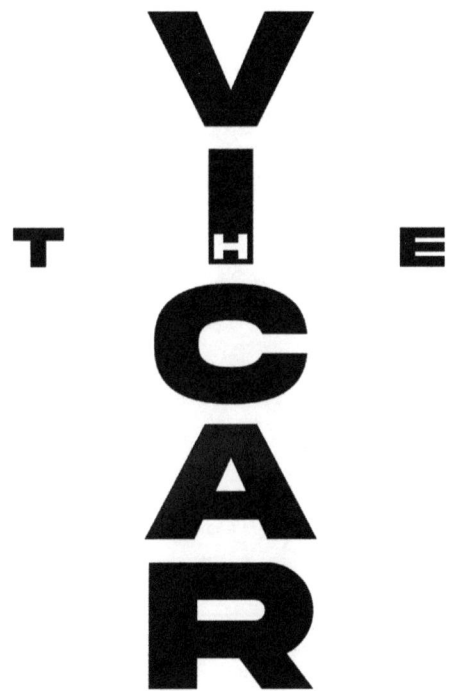

THE VICAR

A NOVEL OF ESPIONAGE
A. J. CHAMBERS

BLACK STONE
PUBLISHING

Copyright © 2023 by A. J. Chambers
Published in 2023 by Blackstone Publishing
Cover and book design by Luis Alejandro Cruz Castillo

All rights reserved. This book or any portion
thereof may not be reproduced or used in any manner
whatsoever without the express written permission
of the publisher except for the use of brief quotations
in a book review.

The characters and events in this book are fictitious.
Any similarity to real persons, living or dead, is coincidental
and not intended by the author.

Printed in the United States of America

First edition: 2023
ISBN 979-8-200-91810-2
Fiction / Thrillers / Suspense

Version 1

Blackstone Publishing
31 Mistletoe Rd.
Ashland, OR 97520

www.BlackstonePublishing.com

*This book is dedicated to
my family. Without your love and support
this book may never have been written.
And
the late great John le Carré,
whose works continue to be an inspiration.*

*Special thanks to
my agent Doug Grad and my editor Patrick LoBrutto.
Your friendship and encouragement kept me on the right
track even when the words were difficult to find.*

AUTHOR'S NOTE

Martin McGuinness died of amyloidosis on March 21, 2017, at the age of sixty-six. As a former leader of the Provisional Irish Republican Army (PIRA, or IRA as it was more commonly known) and an Irish Republican Sinn Féin politician, McGuinness was known as someone you didn't cross lightly, ever. It surprised many that he was one of the main architects of the Belfast Agreement, better known as the Good Friday Agreement, in 1998.

Perhaps McGuinness had come to the realization that the armed struggle against the British government was futile, as Great Britain would never relinquish control of the six counties of Northern Ireland. Or maybe he was just tired of all the death. Whatever his reason, the peace, for the most part, has held. He later served in various positions within the Northern Ireland Assembly, culminating in his appointment as deputy First Minister of Northern Ireland.

With his death and the threat of a no-deal Brexit and all the disruption that this has caused, there is a real concern within the intelligence community that the New Irish Republican Army (NIRA) may expand its terror campaign and try to take advantage of the situation.

According to the British government, her security services, and the United States government, none of the following events ever happened.

The names and places described have been changed to maintain their anonymity.

"Oh! What a tangled web we weave,
When first we practice to deceive."
Sir Walter Scott

1

BELFAST, 1989

To ask for a black and tan was tantamount to suicide in this Catholic establishment, so Terrance Patrick Nolan, or Terry to his mates, took another deep swallow of his room-temperature pint of half-and-half and continued to observe the man he'd been sent by MI5 to remove from the living almost eleven months earlier.

Cigarette smoke hung in the air like a smog of 1950s London. Not that it bothered Terry; he was adding to the haze in Barry's Pub with his own chain smoking.

It still amazed him that his cover as a freelance photojournalist had held up for as long as it had. For him there were no fancy James Bond gadgets, no Walther PPK to produce and save the day. Aside from the Browning Hi-Power carefully taped under the wardrobe in his boarding house room. Hell, he was even using his real name.

Two years ago, after he was recruited to MI5 from 14 Intelligence Company (commonly known as The Det in the British Army), the powers that be had insisted he build a cover based on his real background. Their reasoning was that not only did he have excellent lineage but it would also be hard to screw up during idle conversation or, God forbid, interrogation. The only thing that had been scrubbed from his background was any mention of him being in the British Army. So he had morphed into Terry Nolan, a photojournalist who let it be known that he had some sympathy for the Irish struggle to kick the British out of the six counties of Northern Ireland.

Raised by Irish Catholic parents on a council estate in south Manchester barely two miles from Manchester International Airport, Terry had grown up listening to the old rebel songs from the glory days of the IRA. It came as no shock when he learned at the age of six that his grandfather had fought with the IRA in the Easter Rebellion of 1916. What was slightly confusing was that his father had served with distinction as a senior NCO pilot in the Royal Air Force during and after World War II. Around the age of eleven, he'd asked his dad why he still listened to rebel music. His father had sat him down and given him a history lesson. He explained that he was very proud of *his* father's fight to free his country and how he'd sided with the lawful government of Ireland during the Irish Civil War of 1922. Terry's father had also expressed his disgust with what the IRA was doing in the north. At that moment, Terry decided he would become a soldier.

So here he sat, back against the wall in the far corner of the busy pub, watching Kieran Martin, whose Bristol pub bombing had resulted in the deaths of thirty-eight people, twenty-four of whom were teenagers returning home from a school outing. The outrage felt by the rest of the nation had reverberated throughout the halls of power. There had even been some calls for the prime minister's resignation. Of course, that wasn't in the cards—no one in Maggie's Conservative Party had the balls to call for a vote of no confidence—but it had cost the secretary of state for Northern Ireland his job. The prime minister had vowed to bring the perpetrators to justice and, over many months of interrogations, threats and, in some cases, payoffs, they had gotten a name. The problem was then finding the perpetrator, Kieran Martin, who had gone to ground. And that was where Terry had come in.

Now, two streets off the Falls Road, in this second-rate bar that smelled of slightly rancid beer and sweat and where the likes of Martin were considered heroes, Terry had finally found the bastard. He doubted the man had paid for a drink in the twenty months since the attack. Terry would make sure that the glass of whiskey Martin had just finished with a flourish would be one of his last.

After seeing his quarry enter an hour earlier, Terry had made an excuse to the others at his table and headed for the bathroom. What they didn't see was the phone call he made to another MI5 operative, who was acting as his cutout under the guise of a "lady friend," asking when she was going to join him for their mythical date. She, of course, had feigned a headache and immediately passed on his location to others tasked with carrying out Martin's removal. Terry would have dearly liked to have been responsible for the man's demise himself, but his boss had been worried about mission success and his operative getting his ass out alive. If all went as planned, Martin's death would be attributed to the Ulster Volunteer Force. Hell, it wasn't as if the bastard hadn't killed a few Protestants in his day, so Terry was sure they were going to be happy to take the credit.

He returned to his table complaining about how the girl he had met at the library while researching his book, a good Catholic girl of course, had stood him up. There were a few joking comments about him not getting his end away by the lads at the table, and he was quickly dispatched to buy a round of whiskeys to help soothe their collective sorrows at his loss. Approaching the bar, he just couldn't resist the temptation and eased his way through the crowd until he was standing shoulder to shoulder with Kieran Martin. He raised his voice over the hubbub, laying on his best thick Manchester accent, and ordered five doubles of Jameson.

He couldn't help but smile slightly as Martin's head spun in his direction at the sound of his voice.

"What the fuck might an Englishman be doing in these parts?" he hissed.

"Why, what's it to you, mister?" replied Terry.

"I'll tell you what's it to me, you British bastard, right before I blow the back of your fucking head off. Now answer the fucking question."

Terry looked down as he felt the pistol jammed under his ribcage.

Maybe this wasn't such a good idea after all. "I'm sorry, Mr. Martin, no disrespect intended, it's just I thought all those questions were done with. My name is Terry Nolan. I'm over here writing a book on the Troubles from the Catholic perspective." He held out his hand, which was totally ignored.

"So, Mr. Writer, what brings you into my bar? You have some sort of death wish?"

The gun remained firmly in place.

"Just out with some friends, Mr. Martin." He noticed a quiet had settled over the bar and raised his voice a little. "Also, Mr. Martin, my grandfather was in the 1916 IRA uprising while yours was shitting himself hiding in some pub and, if that doesn't count, maybe you'd like to take it up with my friend over there, Ciaran Sullivan." He gestured over his shoulder with his thumb and leaned a little closer and whispered, "I believe her father is an area commander, which makes him your fucking boss."

Martin looked over at the young lady who had turned to face them, and Terry saw the slight flicker of fear in his eyes.

"Now if you'd care to take your fucking gun from out of my ribs I'll be paying for my drinks."

It vanished as quickly as it appeared. "My apologies, Mr. Nolan. A man in my position can't be too careful. I hope you understand."

"No problem, mate." He was about to pay for the drinks when a twenty-pound note appeared on the bar.

"Please, let me get those for you. It would be my pleasure to buy a round for the grandson of a man who fought for the cause."

"Well, thank you, Mr. Martin. That's very much appreciated." He gathered up the drinks and headed back to the table. He wanted to burst out laughing but figured a large grin to his friends would suffice.

"Is everything okay, Terry?" asked Ciaran, touching the back of his hand.

"It is now," he replied and smiled at the irony. *I just got bought a drink by a dead man.* He raised his glass and looked over at Martin, who was still looking in his direction. "*Sláinte.*"

2

BOSTON HARBOR, PRESENT DAY: APRIL 2018

Terry awoke with a jolt, as was his way, and immediately reached for the glass of vodka that sat by his bed. After he took a healthy swallow, the next urgent task was to fire up a Marlboro Red, which he lit with his ancient Zippo bearing the insignia of his British Army regiment. It was the one relic from his past that he was loath to relinquish. His masters would have been furious if they had known he had brought it with him across the pond, but he was of an age now that he was more inclined to tell them to shove their displeasure up their combined asses than to bow to their whims.

Christ, it was hot, especially for the beginning of April. After taking another gulp of vodka, he wiped his face and chest with the damp bar towel that was hanging off the side of his bed. Glancing at his watch, he saw it was two forty-five in the morning. He sighed and lay back listening to the gentle slap of the waves against the hull of his 2005 thirty-eight-foot Catalina sloop. *If only the goddamn AC unit wouldn't keep fucking up, it would be perfect.*

After the Irish gig, he had floated in and out of various departments and undercover operations in and out of Ireland until this job had come along. It wasn't that it was a bad job, or even dangerous—it was just so fucking boring. His cover was that of a political reporter for the *Guardian* back in the UK. This had been his ongoing cover even when he was home, as it allowed him a great deal of access to people he was "looking into" without raising eyebrows. Hell, he was so good at it now that he even filed actual stories instead of relying on others back at headquarters to do it for him. His current assignment by MI5 was to run half a dozen agents and paid informers in Boston and New York. These individuals were working closely with former IRA and Sinn Féin members supplying drugs and other items, such as small amounts of weapons and explosives, to their colleagues in the New Irish Republican Army back in Northern Ireland. He also had one agent, an American of Irish descent, he had cultivated years earlier in the UK. These people were known as his "Parishioners" and he, as his position was commonly referred to, their "Vicar."

It constantly amused him how people thought the IRA had suddenly held up their hands after the Good Friday Agreement and ran home to their mothers. These guys were hard-core and responsible for most, if not all, of the drugs that came into the north and south of Ireland. They also controlled a great deal of the prostitution, or at least took a cut from the pimps getting their hands dirty. And then there was the protection racket. It was like they'd become the Irish Mafia. *I guess even supposed ex-terrorists have to make a living.*

He snickered lightly at his wit and took another drag on his cigarette, then stubbed it out in the half-full ashtray. He sighed as he turned onto his side. The need for more information about any potential NIRA activity had increased recently due to the death of Martin McGuinness, the former deputy First Minister of Northern Ireland and Sinn Féin's political leader. What most people tended to gloss over was that McGuinness had also been a member of the seven-man IRA Army Council and an active terrorist for years. He had vehemently denied any direct involvement with the IRA, but then he would have, wouldn't he? The two things he had done that had stopped the Troubles in their tracks—well, for the most part—was acting as Sinn Féin's chief negotiator for the Good Friday Agreement and personally overseeing the agreement's arms decommissioning phase. Again, given his stature within the organization, he was about the only one who could have carried it off. Now, after his death, there were whispers from both sides of the pond that there was a push, by some, to start the whole shooting match all over again. Nolan touched the large scar that ran partly around his abdomen.

"Wouldn't that be just a bundle of laughs?" he mumbled sarcastically.

Things weren't all bad, though. His people back home had just coordinated a major cocaine bust with the Garda in Dublin based on information gleaned from one of his Parishioners right here in Boston. *At least that will put a dent in their fucking wallet.* He closed his eyes and reluctantly drifted off to sleep and the nightmares that awaited him.

The iPhone on his nightstand buzzed gently with an incoming text.

Please help me, I think I'm burned.

3

BELFAST, 1989

About twenty minutes before closing, Kieran Martin and two of his Provo mates knocked back their pints and started heading toward the door. Terry watched in disgust as hands were shaken and backs slapped. Some patrons even cheered as Martin left the building. Once he was out the door, less than five seconds passed before the hail of bullets impacted the building. There were shouts and screams as everyone inside hit the deck. Pint glasses shattered on the floor and people pushed over tables in their effort to get away from the door and windows. Terry reacted a little slower than most, maybe because getting shot at had become something of an occupational hazard in his years in The Det. He felt Ciaran's hand on his arm pulling him down on top of her.

"Terry, what the hell are you thinking?" she chastised in her broad Belfast accent. "You could have got your head blown off."

He tried not to smile at the irony of her statement. "I'm sorry," he yelled over the screams. "I guess I kind of froze."

As if a switch had been thrown, there was a screech of tires and then, apart from the whimpering coming from a number of the patrons, all was silent.

Terry started to get to his feet, but Ciaran had a death grip on his arm. He slowly pried himself loose.

"Don't go out there, Terry, they may be waiting."

"It's all right, Ciaran, I think they're long gone."

As he walked toward the steel-reinforced front door, all the eyes in the bar following his progress. He slowly pushed it open, pretending to show fear. After all, his own people were unlikely to blow *his* head off. *I bloody well hope they don't.*

The carnage that the four-man Special Air Service team had inflicted on Martin and his mates was spectacular. The bomber's head had been blown apart—actually, shredded was a more accurate description. Like a cabbage being turned into coleslaw. His two comrades were in an equally mangled state. Terry nearly burst out laughing at the large UVF letters spray painted in bright orange on the wall behind the bodies. *You really have to give it to these SAS lads—they sure like to do things with a flourish.* He felt a presence next to him and turned to see Ciaran staring down at the bodies. She was crying at the sight, which saddened him. *How can you fucking cry for a sick piece of shit that murdered children?* He wanted to say something, but all he could do was switch off the sickness he felt welling up inside at her reaction and maintain the role he'd been chosen to play.

"Those fucking Protestant bastards," she mumbled.

He took her shoulders in his hands and gave her a gentle shake to get her to look up at him.

"Ciaran, you need to get everyone out of the bar. Those Royal Ulster Constabulary fuckers will be here any minute and God knows what shit they'll pull, especially given who your father is. Okay?"

He really wouldn't have minded seeing most of the bar's clientele, besides the group he was out with, rounded up like sheep by the Royal Ulster Constabulary police and thrown into the hellhole known as the Maze prison, but he also had to get the fuck out of there himself. His job was now done. As the people in the pub scattered, he slowly made his way half mile to the prearranged pickup.

God, he felt good. *I'm finally going to get out of this shithole.* There would be a raid on his lodging house in the morning, primarily to retrieve the gun he had stashed under the dresser but also to bring in a couple of the male residents that were "up from the south of Ireland" and had possible ties to the Irish National Liberation Army, another hard-core terrorist group. All that would be left for him was to be debriefed and then head off on some well-deserved leave, possibly to Spain or Greece.

He finally reached the burned-out corner store where the meet was scheduled and, stepping through the shattered glass in the doorway, settled down to wait. At the back of the shop, the darkness enveloped him like a welcomed blanket. As his eyes adjusted, he noticed an old paint bucket and took a seat after lighting a well-deserved smoke. He was on his third cigarette when he saw a beaten-up Ford Sierra with its lights off pull up across the street from the shop. He rose and, keeping to the shadows, made his way slowly toward the blown-out windows of the store. He had to be sure it was a Q car; he wouldn't have been the first operative to make the mistake of approaching what they thought was a pickup only to find a couple making out. The passenger door opened and a man started walking in his direction. By now he was close enough to the first car that he could see its backup parked twenty feet behind. He began to breathe a little easier. The man stopped in the middle of the street and waved his arm in a "come here" motion.

"Get a move on, Terry, we've got a shitload of beer waiting for you at base."

He laughed and started to walk through the doorway. "Holy shit, Bullet Bailey. As I live and breathe, what the hell brings you out of your cushy hideaway in Derry?"

It was rumored that Color Sgt. Steve Bailey had once emptied one hundred rounds from a general-purpose machine gun into a chimney stack that an INLA sniper had been hiding behind. As the sniper's lifeless body slid off the roof to the ground, Steve, whose GPMG was now empty, stuck his hand behind him, palm up, and yelled for more ammunition so he could keep shooting the guy. Hence the nickname "Bullet." What Nolan could have told those who whispered the story behind the color sergeant's back was that he had been there and it had actually been *two hundred* rounds. Furthermore, yes, he had been given another hundred rounds just in case the corpse twitched.

"Hey, watch your mouth, mate. I'm a sergeant major now. Anyway, they thought you might be so brainwashed by these assholes that you might need a familiar—"

The flash and loud bang of an RPG being fired caused Terry to duck slightly, but at only thirty meters away the impact on the car was almost instantaneous and devastating.

Before he knew what was happening, Terry was thrown back through the door by an explosion ripping apart the car. He lay for a second trying to figure out what the hell had just happened before raising himself gingerly onto an elbow. He shook his head, not only from the concussion he had most certainly suffered but also from trying to clear the damn ringing in his ears. The car was gone, probably from the secondary explosions of the gas tank and all the weapons and ordnance carried in Q cars. He sat up looking for Bullet but couldn't see anyone. *Where the fuck are you, mate?* He wiped his face checking for a head wound. His face was wet, and when he looked down at his hand, he was horrified to see flesh and brain matter. Checking out the front of his clothes, he finally ascertained what had happened to Bailey, as he was covered in his remains. Getting to his feet, he tore off his jacket and threw it violently against the wall. He wanted to be sick, desperately needed to be sick, but forced himself to take three deep, shaky breaths to try and hold it together. He looked up just as the stun grenade dispensers from under the second car fired. Spinning away, he covered his ears while opening his mouth and tightly closing his eyes. Even then the bangs were deafening and the light blinding. As he turned back toward the door, he saw tracer rounds being fired at the waste ground next to the derelict store.

Through the fog of his concussion, he heard a voice from outside. "For fuck's sake, move it, Nolan."

He saw two objects land on the ground just past the shop, then heard a pop and hiss as red smoke filled the street. He stood in wonder watching the cloud as it drifted through the broken windows of the shop. Just then his head seemed to clear, and the veil of confusion lifted.

"Get it together, dickhead," he mumbled. "If you don't get to that car, you're fucked."

He half stumbled, half ran through the red smoke into the street toward his three saviors standing in the open doors of the second car and firing like hell in the direction of the ambush. He was nearly at the car when he felt a searing pain as a bullet struck him in his side, spinning him onto the ground. He wanted to scream but he knew agony was a luxury he didn't have time for. Regaining his footing, he dived headfirst onto the back seat as the car sped off into the Belfast night, its occupants still letting fly with everything they had.

As they drove through the city, the soldier sitting next to Terry desperately applied a field dressing to his wound and, once that was accomplished, shoved a lit cigarette in Terry's mouth. The pain kicked in with a vengeance and he moaned. He felt the stab of a needle in his thigh and within seconds the morphine began to do its job. *Man, that's pretty good.* He felt his mouth smile slightly. He was about to thank his savior, but he could see the man was in no mood for thanks.

"What the fuck went wrong, mate?"

The only answer Terry could manage before drifting off into oblivion was, "I wish I fucking knew."

4

BOSTON HARBOR, APRIL 2018

Terry awoke gasping for air, the scar on his side burning in agony. Blinking in the half light of the predawn he realized he was holding the Walther 9mm that usually resided under his pillow. The whole gun under the pillow thing was a bit clichéd, maybe, but if it kept his ass upright, he didn't care. The nightmare was a frequent companion of his troubled sleep as he relived the events that had occurred all those years earlier on that Belfast street. He could still see Bullet's face and the awareness of his own unavoidable death that had, ever so briefly, flashed in his eyes.

Terry placed the 9mm next to him on the sweat-soaked sheets and touched the small Saint Christopher medal that had hung permanently around his neck for the past eighteen years. He kissed it gently before letting it fall back into place. It was something he did every morning; it had nearly become a subconscious action. Nearly, but not quite. He reached for the now-dry bar towel and buried his face into it. Unfortunately, any relief that the coolness of the damp towel had brought him earlier had long passed. Dropping it, he picked up yesterday's T-shirt off the floor and pulled it on, more to help dry the perspiration from his body than for any need for decency. Looking at the nightstand he had put together from IKEA, he noticed that his alarm clock was off. He swore and gave it a slight thump. *Goddamn shore power plug had come loose again.* He was tempted to reach for the sliver of vodka that remained in his glass. *I need coffee and a piss but not in that order.*

Rising slowly from his berth, he stretched like an athlete preparing for a marathon. The aches and pains caused by years of damage in far-flung areas of the world protested loudly, but he ignored their call to rest. Feeling refreshed, he walked the four short steps to the door of his en suite head. It was one of the features he particularly liked about this boat. Once his cabin door was locked, four deadbolts securing the door on all sides with a simple turn of the key, he had no reason to leave the cabin to perform any late-night ablutions. The door also contained a peephole that he always checked before opening.

Having completed his first major task of the day, he now focused on his second, a much-needed French press coffee. He gave the main part of the cabin a cursory glance through the peephole, opened the door, and stepped into the galley, ducking through the doorway in the bulkhead.

Something was off. Maybe it was the faint sliver of light coming through the main hatch that led down to the cabin, or maybe it was the door leading to the guest quarters and engine room that was ajar. It was neither. He heard his assailant draw in a deep breath just before swinging something at Terry's head.

The weapon brushed through his hair and crashed into the galley's upper cabinets. Terry continued ducking and went into a tight forward roll. Quickly gaining his feet, he turned to face his assailant. The weapon, an expandable baton, was in full swing again, his attacker having taken a couple of steps toward him after missing with his first attempt. Now that Terry was facing the man, he easily avoided the blow while simultaneously snatching the ten-inch, ultrasharp chef knife from the block that was sitting next to the cooktop. Bending his knees slightly into a fighting stance, he pointed the gleaming blade at the man.

"Let's go, asshole," he said calmly.

His assailant, who was dressed head to toe in black, including a balaclava and leather gloves, took a step backward.

"Fuck you, Nolan, you British bastard. Some people would like a word, so drop the knife before you really get hurt. You never know, they may even let you live," he replied in a thick Belfast accent.

Terry remained silent. His attention was focused on the man's eyes, watching for a flicker of doubt, an opening. Then it happened.

His attacker looked from the knife to the main hatch to his own weapon and back to the knife.

Terry smiled. "You're fucked, mate."

There wasn't enough headroom for the man to throw the baton overhand, so he pitched it at the MI5 agent sidearm. Terry easily knocked it away with his forearm and took a step closer as the weapon slammed into the stairs leading down to the main cabin.

His assailant reached behind his back and clumsily tried to retrieve the gun that was obviously shoved too deeply in the waistband of his pants. Terry sprang at him.

Clasping his left hand over the man's mouth he pushed back his head, exposing the throat and lower jaw. Despite his struggles it was a simple task for Nolan to dispatch him silently with a quick thrust of the knife up through the soft flesh under the jaw and into the brain. He let the now lifeless body slip to the floor. *Should have cut the fingers off the glove of your gun hand, dumbass. You might have stood a chance.* He spat on the body in disgust.

Phut. Phutphut.

Terry dived through the door of his cabin and rolled to his left as the silenced bullets slammed into the wall, inches from his head.

"Motherfucker," he mumbled, retrieving his 9mm from the bed. "Should have known the fucker wasn't alone."

He got to his feet and looked through one of the holes left by the bullets. The man was dressed the same as his first assailant but was stockier. He was moving slowly, cautiously through the main cabin . Terry took a step back and opened fire through the wall, rapidly dispatching eight rounds. He heard the man crumple to the floor.

Squatting down, Terry glanced around the side of the open doorway. The second attacker was sprawled across the floor, groaning in pain. Terry straightened up and slowly approached the wounded man.

He'd managed to hit him three times, center mass. *Not bad for a blind shot.*

Kicking the dying man's gun away, he squatted down and lifted the balaclava. The assailant was in his late forties to mid-fifties, with a full light-red beard. The face was that of a man from a life of hard drinking and smoking. It was unkempt and weathered like old rough leather. He coughed away the blood that was filling his mouth, desperately trying to fend off death. Hatred for Nolan burned in his eyes.

"Who sent you?" asked Terry.

"Fuck you," he replied defiantly, coughing once again.

Terry pushed his thumb into one of the chest wounds, pinched the skin and twisted. The scream filled the cabin. Terry released his grip. "It's up to you, mate," he hissed. "You can go to your God peacefully or screaming." He twisted again, not waiting for an answer. The screaming began again. Terry kept the pressure on longer this time before releasing his grip.

It wasn't that Terry took any pleasure from the pain he was causing; he didn't. Sad to say, he had learned very early in his career that sometimes it was necessary for good men to do bad things.

"Now. Who fucking sent you?"

The man was gasping for air, the hate in his eyes replaced by fear. Death was coming. Terry didn't have time for niceties. He twisted again.

After the scream faded, replaced by a desperate panting for air, Terry asked softly this time, "Who sent you?"

"I don't know."

Terry was about twist the wound again, but a panic appeared on the man's face. "Please. Please don't," he begged.

"Tell me what you know."

"It was someone in New York. Someone who knew you in the old days in Belfast. They wanted you alive if possible. That's all I know."

Terry knew this was the truth and no matter how much pain he inflicted he would get nothing more. He withdrew his thumb from the wound and clasped his hand over the man's nose and mouth. The assailant's eyes widened but there was no struggling, no attempt to remove Terry's hand, and he slipped away into oblivion.

Terry stood and looked down at his now-dead attacker, shaking his head at the waste of life. Then a thought that had been stuck in the back of his mind ever since the man had shot at him became clear.

"Just what the hell were you doing back there?"

5

LONDON, 1989

The hospital in Belfast had quickly patched Terry up before shipping him back to London on a C-130; he was the only passenger. Another week was spent in another hospital being fussed over by nurses in a private room. During this time, Terry had been seen by a couple of shrinks and had a few light debriefings by some nameless inquisitors, all pleasant and friendly, which didn't fit their usual rubber-hose MO. Everyone finally seemed satisfied by week's end that he wouldn't bleed to death or wind up swinging from a homemade noose, so they released him into the clutches of his masters.

Terry thought it was a bit melodramatic that they had brought him by government car to a safe house outside the city in the New Forest. To describe it as a house was a vast understatement. It was more along the lines of a Tudor mansion, complete with walled grounds and automatic wrought-iron gates.

Upon entering he was shown to his room by a butler, of all things, and informed that dinner would be served at seven. Until then, Terry was free to explore the house and garden at the rear. He was also told to stay out of view of the street at the front of the house. The butler told him he would find a complete wardrobe of clothes in his size in the walk-in closet. *What the hell is this? Why so much fuss?*

After a gloriously hot shower and much-needed shave, he changed into black pants and a slate-gray shirt. There were beautiful silk ties in the closet, but he had a severe aversion to wearing anything around his neck after his years attending Catholic schools and wearing mandatory uniforms. Feeling more like himself than he had in months, he set out to explore the house and soon discovered the snooker room along with its fully stocked bar. Helping himself to an Absolut on the rocks with a twist of lime, he selected a cue from the rack and proceeded to play a lazy game of snooker. He sunk a rather fine shot in the bottom left pocket, leaving himself an easy black in the opposite corner.

"Nice shot, Nolan."

He turned to face the person who had interrupted his tranquil afternoon. Before him was a man in his late thirties wearing a light tweed suit. *If that isn't from Savile Row, I'm Greek.* He was slightly overweight with dark graying hair. It was his eyes that stood out to Nolan. They had an ice-blue intensity that would deter the average man on the street from messing with him in any way. He immediately knew this was a man who could read your very soul. There was also a hint of mischief that matched the slight smile that had appeared along with his outstretched hand. *Military, definitely. Undoubtedly a Sandhurst man.*

"Sorry to startle you, old boy," he said pleasantly. "You can call me Robert, or just R for short."

Nolan shook the outstretched hand, the grasp firm but not overly so. One could have described the handshake as "honest."

"No, no problem at all, sir," he replied. He guessed that very few people called this man Robert to his face, and he figured the name normally had the word *Sir* in front of it. "Could I fix you a drink, sir?" *After all, why not, as it is most probably his liquor behind the bar.*

R checked his watch and smiled. "Thank you, Nolan. I'll take a gin gimlet. You do know how to make a gimlet, don't you?"

"Absolutely, sir. Bombay Sapphire to your liking?" It was.

While Terry made the gimlet and refreshed his own drink, R removed his jacket and tie and hung them on a coat hook. R then methodically rolled up his shirtsleeves to halfway up his forearms and selected a cue from the rack. After looking down its length to check it for straightness, he picked up the chalk to ready the tip.

"Fancy a quick game, Terry?"

Nolan placed the freshly made drinks on one of the side tables dotted around the wood-paneled room and smiled at the officer's use of his first name. *So now the debrief begins.*

"It would be my pleasure, sir."

Racking the balls, Terry watched R take a sip of his drink and nod approvingly. *First test passed.*

"I think it's your break, sir," Nolan said while he chalked his cue tip.

R bent over to break. While he took aim, the questioning began. "So, how are you feeling?"

"Oh, pretty good, sir, considering."

"Not too much discomfort then?" asked R after breaking the balls and sinking a red while leaving himself an easy blue in the side pocket.

"No, sir. Totally fit and ready to go."

The officer looked at him and smiled. The smile was that of a father proud of a son.

"That's the spirit, Terry. But I think we'll give you a little R and R before sending you back out there. If that's all right with you?"

He knew an order when he heard one. "No problem, sir."

"Good, good. I read the reports and the statements you made in the hospital. But perhaps if you wouldn't mind going over everything that happened again? It would be most helpful."

It was one of those orders framed as a request that officers loved to use. Terry began to tell his story, showing zero emotion from the time he arrived in Belfast to the culmination of his assignment with the removal of Kieran Martin. R allowed him to speak with very few interruptions, all the while playing one of the most flawless games of snooker Terry had ever seen. Just as Terry finished, R sunk the final black. Looking down at the now-empty table apart from the solitary white awaiting its next game, R nodded and smiled before returning the cue to the rack.

"And the ambush afterward. What occurred, exactly?"

Terry was about to answer when there was a faint knock on the door and the butler appeared.

"Dinner is served, sir," he announced.

"Ah, thank you, John," replied R. "We'll be right there." He turned to Nolan. "Let's go and see what magic Cook has conjured up. We shall continue our chat after dinner."

The meal was classic upper-crust British fare, not the tourist garbage that was served in the cities, but high-end country food, full of flavor yet simply prepared. Over a steaming bowl of potato leek soup, Terry took the opportunity to glean more information about his host. It turned out that the house had been in his family since the seventeenth century and that R saw himself more along the lines of a caretaker rather than an owner. He spoke rather dispassionately, as if showing a tour group around his home, about the various paintings that dotted the walls around the dining room. The original heavy oak table, where they now sat, that could seat thirty.

For the main course, John appeared with a pair of roasted wood pigeons with walnut sauce and pan-roasted vegetables. Terry commented how delicious it was, but he couldn't help wishing he had a nice and familiar Holland's meat and potato pie with mushy peas, chips, and gravy. R continued to talk about the paintings of his ancestors that lined the hand-carved main staircase and the upstairs landing. Terry didn't fail to notice that throughout the officer's reminiscences about his family he made no mention of the family name. Everything was Sir Edward or Lady Philippa but never a hint at a surname. He guessed rightly, as he later discovered, that no mention of this house existed on any national historic registry and that R himself was not someone about whom inquiries would return any answers.

After a dessert of treacle pudding with lashings of hot, rich custard that, for Terry, brought back memories of loud public-school dinner ladies and trying to charm them for extra custard, they withdrew to the stone-flagged terrace and the crisp night air. They both carried with them large glasses of brandy and fat Cuban cigars. They sat silently for a few minutes in slightly worn white wicker armchairs, contemplating the stars and the wisps of cigar smoke drifting toward them. As if unwilling to insult the serenity of the moment, R quietly spoke.

"The ambush, Terry, tell me about the ambush."

Terry sighed, took a long sip of brandy, closed his eyes, and proceeded to recount the nightmare that was now an unwanted component of his dreams. This time there were no interruptions from R. Terry described everything in minute detail from the time he left the bar up until he'd been given the shot of morphine in the back of the Q car. After he had finished, R hesitated as if choosing his words carefully.

"And you're sure you weren't followed?"

"Absolutely, sir, not a chance."

"So that means they were waiting."

"Or just bloody lucky," mumbled Terry.

"You cannot seriously believe that." It was a statement, not a question.

"Not really sir," admitted Terry.

"Then back to my previous point, they must have been waiting."

"Yes, sir," Terry whispered.

"Then I must ask, Terry, who did you tell?"

"Absolutely nobody, sir. I didn't breathe a word."

"Then it must have been Sergeant Major Bailey, as he was the only one who knew the exact location of the pickup in advance. The others were only informed of the details minutes before the cars started rolling"

"I'm sorry, sir, but not a chance. Steve was a pro. Hell, he wouldn't have even breathed a word to his wife."

"Then who? Come on, Nolan, you must have had some thoughts on this."

Terry was getting angry. "I wish I fucking knew! Sorry sir, but I've been playing this over and over in my head and the only logical thing I can come up with is that it had to be someone on this end."

There was silence as the accusation against MI5 hung in the air. Both men contemplated the incomprehensible dread of what that could mean for the service.

"Are you suggesting that we have a mole?"

"No, sir, not at all. It could have just been someone speaking out of turn or, oh hell, sir, I just don't know what to think."

Then came the one question that Terry had been dreading. "Tell me about the girl."

As soon as he spoke, he knew that his reply was too quick, too defensive. "What girl?"

"Oh, let's not ruin a perfectly good evening, Nolan. I would rather part as friends and not have to involve my inquisitors and their unpleasant methods. So I would appreciate it . . ." R took a breath. His face became cold and his body seemed to stiffen as he raised his voice almost to a shout, ". . . if you would not fuck me around and tell me about the fucking girl!"

6

BOSTON HARBOR, APRIL 2018

There was a need for urgency now. The second assailant may have used a silencer but Terry sure as hell hadn't. Given the thin fiberglass hull of the sailboat, he figured anyone awake at this hour must have heard something. If they had and were inclined to get involved, he figured he had eight to ten minutes before the Boston PD were sniffing around trying to figure out if the caller had been correct in their assumption of gunshots or just seen too many episodes of *Criminal Minds*.

He searched the body of the big guy first and came up empty. Moving to his companion, he found the same, apart from a set of car keys with an alarm fob. He slipped them into his pocket, planning to give the car a once-over as he was leaving the marina. He relieved the body of the SIG Sauer. This one didn't have an attached silencer, which he had rightly guessed was tucked away in the waistband. He ejected the clip and put it in his pocket. Returning to the other body, he ejected the magazine from the silenced weapon and loaded a fresh one, then headed for the guest cabin. Tucked away in the corner of the room was a small hatch that led to the engine compartment. It was open.

Turning on the light, he couldn't help but notice the explosive device stuck to the side of the diesel tank that fed the engine. *I fucking hate bombs.* He knelt down in front of it to get a closer look and was not at all happy with what he saw. The trigger mechanism for the device was attached to four blocks of C-4, and there was a built-in timer that was ticking down from twenty-one minutes. He reached up to see if the bomb could be easily removed from the diesel tank when he saw the mercury trembler switch tucked in behind the wires leading to the back of the trigger mechanism and what he presumed would be the detonator. It was an antitampering device. *I guess I'm going to be looking for a new boat.* The timer clicked down to twenty minutes. *Time to fucking go, Terry.*

He backed away from the device and ran toward his cabin, counting down the minutes as he went. He threw on a pair of jeans and a loose-fitting golf shirt then grabbed socks and his lace-up brown leather Sketchers.

Seventeen. C'mon, move your ass before the cops arrive, dammit.

He pulled out his go bag from the floor of the closet and tossed it on the bed; then, taking a knee, he reached into the closet and pressed down on the right corner of the floor. There was a slight click, and the floor came loose.

Sixteen.

Pulling out the metal lockbox that he had stashed there when he first came to the States, he took a deep breath and dialed in the combination on the lock. It didn't open.

Fifteen minutes, shit, shit, shit.

He wiped the sweat from his brow and dialed it in again. This time it worked, and he breathed a sigh of relief. Inside there were three slightly used passports, one from New Zealand, one British, and one Swiss—no one ever fucked with the Swiss—in various identities. With each passport there were corresponding driver's licenses as well as American licenses from Illinois, California, and Florida. There were also credit and debit cards to match each identity. Underneath these items was twenty-five thousand dollars in used hundred-dollar bills, nonconsecutive and impossible to trace. He pulled out another Walther 9mm with a silencer along with five full fifteen-round magazines. Lastly, he grabbed a small handheld night-vision device that resembled a one-inch-diameter flashlight but with an eyepiece at one end. All this went into the go bag along with his other Walther and his attacker's silenced 9mm SIG Sauer.

Thirteen.

He was really moving now. He snatched his phone along with the charger off the nightstand and grabbed the bag off the bed. He was already punching in the six-digit security code on the phone with his right thumb and was through the door into the main cabin when he stopped abruptly. The text message from his agent in New York shook him.

Please help me, I think I'm burned.

Shit! How the hell had they cottoned on to Shae?

He snapped out of the shock of seeing the message.

Twelve.

Opening the camera app on his phone, he took a couple of quick photos of his attackers' faces. Running up on deck, he tossed his go bag on the floating metal dock and said a quick prayer before turning the key to start the engine. After a couple of spluttering tries it sprang to life. "Thank you, Jesus," he whispered.

Ten.

He had to get the boat away from the dock and the other boats moored in the vicinity. *God knows what damage four blocks of C-4 will do, but it sure as hell won't be pretty.* Jumping down on the dock he untied the fore and aft lines from their moorings and jumped back on board. Now for the tricky bit.

Eight.

Putting the gearbox in reverse, he carefully backed out of his slot that thankfully was near the far end of the dock. Then, pulling slowly forward, he moved the boat as close to the dock as possible without bumping into it too roughly and causing the package belowdecks to go bang.

Six.

He tied off the wheel so the sailboat would head straight into the open water of the main channel and pushed the throttle fully forward, then made a mad dash to jump onto the dock. He made it, barely, and rolled roughly on the metal walkway. Picking up the go bag, he ran like hell past the other moored boats for dry land and the parking lot. Despite his mad dash he chuckled. *If the gunshots don't wake the lazy bastards in their boats, then this sure will.* He was crying with laughter by the time he reached the parking lot.

Four.

He pulled out the car keys he had taken from his assailant and rapidly pressed the unlock button on the fob. It took him a second, but he eventually saw the brake lights blinking on a car in the far corner of the lot. On the way he passed his own Ford F250 but gave it a wide berth. *You never know, they may have left a little surprise under the hood.* Reaching his attackers' car, an ancient white Toyota Corolla, he threw his go bag on the back seat and opened the driver's door.

Two.

The explosion lit the harbor as if someone had just thrown on a light switch. *Fucking hell, guess my count was off.* He took a second to watch the flames spread over the water. There was no boat to sink—it was just gone. Within seconds, the wail of the Boston PD harbor patrol sirens was waking those who had somehow slept through the explosion. He drove out of the parking lot, heading for Boston South Station to catch the next Acela high-speed train to New York. He couldn't fly, not with all the arms and cash he was carrying, and he sure as hell wasn't driving this piece of crap five or six hours plus; the train would give him the opportunity to make some calls to his other Parishioners and try and get to Shae. He parked the car five blocks from the station and searched the glove box. "Well, what do you know?" he mumbled as he pulled two IDs from underneath the car's manual. Both were from New York but were unlikely to be kosher unless his now disintegrated attackers were completely stupid. He smiled. Most criminals were not high on the IQ testing scale. Slipping the IDs in his pocket, he grabbed his gear and ran for the train.

7

LONDON, 1989

Terry sighed as he looked off in the distance, not trusting himself to look in R's direction in case he gave something away. The story he was about to tell was definitely not the whole truth.

"You mean Ciaran."

"Well, I don't mean the Queen of bloody Sheba, do I, Terry?"

"No, no, of course you don't . . . sir." He tried not to make the delay in adding "sir" too disrespectful. Even though he felt like telling his boss to go to hell, it just wasn't done, and orders were orders. "What would you like to know?"

"Let us start at the beginning. When and how did you meet?"

"I'd been in-country about six weeks when I was introduced to her by a friend in a pub."

R interrupted quickly. "Which friend?"

"Patrick Walsh."

"And how did you know Walsh?"

"Met him and a couple of his mates playing darts." Everything seemed to revolve around the pub in Belfast, not unlike his hometown of Manchester. "We got to talking about why I was in Belfast, and he was intrigued. Pat even offered to give me any help I might need, especially with arranging interviews I might want to do with some of the older people. It seems they might be a little hostile to being approached by a Brit." He smiled. "To be honest, sir, he was a godsend with helping me maintain my cover story, plus he seemed to know everybody. Hell, there was this one night after I'd known him about a month when he took me to at least a dozen pubs and introduced me to all the landlords and anyone who was anyone. The general consensus was that if I was friends with Pat then I was someone they could trust."

"Any terrorist connection that you know of?"

"I don't think so. He didn't seem to command that respect, that fear the locals have when those guys are around. I know he knows who most of them are—he even pointed some of them out to me as people to avoid."

"So, he was your source for that information you passed along. I think we need to have a word with him." R studied Nolan's reaction intently. "Maybe he could become an informer?"

"Not a chance, sir. He wouldn't last a week before he blew his cover. We'd find his body on some country road wired with explosives. He's actually a nice guy. If I thought we could get him out without attracting attention, I would suggest that. As it is, if my cover was burned, he is going to be torn to shreds by IRA interrogators, and the only thing that might save him is that he knows bugger all."

R shrugged. "Sorry, Terry, that's not your problem anymore. Anyway, we've been keeping a distant eye on them, but now that you're out, it's time to rattle a few cages. Now, back to Ciaran Sullivan. You are saying that Walsh just took it upon himself to introduce you?"

"No, sir, she was with a couple of her girlfriends that he knew. They ca—"

Again, R interrupted. "Were they already in the pub when you arrived or did they come in later?"

This is when he started to bend the truth. Terry knew what R was getting at. He was trying to figure out if the seemingly chance meeting had been arranged. What Terry didn't tell him was that he had seen Ciaran a few weeks earlier shopping with some friends near the city center and had been intrigued. The sky had been a dull gray, which seemed to make him notice her even more. Her hair was long, past her shoulders, and had a slight curl to it. Even though it was black, it seemed to shine in the light. But what really got to him was her laugh. When she laughed at her friend's joke, it was as if the whole street seemed to rejoice. Unlike most of the locals, who tended to have a permanent pasty-white complexion, her skin had a light olive glow. He remembered thinking that there must have been some Spanish blood in her lineage. He had asked Patrick about her, but his friend had quickly claimed to have no knowledge of who she might be. He had known his friend was lying but, for the life of him, couldn't figure out why. Terry found out much later that Patrick knew who her father was and of his reputation, so was just trying to protect the man he considered a friend.

"They arrived after we did, sir."

"But you must have known who she was."

"Actually, not until later in the evening."

"Her father is the local Belfast commander. Surely they covered this in your briefings, for Christ's sake."

"Sorry to disappoint, sir, but no. Obviously I knew of her father, but they glossed over his family in the briefing. The only thing of consequence that they mentioned was that his wife had been killed back in '81 in an attempted assassination by the UVF."

R made a tight fist with his right hand. "I'll be sure to have a word with our briefers about that. So, when you found out, you pursued her anyway?"

"I looked on it as a possible way to gather information and, through her group of friends, unhindered access to the social scene." That, of course, was total shit. He pursued her because she was, in his mind, perfection, and the fact that she was into him was icing on the cake. He had "accidentally" bumped into her when she was leaving the bathroom in the pub and somehow summoned the nerve to ask her out. She had looked around nervously to make sure no one was in earshot and told him to meet her the next day at the Queen's University library. He had found her with her nose buried in one of the Greek classics and she had followed him down one of the rows. She had wasted no time in kissing him passionately, which had thrown him for bit of a loop. It was then she told him her father would quite literally have him shot if he found out they were dating. After the kiss she had planted on him, he really didn't care. Their surreptitious affair had been consummated that very weekend at a small hotel in the countryside away from prying eyes.

"You kept the relationship secret?"

"Absolutely, sir. After all, I don't have a death wish."

"Was she of any use?"

"Not really. Her father keeps his dealings very separate from his home life."

"Why not end it if she was a dead end?"

"It doesn't pay to piss off the daughter of a Belfast commander, sir."

R burst out laughing at that and Terry gladly joined in.

"You could have ended up with your balls on your chin, laddie."

"Precisely, sir," he replied, trying to suppress the grin that was rapidly spreading across his face.

"Well, you certainly must have left an impression."

"How so, sir?"

"You should know that, in an attempt to protect your cover, we have you listed in the intensive-care burns unit of the Royal Victoria Hospital. The story goes that you ran into the same chaps that took out Martin, and just for shits and giggles, after shooting you, they poured a little petrol over you and struck a match. After all, we had to have a reason for your absence."

Bloody hell, she must be frantic. "What's that to do with Ciaran, sir?"

"It seems that after she found out where you were, she's barely left the hospital. Although she's not been allowed in your room, with the excuse that they have to maintain a sterile environment while keeping you in an induced coma."

Nolan closed his eyes for a second when he realized what the cover story meant to his future. *I'm sorry, my love. I'm so very sorry.*

"The problem, Terry, is that we can't really know if your cover was blown or if they just got wind of the pickup. I am personally leaning toward the second explanation because if they had found out who you were, you would have been dead weeks ago. We most probably would have found you in an alley after being beaten and then capped in the back of the head."

He could feel the anger building, but he maintained control, barely. "Who knew I was in Belfast, sir? I'd like to have a little word with them . . . if you wouldn't mind."

"Not necessary or warranted, Nolan. They have already been . . ." He paused as a thin smile crossed his lips. "Interviewed."

Terry knew what it meant if the head of the inquisitors got his claws into you, and it wouldn't have been a pleasant experience.

"There were only about ten people who knew where you were and what you were up to. Even the PM didn't know. She didn't want to know."

"Then there is a mole. I would be more than happy to help find the bastard."

"I'm sorry, Terry but that's not your job, it's mine," R replied testily. "I guess the big question is what we do with you now. I'm afraid you are going to succumb to your injuries and then we will fly back your remains. There will be a closed casket at your funeral and a cremation, of course. Can't risk someone doing a little late-night digging and making sure it's really you down there, can we?"

"What about my sister? She'll have to be told that I'm not really dead."

"After the funeral. Thing is, Terry, there needs to be a touch of realism to sell this and grief, real grief, is a great selling point. Does your sister know what you were up to?"

"God, no. She thought I had left the army when I joined Five. I told her I was planning on writing a book about the Troubles and how the Catholics had been screwed over for years by the Protestants. I informed her I was going to be living in Belfast while doing the research—she said I was out of my mind, by the way—so we are good there. It's just the British Army stuff you need to talk to her about. I would like her and her family put in witness protection after a short while and shipped off somewhere like Canada or New Zealand. After all, we can't risk the chance that I had been burned and not just in the wrong place at the wrong time."

"We can arrange that. I will even have some of our lads set up some covert surveillance until we can make the move."

"So what have you got planned for me?"

"Obviously, Belfast is out of the question as well as Northern Ireland in general, at least for a few years. First, I think we should send you on a nice, long leave for a couple of months. We have a place down in the Turks and Caicos Islands on Providenciales that is available. It's bloody nice. It's right next door to a new all-inclusive resort on Grace Bay, which you will have access to so you won't need to lift a finger." He reached inside his jacket pocket and pulled out an overstuffed manila envelope, which he handed over.

Terry looked inside and found a new passport, birth certificate, and driver's license in the name of Terrance Williams, as well as credit cards, a checkbook, cash, and an airline ticket. "At least I get to keep my first name, sir."

R smiled. "Thought you might like that, son. It's for practical reasons. We've found that it's much easier not to fuck up during conversation if you keep it."

"So, when do I leave?"

"In a couple of days. I have to head back to London tonight, so I'm afraid I won't be around, but feel free to have the run of the house until then. One of our people will drive you to Heathrow."

Both men stood and R shook his hand, warmly. "It has been a pleasure, Terry, and thanks for doing one hell of a job."

"Thank you, sir."

R started walking back into the house then stopped and looked at his agent. "This Ciaran business. I can't emphasize this enough. If you try and make any contact with her or anyone that she knows, not only will you be putting her life and the lives of others that knew you in danger, but you will be done with us, on your own, and that includes your sister's family. You know what that would mean, yes?"

"Yes, sir. I'd be truly fucked, sir."

8

ACELA TRAIN TO NEW YORK, APRIL 2018

After spending thirty minutes observing the station to make sure he didn't have any unexpected surprises waiting for him and that he could board the train without security checking his bag, Nolan sat in the rearmost train car and in the rearmost forward-facing seat. It was something he had done for years and now was second nature. Like a mafioso, when he went out to eat, he always chose the table at the rear of the restaurant, in a corner, near the kitchen. He wanted to know the comings and goings of the other patrons and have a quick exit from the building; no point making it easy for anyone who might want to mess up his day. Being on a train was a little different, but not by much. The easy exit wasn't really an option but at least no one could approach him from the rear. And he would spot a frontal assault coming from half a car-length away.

He had bought the obligatory Starbucks coffee, a venti macchiato loaded with sugar for energy, as well as a bacon, gouda, and egg breakfast sandwich. He wolfed down the sandwich and drank a third of the coffee before starting the day's urgent tasks. First he had to send out a warning flare to his other Parishioners. Given that his boat had been compromised and his attackers—presumably remnants of the IRA—knew his real name, he had to be sure his Parishioners were safe. Terry dug out one of the cell phones from his duffel and a number of SIM cards that were in small labeled Ziploc bags, one for each agent. Inserting one of the SIMs he sent the first text message.

> Hi Michael, are we still heading up to Moosehead Lake this weekend for a few beers and hopefully some good fishing?

Now I have to wait fifteen minutes. If everything was okay, the reply would be, "Sorry buddy I can't make it. I have to help the father-in-law with some stuff at his house." If the shit had hit the fan, the reply would be, "Great, looking forward to it," or no reply at all. In this case, after fifteen minutes, nothing, so against protocol he gave his Parishioner another ten—still nothing. "Oh shit," he mumbled before quickly removing the SIM card and tossing it back in its Ziploc.

After three more tries with different messages to other Parishioners and still no reply, he knew they had all been burned. *Goddamn it! What the hell is going on?* Putting his frustration aside, he tried the others with similar results. *How the fuck could they all have been burned? It's not like we ever really met in person.*

And they hadn't, except once when he had first come over to the States. These people had been on the payroll for a very long time and been run by various Vicars, who, for security reasons, he didn't know and didn't want to. Terry was old school when it came to making contact. Any monies paid were sent to various overseas bank accounts. Those payments were then transferred by the Parishioners in small amounts to US banks, but not the banks that held their regular accounts. All communication was done by dead drop or brush past, which he was excellent at. All brush-past contact was carried out in locations that were packed with people, such as baseball or football games, or the subway. These passes and dead drops were arranged with various signals such as chalk marks on a lamppost or mailbox or a flyer on a notice board. Terry even placed messages in the articles he wrote if it was urgent. On rare occasions, he used the classified sections of local papers that were impossible for anyone to read without the one-time keys his Parishioners had been supplied.

He knew some Vicars used email and other online messaging applications, but he didn't trust them. He had an inkling of what the Government Communications Headquarters in the UK was capable of, and he felt certain that the NSA was ahead of them in the game of snooping into other people's mail.

He sat for a second and considered his next move. Obviously, he had to call headquarters and report his predicament, but he was beginning to get that what-the-fuck-happened feeling that he'd had after nearly getting blown to shit in Belfast back in the day. *Please, God, don't let this be a bloody mole.* But even if there was a mole, how the hell had they found out about Shae?

Unlike his other Parishioners, Shae was completely off the books. Only two people knew about her, himself and K. R had steadily climbed the ranks and was now director general of MI5, a position that traditionally was known throughout the organization as K. *And I sure as hell know K isn't a mole.*

Terry and Shae had met in 2014 completely by chance in an out-of-the-way Thai restaurant called Archa off the Highgate Road near Hampstead Heath. He had been told about the place by a reporter friend and decided to give it a try. After being shown to a table, at the rear of the restaurant per usual, he had looked up from the menu and was surprised to see a fellow member of MI5 sitting with a gorgeous blond. There was something about her that brought back memories of a better time, but also a time in his life of terrible sadness. He had thought about walking over to their table and saying hello, but they seemed very engrossed with each other's company, so he had decided to give it a pass. Through snippets of their conversation he had gathered that the girl was American—somewhere in the Midwest was his guess—and she was wearing a ring. It didn't seem to be a wedding ring or an engagement ring. *I wonder if she's been checked out by our masters.* He was halfway through a huge bowl of the most delicious tom kha soup he had tasted in years when his fellow agent noticed him.

At first there was shock as the couple quickly spoke quietly with each other; then, surprisingly, they both rose and approached his table.

"Hello, Terry." He was still using the name K had given him, but he'd become Terry Williams, his permanent identity now. "Not on the job, are you?"

Terry laughed. "Sorry to disappoint but no, not tonight. Just out grabbing some delicious Thai food."

"Good, that's good. I'd like you to meet a good friend of mine. Shae, this is Terry Williams, he's a reporter mate from way back. Terry, this is Shae."

Terry stood and shook her hand. "It's a pleasure to meet you, Shae." He raised her hands and took a good look at her ring. "I guess you may be a little closer than good friends." The young lady blushed and Terry laughed again. "Don't worry, guys, your secret's safe with me." He was looking in the eyes of his fellow operative when he spoke.

"Thanks, Terry, I appreciate that," replied his compadre. "Shae, can you give me a second? I have to have a little chat with Terry for a minute."

The girl flashed them both a smile and returned to their table. Terry sat and took another mouthful of soup before speaking.

"Are you out of your fucking mind?" he hissed. "A goddamn Yank, you're fucking engaged to a Yank. Our masters will lose their goddamn minds."

"I know, I know," replied his friend. "I didn't mean it to happen, it just did."

"I presume you haven't reported this relationship."

"Not yet, no."

"Jesus, they are going to eat you alive. As for her, you better hope there's nothing, I mean *nothing*, that will come back on you."

"There isn't."

"I bloody hope so." He suddenly felt sorry for them both as he remembered his affair with Ciaran more than twenty-four years ago now. *What the hell, what the heart wants the heart hopefully gets.* "Listen, they aren't going to find out from me, okay? Just get it sorted before you get crucified."

"Thanks, Terry, but there's another reason I want to talk to you."

"What might that be?"

"I'm leaving tomorrow to spend some time with our friends in the north."

Terry wiped his hand across his face. "Please tell me she doesn't know what you do for a living."

"Do you think I'm mad? Not a chance. She thinks I work as an assistant to a member of Parliament who happens to travel a great deal."

"That's something, at least. So what do you want me to do?"

"As I was saying, I'm traveling with a team back to Londonderry in the morning. We've been working with the Police Service of Northern Ireland tracking an arms and drug shipment coming over by boat from New York and destined for our NIRA friends. It's due to arrive in four days and our intention is to track it to its final destination, then have our police friends roll in and bust the lot of them. MI5's job is to interrogate the people on the receiving end before their lawyers get involved and try and locate the source in the States. I should be back in a couple of weeks."

"You really shouldn't be talking to me about this, you know."

"I have to talk to someone and my direct superior is out of the question."

"Okay, I'll let it slide this time. Anyway. It sounds easy enough. So what's the problem?"

"If something should go wrong, I want you to let Shae know. She's . . ."

"Let her know. Let her know what, for Christ's sake?"

"I don't know, make something up. Tell her there was a traffic accident or something. Just don't leave her in the dark. She deserves better than that."

He could have said no, said they were nuts, but he couldn't do that. At least Ciaran had the closure of a funeral, but Shae never would if the operation went to shit. "Okay, I'll take care of it. How do I get hold of her?"

"She's a student at the London School of Economics. One year left of her masters. Last name: Cochran. That should be enough for you to find her."

"Fine. You can both buy me dinner when you get back, okay?"

"Absolutely, and thanks."

"Yeah, yeah, yeah. Now get back to your date."

And of course, as things tend to do when fate is challenged, the operation had gone to shit. When the team had moved in, they'd been ambushed and cut to pieces.

9

PROVIDENCIALES, TURKS AND CAICOS ISLANDS, 1989

It had been two weeks since Terry arrived. R was right—the place was stunning. By day he lay out on the beach and read some Stephen King or just enjoyed people watching while trying not to think of Ciaran, which for some odd reason was becoming easier by the day. *Maybe it was just something to keep my head straight while I was so deep undercover?*

His side was healing quite nicely. R had even arranged for a nurse to come in daily and redo the dressing after he showered. The nurse, a matronly Black lady who was a real charmer as long as you followed her instructions to the letter, had told him he wasn't allowed to swim in the ocean yet, too much chance of infection. And just for giggles, she'd told him that infection wouldn't be a problem as the sharks would eat his ass anyway. Two more weeks and he'd be good to go, so he could wait. For meals he strolled over to the resort next door and would dive into some conch chowder and spiny lobster salad for lunch. Dinner usually consisted of the fish of the day, lightly grilled with salad and fruit so fresh it tasted as though it had been picked only minutes before being served. Days weren't the problem; it was the nights.

His recurring nightmare had decided to come on full force since his arrival. The first night he'd been awakened by banging on his door after resort security had been notified of the screams from an alarmed neighbor. Terry had sheepishly slipped the guard twenty dollars and then promptly closed his shutter-style windows. This continued until he found himself visiting the bar one night at the resort, and after many fine rum-based cocktails, he hit the sack and slept like a baby. The nagging hangover wasn't necessarily pleasant, but at least he managed to get eight hours' rest. Unfortunately, his alcohol-induced slumber had failed him after a week, so he had increased the amount of his home cure to the point that he found himself stumbling back to the house and passing out on the couch. It seemed to work wonders, except now he felt like total shit the next day.

It was a few days later, and five or six cocktails into his evening, when Terry first spotted Amanda. He was sitting at the far corner of the poolside bar surveying the resort's boisterous crowd when their eyes met. Usually he would have looked away, but there was something about her that seemed to hold his attention; it was as if, even if he had tried to look away, some unseen force would have prevented him. She was a slim woman who appeared to be in her early twenties and was wearing a thin cotton sundress. Her blond hair, most assuredly not from a bottle, was shoulder length and held back from her face with a small tortoiseshell clip. Unlike the rest of her female companions, of which there were four, she wore no makeup apart from a light application of lip gloss. She had a very light tan—obviously a new arrival in paradise. To even the casual observer she would be considered a stunner. When she slightly smiled at him, the spell seemed to be broken, and he returned her acknowledgment with an embarrassed grin before refocusing on his industrial-strength mojito.

As the evening wore on and he got more and more inebriated, he noticed that every time he looked in the girl's direction, she seemed to be looking at him. By now the evening had worn on so long that he would have been incapable of striking up a conversation with her even if he wished, so he decided to call it a night. As he stood up to leave, he realized that on this particular evening he had overdone it even by his recent standards, and as he reached for the bar to steady himself, he stumbled. The high barstool next to him fell to the floor with a loud bang and he almost joined it but for the swift hands of a passing waiter. His embarrassment seemed complete when he noticed that all conversation in the bar had ceased, apart from some whispers. Regaining his balance and focus, he looked over the crowd and was met by stares of displeasure, apart from the angel—as he now thought of her. She seemed sad. Not because he had failed some kind of female test of etiquette and behavior, but rather for *him*, for his *pain*. It was at that moment, as he walked gingerly from the bar, in his inebriated mind he fell head over heels in love with her, loved her for her kindness, her soul. But how would he ever get to know her, to know if his love was real, after the night's performance?

Waking the following morning, the first thoughts that crossed his mind were Tylenol, coffee, and the girl, in that order. Terry gulped down coffee and Tylenol, then proceeded on his usual five-mile run. Eventually, he would increase his fitness regimen to ten miles, but for now, he was still recuperating from his injury. Some may have thought him nuts for even attempting five miles given that he had just been shot, but there was nothing worse than showing up after a leave and being out of shape, and three months of hanging out in the Caribbean was guaranteed to screw up his fitness level. After a shower and a visit from his nurse he settled down at the resort's outdoor restaurant and ordered a hearty, English-style breakfast. Walking past the pool on his way to the magnificent white sand beach and its pure turquoise waters, he spotted his angel with her friends sunbathing on the far side of the pool deck. He stopped walking and just stared, not in some creepy way but as if his mind had completely frozen. As if guided by some sixth sense, she lifted up her sunglasses and smiled slightly at him, and Terry quickly scurried off to the beach like a nervous adolescent seeing his first crush.

He tried to read *The Cardinal of the Kremlin* by Tom Clancy, but he found himself staring at the page without taking in a word. He hoped to man up at lunch and introduce himself, but he was given a reprieve when there was no sign of her in the restaurant, and he consumed his conch salad in silence. He wondered if he was on the rebound from Ciaran, but as he thought about it, he realized that episode of his life was best left where it belonged, in his past. Anyway, it wasn't as if Ciaran had ever known the real him. How could she have? After an afternoon sailing excursion he returned to his temporary home, showered, and changed for his evening meal. At dinner he ordered his usual forty-four-gallon drum mojito (or fifty-five-gallon drum, as the oil barrels are called in the States), followed by a double order of the conch fritters, the grilled lobster with crab stuffing, and fried yucca. He had just started in on his second fritter, dipping it in the spicy mango sauce that was served on the side, when he felt a presence over his right shoulder. He quickly turned to see his angel looking down at him, smiling.

"Looks good," she said pleasantly.

"Excuse me?" he stammered back.

"The food," she replied. "It looks really good."

"Thanks. I mean yeah, it is. Would you like some?" he gestured at the plate of food. It quickly crossed his mind that she was English. Her posh accent was the tip-off. He had wondered if she was American or Scandinavian but no, she was a Brit through and through.

"I don't mind if I do." She placed her left hand on his shoulder and took one of the bite-sized fritters, dipped it in the sauce, and popped it into her mouth. Her eyes closed and she made a sound of appreciation as she chewed. Her hand remained on his shoulder.

He smiled broadly and shook his head. *This chick has balls.* He laughed and she joined in.

"I meant would you like to join me."

"I know," she replied cheekily. "Maybe later. I have to hang out with my friends for a while."

She was turning to leave when he quickly took her hand as it moved off his shoulder. It was soft, delicate, and cool to the touch. "At least tell me your name. After all, we have broken bread together, so to speak."

She paused for a second as if mulling over whether to divulge state secrets to a foreign agent. She smiled at him again and touched his shoulder with those oh-so-delicate fingers. His heart stopped in anticipation.

"Amanda. Amanda Clay." She began to walk off.

"Don't you want to know my name?" he almost begged.

"I already do, Terry," she replied over her shoulder.

10

ACELA TRAIN TO NEW YORK, APRIL 2018

"Fuck!" Terry stared at the phone for a second, simultaneously wanting to redial and smash it. He did neither. Seconds earlier he had called Shae's number using a special SIM card whose number would mimic that of her parents' home number on her caller ID. He had left her an abort message, supposedly from her father, using his best midwestern accent, as they were originally from Lansing, Michigan. Now, per tradecraft, he had to wait fifteen minutes for her reply call or text, but he had that same dreaded feeling that none would be forthcoming. The question he was asking himself was what the hell would he do now?

It sure as hell wasn't going to be, as procedure dictated, to call his panic number, which would then patch him through to Operations for either additional manpower or extraction. He was going to call K directly. Very few people were able to reach K directly, and Terry was one of them. This was precisely how he had contacted K regarding bringing Shae into the fold.

As requested by his now-deceased fellow agent, Terry had contacted Shae, under his guise of being a reporter, and informed her of her fiancé's death. Instead of going with the suggested car accident, he had told her it was a mugging gone wrong as his friend was walking back to the hotel after having a few beers at a pub nearby. He had even shown her the newspaper report of the incident that had been planted by MI5. There had been many tears shed at the old London pub he had taken her to. It was always best to do these kinds of things in public so he could avoid any hysterics and get the hell out of there as quickly as possible. But he hadn't. They spent over four hours together having drinks, talking about her late fiancé and her significantly altered plans for the future. There had been tears at first but no wailing, no scene; she cried softly as she drank her gin and tonic. She told him that after finishing her studies she planned on moving to New York and becoming a Wall Street star. True to her word, she had.

Terry had kept in touch with her over the years, sending the odd birthday and Christmas card as well as checking in by phone every so often. He wasn't sure why he'd done it, but there came a point, completely by chance, that it would prove most fruitful. It had been just over three years since her return to the States when MI5 had heard chatter that NY&E Investments, an investment house in New York, had been responsible for the arms shipment and ambush that had resulted in the murder of Shae's fiancé. NY&E was a privately held company with around 2.5 billion dollars in assets. They had popped up on the scene twelve years earlier, and within three years had become a powerhouse on Wall Street. They had even weathered the crash of 2008 surprisingly well. Thanks to a stellar reputation, they had attracted the brightest and the best, as far as their young traders were concerned. Shae was one of them. He remembered that she had mentioned years earlier that she would be joining the firm. This had set the wheels turning in his mind.

The first thing he decided was that if he could bring her into the fold as a Parishioner, she would have to be completely off the books. To accomplish this, he had reached out directly to K. His former inquisitor had kept in close touch with him over the years and a mentor-student relationship had developed. K had been intrigued with the idea of having Shae on the inside but was unsure of how to secure her cooperation. Terry had replied with four words: "Tell her the truth." At first K had nearly chewed his head off.

"Are you out of your fucking mind? You really mean to tell her the details of her fiancé's death. That's insane."

"Not really, sir. You weren't there when I told her the cover story about what had happened. Shae was more mad as hell than sad. I really think she would do anything to help us if I told her the truth. I could have her sign the Official Secrets Act if you like, but that won't mean anything, what with her being a Yank and all. Anyway, that would involve leaving a paper trail."

"You do realize this could totally bite us on the ass. If you are honest with her and then she loses it when she hears the truth—loses it because of the cover up—and then goes to the press . . . ? Christ, the negative publicity, the damage it could cause? It isn't worth contemplating."

"She's not the type, sir. Believe me, it's worth a shot."

And so, that evening, Terry was on a British Airways flight to New York.

He checked into a one-bedroom suite at the Plaza, and through casual conversation at the front desk, let it be known that he was a representative of a large London brokerage house on a headhunting trip. When he called Shae later that day and told her he was in the city for a few days, she immediately insisted that he meet her for dinner. She'd suggested Keens Steakhouse, but he said he knew of a small Italian place called Salumeria Rosi on the Upper West Side that served the most amazing pasta alla chitarra con carbonara. It was only available as a Saturday special on the menu, but Terry knew the owner and was allowed to order it any day of the week. They had decided to meet there that evening at eight. Dinner had been exquisite and their conversation enjoyable. When they were drinking coffee and a glass of grappa after their meal, he informed her of his ulterior motive in wishing to meet, but she would have to come back to the Plaza with him to discuss it further.

When they arrived at his room, he ordered a large pot of coffee from room service. Then, as Shae looked on with curiosity, Terry switched on a gadget designed to defeat most listening devices—he had already swept the room upon his arrival, but you couldn't be too careful. Before she could ask him what that was all about, he proceeded to tell her what he really did for a living and what had happened to her fiancé, right down to MI5's suspicion that NY&E had been involved. After he had finished, she helped herself to a cup of coffee and, without hesitation, asked what he needed from her. He asked if she could take a week's vacation in a month and join him at a secluded cabin near Acadia National Park in Maine for a full briefing and instruction in tradecraft. Again, without hesitation, she had agreed.

That had been almost two years ago. Now she had probably been burned. He picked out a different cell phone from his bag. This one contained a very high-end scrambling program, and he dialed K's number from memory. After three rings K answered.

"K, it's Terry . . ."

"Terry, thank God, are you okay?"

11

PROVIDENCIALES, TURKS AND CAICOS ISLANDS, 1989

Terry hoped to spot Amanda during the evening, but she was nowhere to be found. Despondent, he resumed his usual position at the corner of the bar and proceeded to drink even more heavily than usual. He lit a cigarette and was about to unsteadily make his way back to his villa when she appeared by his side.

"Hi, Terry," she whispered in his ear.

He turned quickly, which resulted in him nearly falling off the barstool. He wanted to say something endearing, but his mouth couldn't seem to coordinate with his brain, and all he managed was a mumbled, "Hello."

"You really shouldn't do that, it's very bad for you," she said, pointing at his cigarette.

"What?" he muttered.

She reached over and took the cigarette from his fingers and stubbed it out in the semifull ashtray that sat next to his nearly empty drink.

"Oh."

She sensed his predicament and suggested they escape the noise of the bar and take a stroll on the beach.

Embarrassed at his condition, he tried to get his shit together but failed miserably. The result being that he had to lean heavily on her to make it out of there without crashing to the red tiled floor. The two minutes it should have taken to reach the fine golden sands of Grace Bay took ten, much to the amusement of the other patrons. Amanda, for her part, fixed them with an angry stare, daring them to say anything, until they looked away sheepishly.

Upon reaching their destination, directly in front of where he was staying, he sat down on the cool sand and desperately tried to focus on the dark, moonlit ocean as she sat down next to him. They sat silently for a few minutes, him not daring to risk conversation, her wondering what was troubling him so much that he was drowning himself in alcohol on a nightly basis.

She needed to make him at least somewhat coherent and knew of only one way to achieve this. Standing, she kicked off her shoes and dropped her dress slowly to the sand, revealing her white panties and pert pale breasts. Kneeling in front of him so that he could see her clearly, she took him by the hands.

"Terry, it's a beautiful evening, let's go for a swim."

Even in his drunken haze, he recognized this as an order more than a suggestion and, with her help, slowly rose to his feet. He wanted to kiss her so badly, to wallow in her beauty, but he was in no condition and did not trust himself to succeed in the manhood department. She helped him out of his clothing until he was down to his boxers, then she stood on her tiptoes and gently kissed him on the lips. The touch of her mouth on his partially broke him out of his drunken stupor, and he was surprised to feel himself immediately react down below. Reaching up, he gingerly touched her left breast and felt her nipple harden slightly. She let his hand linger there for a moment before reaching up and slowly, reluctantly moving it away. Interlocking her fingers with his, she turned toward the ocean.

"Come on, Terry, this will do us both a world of good."

Maybe it was the fresh air, the kiss, or seeing her partially naked in the moonlight, but his head seemed to clear a little, and he made it to the water's edge without falling on his ass. She was already up to her waist when she dived into the surf. She reemerged on the far side of a crashing wave with a yelp of joy.

"Come on in, it's lovely," she yelled. "Or are you chicken?"

It wasn't so much the taunt that drove him forward, diving ungainly into the surf, as it was the sight of the rivulets of water dripping off her wet hair and running down her perfect body.

"Bloody hell!" He gasped for breath as he resurfaced. He swam a couple of strokes over to where she was standing and stood in front of her.

"Beautiful, isn't it?" she said softly, looking up at the moon and the stars.

He just continued to look at her. "Yes," he whispered.

She turned toward him, and a smile crossed her face when she realized he was looking at her. Reaching up, she placed her slender arms around his neck and interlocked her fingers. "You're so silly," she purred before kissing him for so long it took his breath away.

Everything was fully functioning now, which may have been her ulterior motive from the moment she suggested they go for a swim. Without a word and without taking her eyes off him, she reached under the water and pulled down his boxers so they were around his knees. Then she pulled herself up, wrapping her legs around his waist. "Give me a hand," she whispered before kissing him again.

Putting his hands underneath her firm buttocks, he realized she was still wearing her underwear. Pulling them to one side, he held himself close to her, and she slowly lowered herself onto him.

"Lovely," she moaned when she had reached the base.

Slowly, at first, she began to move, keeping her eyes locked on his. For one brief second, he remembered his nurse's warning about being eaten by a tiger shark, but he didn't really care anymore. She kissed him again and began to speed up her gyrations. He moaned loudly and grabbed at her butt in desperation, wishing it wouldn't end but knowing he couldn't last much longer. She let out a cry of pleasure and he knew she couldn't either. When they both came it was as if every fiber of his body was electrified and the charge was coming from her. He let out a loud cry as he finished and was gasping for breath even though he had done little of the work. A thought flashed through his mind. *What the hell just happened?* He expected that she would release her grip around him and lower herself down, but she stayed exactly where she was, with him still inside of her, resting her head on his shoulder, not saying a word. He was about to speak, feeling the need to say something, anything, when she lifted her head off his shoulder and put her finger to his lips.

"Think you could do that again?" she asked, starting to move on him.

"Perhaps," he mumbled.

And so they began their lovemaking all over again.

When they were finished, they walked hand in hand to the beach and lay down in the sand, not speaking, her head nestled on his chest, just looking up at the stars. She ran her finger over his scar, the dressing long claimed by the ocean.

"What happened?"

"Oh, just in the wrong place at the wrong time," he answered. He could tell she wanted to ask him more, but she held her peace.

After ten or so minutes, she propped herself up on her elbow and kissed him gently on the lips.

"Let's go to bed. It's getting a little chilly."

He nodded, and without bothering to dress, they gathered up their clothes and headed for his villa. After showering together, they made love once more and fell asleep entwined as if any space between them might allow the magic to end.

Around four in the morning, he awoke and bolted upright, screaming, covered in sweat. It took him a full half minute to realize where he was and remember that he wasn't alone. He knew Amanda would be dressed and out the door in under a minute.

Instead, she put her arms around him and lowered him back down to the pillow. Then she rested her head on his chest and began to stroke his hair. "It's okay, Terry, I'm here, I will always be here."

For some reason, and against all security protocols, he began to tell her his story. He described the pain, the utter devastation he felt at the age of fifteen with the loss of his father to cancer. He talked about his mother, about moving in with his older sister, and about how he joined the army at sixteen. He talked about how the army had become his home, even more so when his mother died when he was nineteen. By then he'd been in Northern Ireland for two years, and the things he had seen and done had hardened him, and he hadn't shed a tear at her funeral. He talked about the deep guilt he felt about this and how he wished he had been able to spend more time with her before her death. Then he began to tell her about his mission in Northern Ireland to eliminate Kieran Martin, the man responsible for the Bristol pub bombing. He even told her about Ciaran and how he thought he had loved her but had been disgusted by her tears at the death of Kieran Martin.

His own tears silently flowed now as he told her about the ambush and the death of his friend, Steve Bailey, and how he hadn't been able to attend the funeral because of security concerns. The only thing he didn't tell her about was his debrief with R. When he had finished, he felt totally drained but also at peace for the first time in a long time. She moved up to him and kissed him gently on the mouth, and then held him close as he fell asleep in her arms.

When he awoke the following day, she was not next to him. He glanced over at his alarm clock and was surprised to see it was eleven in the morning; it was the latest he had slept in years. He lit his first cigarette of the morning and was about to get out of bed when she appeared naked in the doorway of the kitchen carrying a large mug of tea. He felt himself reacting to her nakedness, but he ignored it, knowing he had to talk to her about the previous night's confession. After his confession, he felt completely at peace and absolved from his sins. She took the cigarette and put it out in the ashtray on his nightstand.

"Foul bloody things," she said, giving him a stern look.

"Sorry. I guess I'll have to quit."

She smiled her approval and handed him the steaming mug of tea. When she sat cross-legged on the bed in front of him he almost spilled the hot tea all over himself. He took a sip and was pleased to see she had made it NATO style, thick as mud with a little milk and two heaping teaspoons of sugar.

"Good tea," he said with a smile.

She gave him a pleasant smile back. "I thought you might like it that way. It's how my father takes it."

"Your father is in the military?"

"He's a lieutenant colonel in the Household Cavalry."

He realized that, besides her name, this was the only other thing he knew about her. "Oh really, what regiment?"

"The Life Guards."

He knew little about the regiment, but the one thing he did know was that you didn't become a lieutenant colonel as a working-class lad from Manchester. That meant her family had land and a shit-load of money. At present, though, that was the furthest thing from his mind. He had to talk to her about last night and the things he had told her.

"Listen, about last night, I may have said a few things that I shouldn't have. It's really important that you don't talk to anyone about what I said, okay, or I could end up in a great deal of trouble."

Her reaction was not the one he expected: she laughed. "It's all right, Terry, I won't breathe a word. Anyway, my father asked me to keep an eye on you while I was here."

Terry, who had been taking a large gulp of tea, had a brief coughing fit before being able to speak. "He did *what*?"

"A friend of his, someone high up in the government, apparently, found out I was going to be in Providenciales with some friends on a bachelorette getaway and asked him to ask me to keep an eye on you and report back on how you were doing."

"Oh, Christ," he mumbled. "So what the hell was last night, checking me out to see if I was fit for duty?" he asked angrily.

She pouted slightly and he saw tears well up in her eyes.

"God, I'm sorry," he said grabbing her in a tight hug before kissing her cheeks and eyelids. "I didn't mean it to come out that way. It's just that I was shocked by what you said. Please forgive me."

She lay her head on the pillow facing him and draped her long slender leg over him. He felt himself twitch again at her touch.

"Last night, Terry, was me wanting to help the man I have found myself falling for. Don't tell me you don't feel the same way because I've seen the way you look at me."

He blushed. "Oh, I'm done falling, I've already landed with a thud. I was just hoping this wasn't some one-night stand for you."

"If it was, I wouldn't have been here when you woke up."

"Amanda, why me? I mean it's not like I must have made a great impression being pissed every time you saw me. I'm sure I'm not the prize your mom and dad were hoping you would bring home."

She laughed loudly. "Who said anything about bringing you home?" She saw him react negatively and realized she'd touched a nerve. "I'm sorry, darling, I would love to bring you home. To be honest, I just don't know. It's as if when I first saw you, I just knew. As for the drinking, please don't worry about that. I saw my father climb in and, eventually, out of a bottle, especially after his second tour in Ireland. As for a prize, there is one thing you should know about my parents. They are the most down-to-earth rich people you will ever meet. They will just be ecstatic that I've met someone, and when Daddy hears that you are in the military, he will be so pleased."

"I hope so. I can't help thinking that I am at a bit of a disadvantage. You know everything about me, and I don't know much about you. What are your plans for the future? What are you doing now?"

Amanda laughed. "Besides being with you?"

"You know what I mean," replied Nolan.

"I'm at university studying law. I really want to represent people that usually fall through the cracks of the system."

"Hey, that's great. Which university?"

"Downing College at Cambridge."

Nolan let out a low whistle. "Wow, that's very impressive. I might end up married to a famous lawyer."

She smiled and kissed him hard this time, and he couldn't ignore his physical reaction. He tried to roll on top of her, but she put her hand on his chest. "I'm sorry, Terry, I can't, I have to get back and pack. We are supposed to be flying out today for Miami."

"I guess that's that, then," he replied. "You'll be back in England while I'm stuck here alone. Once I get back, I'm sure they'll have some sort of job for me to do."

"How much longer are you going to be here?"

"At least another six weeks."

She reached down with her hand and teased him, moving her hand up and down. He gasped with pleasure. "You could always ask me to stay," she purred before lowering her mouth onto him.

"Oh my God, please stay!"

Quickly she straddled him and guided him into her as she lowered herself down. He lifted his head and sucked on her nipple ever so gently. Now it was her turn to moan.

She pushed his head down on the pillow and smiled mischievously as she began to rock up and down on him. "My bags are already in the spare room," she said before kissing him greedily.

They returned to England six weeks later. Two months after, they were married in a private ceremony on her family's estate in Oxfordshire. R even agreed to be Terry's best man. There was no one else he could ask. And although she wasn't showing in her wedding dress, Amanda was already three months pregnant with their daughter, Miranda.

12

PALACE BARRACKS, COUNTY DOWN, NORTHERN IRELAND, APRIL 2018

In a way, the six NIRA men in the three-quarter-ton British Army Land Rover had been preparing for this mission their whole lives. In reality, they had been training for this particular attack for the last month. They had studied the layout of their objective using photographs, as well as a scale model, and had spent numerous hours honing their skills on the A2 variant of the SA80 assault rifle. They had even practiced refining their English accents to the point that any of them would easily pass for someone who had been raised in the southeast of England.

It was eight fifteen as they pulled up to the main gate of one of the most heavily guarded British Army installations in the United Kingdom. None of them spoke. Although the sun was starting to show itself through the gray clouds overhead, the ground and imposing buildings were still wet from the previous night's downpour. This was Ireland, after all; it wasn't lack of rain that made it so green. Palace Barracks, as it was known, was the home of the Royal Scots Borders, first battalion of the Royal Regiment of Scotland. The battalion was considered specialized infantry and was tasked in a counter-terrorism role. This specialization and the fact that it was a Scottish battalion in Northern Ireland made it a ripe target. The barracks were not exactly an homage to any form of architecture, unless there was a "dull and dreary" movement.

The leader of the six-man NIRA cell, Raymond Boyle of the Special Investigation Branch, was dressed in a slightly worn suit, as was the driver. The other four men in the back of the vehicle wore Military Police uniforms. Nobody messed with the Military Police. One of the guards approached the passenger-side window while another approached the driver's side. There were other soldiers visible, and the NIRA men knew that there would be even more manning weapons, creating a crossfire that would rip them to pieces. The first guard tapped on the passenger-side glass.

Boyle lowered the window.

"Identification," ordered the guard.

"'Sir,'" responded Boyle in a perfect posh southern accent.

"Excuse me?" responded the guard.

"Identification, *sir*."

The man immediately came to attention and saluted. "Sorry, sir, of course, sir. If you wouldn't mind, could I please see your identification, sir?"

"Yes, of course, Private . . . ?"

"Hunter, sir."

"Of course, Private Hunter. Don't worry yourself too much about the 'sir' thing. After all, you weren't to know." Boyle handed over the perfect fake ID.

"Thank you, Captain Boyle. Much appreciated. Could I also see the identification cards for each of your men, sir?"

"With pleasure, Hunter." The other men passed their ID cards to Boyle for inspection.

Another man appeared from a small building next to the main gate wheeling a small mirror on the end of a long handle. He proceeded to wheel the mirror under the Land Rover, checking for bombs. He found nothing and gave Private Hunter a thumbs up. Hunter nodded back in acknowledgment.

"Can I ask where you are going, sir?"

"I need to see the lieutenant colonel on an urgent matter. Can you give me directions to the battalion office?"

"Absolutely, sir." The private handed back the IDs and proceeded to give them directions, which of course they didn't need. As they drove off, he snapped a smart salute. Boyle nodded in recognition and smiled thinly.

As Boyle raised the window, one of the men in the back laughed slightly. "Bejesus, Raymond. You almost gave me a heart attack when you made him call you 'sir,'" he said in a broad Londonderry accent. The other men started laughing, their nerves getting the better of them.

"Shut the fuck up," hissed Boyle. "You want this over before we even get started?" All the men instantly fell silent. "Make sure you keep to the speed limit, Shaun."

"Yes, sir," he replied. Two of the men in the back snickered.

On their way up to the mess hall for the lower ranks, Boyle pondered how the men with him had ended up where they were. All of them, besides himself, had been in infant school when the Good Friday Agreement had been signed, yet to a man, they hated it and considered it traitorous. They had all lost one or more family members in the Troubles, either at the hands of the UVF, the British Army, or the Royal Ulster Constabulary, and they'd been constantly reminded of this fact throughout their youth. That they were even part of this suicide mission, which is precisely what it was, was a testament to their dedication. It also didn't hurt in their recruitment that their prospects in life were nonexistent. Boyle had watched his father, mother, and sister blown to pieces in the street by a bomb wired to the ignition of the family car. The only reason he hadn't died was that he had been running a fever, so they had left him in the care of a neighbor while they went to visit his grandmother in Crossmaglen. This was his chance for payback.

As the Land Rover pulled up outside of the lower ranks' mess hall, three of the men opened the back door of the vehicle, stepped out, and slung their SA80s over their shoulders. Then they each reached into the back and picked up gym bags containing grenades and more full magazines. As they closed the door, there were no words of encouragement or good luck. They were beyond that. The only thing uttered was Boyle's reminder to wait for the explosion before moving in on their target. Forty seconds later, the Land Rover was pulling up outside the Sergeants' Mess.

Boyle got out, along with the other man in the back dressed as an MP, slung his weapon over his shoulder, and grabbed his own gym bag. Before closing the passenger door, he reached in and shook the driver's hand. "Are you good with this, Shaun?"

"Be away with you, Raymond, I'm fine," came the reply.

He smiled at the man and was about to say something but changed his mind. He slammed the door shut and stood watching as the Land Rover drove away toward the Officers' Mess with its deadly cargo of sixty pounds of C-4.

He turned to the other man. "Come on, Seamus, let's get this over with."

Both men walked calmly into the corridor outside the Sergeants' Mess and found the bathroom exactly where it should be according to the floorplans they had studied. Each man chose a stall and proceeded to don the British Army–style webbing that was in their bags. They then loaded the magazine pouches and clipped each of the dozen grenades they both carried to the webbing. As they walked out of the bathroom, the windows were shattered by the enormous explosion of the Land Rover being driven directly through the main doors of the Officers' Mess.

As they pushed open the double doors into the main dining room area of the Sergeants' Mess, they were confronted with total mayhem. Men were running toward the windows to see what had happened, and confusion was rife. Both men started lobbing grenades into the mass of senior NCOs before stepping back outside the doors. The explosions began ripping flesh apart. As the last grenade exploded, they stepped back into the room and started spraying the survivors with bullets. The men didn't stand a chance. The living were cut down like chickens in a slaughterhouse. It didn't help that all were unarmed except for one man.

A Provost Sergeant who had just come off guard was sitting at the back of the dining hall enjoying a large mug of tea after his breakfast when the men burst into the room. He watched, as if in slow motion, as the two men started throwing grenades at his fellow soldiers. What saved his life was the large wooden table he'd been sitting at when the explosion at the Officers' Mess happened. At the sight of the two gunmen, he kicked it over, ducked down behind it, and waited for the grenades to explode. He knew they would come back into the room to finish off the survivors, and he had already drawn the SIG Sauer P226 9mm as the two men opened fire. Keeping his head down, he knelt at the end of the table and returned fire, killing one of the men instantly with three rounds in the chest. He turned his attention to the other gunman, but he was gone. He was tempted to make his way after him but looking around at the number of wounded and dying, thought it best to watch over them just in case there were others out there.

Boyle had watched Seamus take the rounds in the chest and he knew he was gone. He decided that instead of continuing the attack on the mess, he would kill as many of the soldiers as he saw outside running toward the site of the explosion. He emptied the rest of the magazine into the room and ducked out of the door. He was reloading as he ran outside into the bright morning sunlight when he came face-to-face with Private Hunter. Boyle smiled at the shock of recognition on Hunter's face and swung his weapon round. Hunter beat him to the trigger and fired five rounds at him, two of which found their mark.

As Boyle lay on the ground bleeding out, he smiled again at the thought of all the songs they would sing about him and his men and the great victory they had won. He knew this was only the start of the latest round of the Troubles, but God willing and the blood of patriots, they would win a united Ireland.

13

ACELA TRAIN TO NEW YORK, APRIL 2018

"Yeah, I'm fine, sir. How did you know?" Terry whispered, just in case a fellow passenger heard him on the phone.

"We received a flash report from GCHQ, Government Communications Headquarters, that there had been an explosion in Boston Harbor. We have also had a number of reports of people—our people undercover *and* their contacts—being found murdered. You're the only one still alive."

"Bloody hell! Are you telling me that everyone is gone? Including our other Vicars in the States?"

"Yes, but that's not the half of it. A number of Police Service of Northern Ireland and British Army bases, including Palace Barracks in County Down and Thiepval Barracks in County Antrim, were hit by suicide bombers driving British Army Land Rovers loaded with explosives. All around the same time that your boat exploded. They even made a play for our headquarters here in London, but our antivehicle measures and some damn fine shooting by our armed police stopped them dead in their tracks. Unfortunately, the driver triggered the bomb before he died, so there is very little immediate evidence we can act on"

"Jesus! Suicide bombers, that's new. How many dead and wounded?"

"Here, we were lucky. A few wounded security officers only, no dead. Ireland is a different matter. They took out the Officers' Mess, as well as the Sergeants' and other ranks' messes at Palace Barracks just as breakfast was in full swing. It is going to be a high body count."

"Any leads as to who was responsible?"

"I bloody wish, but so far nothing. They are obviously making a play for power now that Martin McGuinness is dead. If we don't stop these bastards, and soon, the entire shit show is going to start all over again. We need to pull you out and regroup. No point in losing you as well, especially as they seem to know who you are."

"I can't do that, sir. Sorry."

"What do you mean you can't do that? This is a bloody order. Get the hell out while you can."

"They might have Shae, sir. I'm on my way to New York to see if I can find out what's happened to her." He could almost hear K's thoughts as he pondered what he had just been told. They were the same as his. *How the hell had they found out about Shae?*

K was silent for a second. "Listen, Terry, I know you may feel responsible if anything has happened to Shae, but I have to ask, has this got anything to do with what happened to Miranda? After all, she's not much older than your daughter would have been. That would be totally understandable, you kind of wanting to make amends."

Terry sighed. "No, sir, and anyway, that was a long time ago. You are right in one respect. I do feel responsible for Shae, as I was the one who lit the fuse that made her want to do this. So if there is any chance of getting her out, I'm going to be the one who does it."

"Fine, I can give you twenty-four hours before you get your ass out of there, and for God's sake stay away from our consulate, as the NIRA are most assuredly watching it."

"I'll need at least forty-eight hours, sir. After that I'll let you know."

"No, Terry, forty-eight hours and you're done, got it?"

"Yes, sir." He pulled out the two IDs he had taken from the car earlier. "Sir, I have a couple of driver's licenses I took from my attackers.

I'm going to send you a photo of them to see if you guys can dig up any information about them. The names are probably fake, but could you see if anything shows up on facial ID?"

"No problem. We should have something for you within the hour. Where are the bodies?"

"In very tiny pieces at the bottom of Boston Harbor."

He heard K chuckle slightly. "Good, good. Oh, and Terry, if you do happen to find these bastards who are responsible for the deaths of our people, please proceed with extreme prejudice."

"My pleasure, sir."

Terry hung up and sat back in his chair, wanting desperately to get some shut-eye before he arrived in New York but knowing that was out of the question. The train had made a number of stops—Providence, Rhode Island, and New London and New Haven, Connecticut—even though it was the express. By New Haven, it was starting to fill up. Thankfully, most people avoided the rear carriage, preferring instead to be closer to the front of the train, so they could exit Penn Station quicker. He was about to get a coffee from the café car when the train started to slow for the final stop before New York—Stamford, Connecticut. He sat back down and was casually observing passengers get on board when he spotted three men enter his carriage from the next one down. He pretended not to be watching them—*Thank God for sunglasses*—and saw one of the men tap the arm of the man in front of him after looking in his direction; they quickly sat down four seats away from the back. There was also a slight bulge under the left side of the jacket of the first man.

Shit, how the hell did they find me?

One of the men, who was sporting a heavy, unruly dark beard, looked directly at him; Terry pretended not to notice. Most likely, nothing was going to happen before they arrived in Penn Station. *They'll have people at that end ready to make a grab for me when I leave the safety of the station.* So it was up to him to initiate contact and disrupt their plans. His first priority was figuring out how they were tracking him; he'd only taken a gun and IDs off his previous attackers. He took the Swiss Army knife that was a permanent fixture of his go bag and held one of the identification cards under the pull-down tray. Very carefully he peeled back the plastic coating, then the paper underneath, and voila, there was a thin lithium battery with a tracking chip attached. He didn't destroy it, in case someone was monitoring its signal; instead he pushed it down the side of the seat. He did the same thing with the other identification card.

Next, he checked the weapon. All seemed fine until he removed the magazine and felt inside the butt of the gun. *Son of a bitch, there's one in there as well.* After removing that one, he reloaded the magazine and slowly, quietly chambered a round. He looked around the carriage; by now it was three-quarters full of civilians heading into the city. *No way I can do anything about these muppets yet.* He settled back in his seat and closed his eyes, trying to relax. Now all he could do was wait until they arrived in New York.

14

LONDON, 2000

Miranda was a joy. Terry was still away a good six months of the year, but he was happier than he had ever been. For a wedding present, Amanda's parents had bought them a luxurious three-bedroom flat in London's Kensington district. Terry had been a little perturbed at first, as he wanted to provide for his wife and soon-to-be-born baby girl. Amanda had told him not to be silly; her family was loaded, and she had no wish to live in a one-room flat in Brixton. They had welcomed Terry with open arms, which shocked him to no end given their status, and were overjoyed when Miranda was born.

Amanda's family were not the upper-crust cold fish he had imagined but kind, generous people. Besides Amanda's obvious beauty, she had a kindness about her which, other than from his parents, wasn't something he was used to seeing. Amanda was the sort of person who, if she saw a homeless person, would run into a store, buy them food and, if needed, give them the coat off her back. She and her parents ran a charity that helped homeless families find housing and jobs in the London area and also provided scholarships for kids from low-income backgrounds to attend university. They didn't do it to attract praise and attention, as so many others did; they just wanted to do what was right. Amanda transferred to King's College London to be near to her husband's work and make things easier when their daughter was born. She finished law school and started working for a friend of the family to gain experience, as she planned on starting her own firm in the future.

After Miranda was born, every weekend they could get away was spent in the countryside of Oxfordshire, which was where, at the age of nine, Miranda came down with a slight cold over Christmas and New Year.

They had been walking through the woods to try and burn off a few calories after a spectacular Christmas feast. Glorious trifle and mince pies with lashings of double cream were waiting back at the house, and the evening would be spent playing board games, during which much cheating would ensue, to the obvious delight of all, in front of a roaring fire. Then his daughter complained about not feeling very well.

The family immediately headed back to the house, where Miranda's grandmother smothered her chest in Vicks, gave her a healthy dose of cold medicine, and covered her in a blanket on the couch next to the fire. Within thirty minutes, Miranda was feeling decidedly better, so the board games were broken out of the storage cupboard in her grandfather's study, and the evening proceeded as planned.

The following morning, Boxing Day, Miranda had a slight fever. The family doctor was called; he prescribed antibiotics and some slightly stronger cold medicine. He wasn't about to take any chances with the child, as there was a nasty strain of the flu going around that year—strict instructions were given to keep her bundled up and away from the children in the village. After consuming a mince pie and a glass of sherry, he smiled when he left and told them not to worry, that all would be fine.

They returned to London a week later. Although Miranda was feeling a little better, she was still running a slight fever, so another doctor's visit was arranged where blood was drawn, much to her displeasure, and a further course of antibiotics were given. A couple of days later, Terry was given orders to ship out to Cyprus. Two members of the Special Investigation Branch of the Royal Military Police had been found murdered while they were working a case involving drug shipments into the United Kingdom that, it was thought, involved some members of a British Army unit. He returned home and packed for his flight, told Amanda not to worry, and gave his daughter a big hug and kiss goodbye.

Three days later, he received a call telling him his daughter had been rushed to the hospital with pneumonia and a temperature of 104 degrees and that she was in intensive care. The flight home was the following day, and a car was waiting for him at the airport to rush him to the hospital. By the time he arrived and ran up to the ward to see Miranda, it was too late. She had passed ten minutes earlier.

When he entered his daughter's room, he saw a sight he had grown all too familiar with from escorting the bodies of dead comrades back to the mainland—the family holding each other mourning the loss of their loved one, woven with the trauma and disbelief of what was happening. He screamed at his daughter's doctors and nurses, his anger and confusion tearing at his soul. He could have understood if she had died in a car accident or even a terrorist attack, but to be taken from him by some bug was not something he could wrap his mind around. What had made it even worse was their understanding and their refusal to react to his profanity-laden rant. Eventually, he quieted and sat in the corner of the room, his head buried in his hands as he fought to contain the tears that needed to flow but he refused to allow. He found himself gasping for breath, and it was his wife who came to him and held him while whispering over and over that it would be okay. He knew she was lying, knew it never would be okay. But he gave himself permission to live. He learned to breathe again. The only way he was able to do this was to bury his guilt and loss. It caused an emptiness that remained eighteen years later.

15

ACELA TRAIN, NEW YORK PENN STATION, APRIL 2018

Terry was in the shit, and he knew it. Not only did he have to deal with these three gorillas on the train but he also had to evade their cohorts, who were surely waiting for him at various station exits. He was somewhat familiar with Penn Station, but it wasn't as if he had studied the schematics or anything. As the train thundered across the Hell Gate Bridge spanning the East River, he quickly googled a map of the station on his phone, but that was little help—there were too many platforms and staircases and escalators and levels to know it all in a few minutes. He thought about going through the main station and then into the subway, but all it would take was a few guys covering the platform exits and he'd be stuck down there like a rat in a trap. He could try and make it out of one of the side entrances, but all they'd need would be a few people strategically positioned with long guns, and he'd be done before even reaching the curb. It wasn't as if he could start shooting back, as there were enough of New York City's finest and National Guardsmen armed to the teeth in and around the station to fill Madison Square Garden. There was only one thing to do; he'd have to exit the way he'd came in, along the tracks and out one of the service entrances.

The train slowed and clacked over the maze of switches through the Harold Interlocking—the busiest rail junction in the United States. At the other end of Sunnyside Yard was the tunnel portal that led under the East River and over to Penn Station.

Now all he needed was a distraction or, better yet, total panic.

He had about three minutes before the train stopped at the platform when he saw his chance. A lady with a couple of kids sat across from the three guys. She stood up to get their backpacks and her much larger one from the overhead compartment. The kids' backpacks were retrieved without a problem, but hers appeared to have gotten stuck. Terry was on his feet in a flash, the silenced 9mm SIG Sauer in his waistband on his left hip, offering to help her get it down. She smiled thankfully and took a step back. Perfect. With much grunting and mumbling, more for show, really, as he'd managed to get the bag loose within a couple of seconds, he began pulling the bag down. He slipped the tracking device he had retrieved from the weapon into one of the backpack pockets. He smiled. *That should confuse any welcoming committee at the station.*

One of the men sitting across from them nudged his friend and said, loud enough for him and the woman to hear, "That's the problem with these British bastards, Michael. They aren't worth a shit."

The woman, for her part, glared at them then mouthed the word "asshole" to Terry. He grinned appreciatively and gave the bag one final heave. The effort and weight of the bag apparently caused him to stumble onto the right arm of the man sitting facing his two compadres. This was the one who had a weapon under his left armpit, so Terry knew he was a right-handed shooter. Terry's "fall" effectively put him out of action for a few seconds. Holding the handle of the backpack in his left hand, and using it to shield the view of his right hand and the men briefly from the lady and her kids, he slightly pulled the weapon from his waistband and put one round in each of the men's hearts facing him. *Phut, phut.* Now for the panic. Turning the weapon slightly he placed two rounds—*phut, phut*—into the third man's head, causing it to explode as if he'd been hit by a grenade. Then, in a blur, he put three rounds through the window.

The woman started to scream at the sight of the blood and brains as the Irishmen fell lifeless onto the table in front of him.

"Jesus!" screamed Terry. "Get down, someone's shooting at the train!"

He had already slipped his weapon into his right-hand pocket as he dropped her bag on the floor. He pointed at the window with his left hand; the woman looked, and her eyes went wide. He grabbed the kids from their seats and pushed them to the floor, "Crawl, dammit, get the hell out of this carriage."

She nodded bravely. Keeping her children close, she grabbed her backpack and started to crawl away from the carnage. Other passengers in the train car who had heard the commotion stood up to see what was going on. "Get down on the floor, you bloody fools, someone's shooting at the train." It was as if he'd given an electric shock to peoples' brains; what had been calm sixty seconds earlier was now total panic. People were climbing over seats, over each other, in an attempt to get out of the door into the next car. He heard a yell from further down that someone was shooting at the train. The panic was spreading. Suddenly the outside went dark as the train entered the East River tunnel. Terry reckoned he only had a minute or two before they arrived. He jumped up and flipped the emergency brake switch. The wheels automatically locked with a terrible screeching sound, and within ten seconds, the train came to a shuddering halt. *Now to get the hell out.*

The rear car was nearly empty now, and everyone still there was focused on escape. Terry ran back to get his bag and its precious contents, then pried open the rearmost sliding door. Opening it quickly, he jumped down onto the gravel ballast separating the tracks and ran from the mayhem that he had caused. He figured he had a couple of minutes to get away before the train was swarming with cops. Running like hell toward the tunnel wall at the far side of the numerous tracks. and enveloped in darkness, he headed back toward Sunnyside Yard in Queens. In under a minute, he found what he was looking for—an access door used by maintenance workers. It was locked, but three carefully placed rounds took care of that. Then he made his way through an upward-sloping, dimly lit corridor. Turning a corner, he was confronted with a concrete staircase. Taking the steps two at a time, he continued along the corridor until he reached a heavily painted wooden six-panel door. Trying the handle, he opened the door and entered a maintenance room. There were men and a few women in overalls working on tool benches lining the walls.

Most people would have tried to make their way out of the building surreptitiously, but Terry had learned over the years that confidence can usually get you in and out of most places. So he slung his bag over his shoulder, stuffed his hands in his pockets and, with the odd nod to the people working there, made his way out toward the city streets, scanning for any watchers around Penn Station. He knew he had to head for Shae's apartment, but first he needed to get out of these clothes and shower. He made his way to Macy's to pick up a couple of changes of clothes, shoes, toiletries, an electric shaver, and a decent suitcase before jumping in a cab to head to the Grand Hyatt on Forty-Second Street.

At the hotel, he used his Swiss passport and spoke German at the front desk. After a long hot and then cold shower, he ordered a decent breakfast and a French press coffee from room service before flicking on the TV. He watched the coverage of the shooting for a while, then muted the sound and darkened the room. Terry needed sleep, and he waited for darkness to envelop the city. He operated best in the dark.

16

OXFORDSHIRE, 2000

In order to deal with the death of his daughter, Terry had done what most soldiers do and compartmentalized the pain. Amanda, for her part, was a wreck and couldn't understand why there were no tears, why Terry wasn't angry. Her mother replaced Terry as her rock, which caused Amanda to withdraw further from him. Even then, people were telling him he was going to lose her if he didn't take his head out of his ass, but he wouldn't listen.

The funeral took place at the village church near the estate where the Clay family had worshipped for centuries. It was also where Miranda had been baptized.

The morning prior to the funeral, the undertaker brought the small coffin containing Terry's little girl into the manor house and set her remains in the family's private chapel. Then they did the unthinkable: they opened the coffin. He was furious—how dare his wife's family show her off in some grotesque version of lying in state? He told his wife that he thought it was wrong, but she replied that people wanted to say goodbye, and so he had kept his tongue like a good husband and allowed the show-and-tell. The viewing for all and sundry to see his little angel was between three and seven, and so they sat, like only the English can sit, back straight and shoulders back, as if at attention, which was ingrained in them when they were schoolkids. welcoming the mourners and hangers-on as they arrived in force. There were lords and ladies, earls, members of the cabinet, and even some lesser members of the royal family. It was quite a show. In the front pew, his in-laws flanked their heartbroken daughter. He chose to sit furthest away from the aisle, next to his mother-in-law, who was gently sobbing like his wife. He just sat staring forward, unable to utter a word. All he wished was that the visitors would fuck off and leave them be, but no, they just kept coming like a river of grief.

The only tolerable moment was when R, who had been one of Miranda's godparents, appeared in front of him accompanied by Terry's sister. She, like Amanda, was devastated by the loss. Although Terry and his sister had not spoken directly since she was whisked away into witness protection, R, over the years, had arranged for her to receive letters from the family as well as home movies and videos, so she could keep track of them. That she was here now was a testament to how worried R was for his agent and friend. Terry rose from his seat as if on autopilot, and his sister hugged him, hard, sobbing into his jacket the whole time. He had barely been able to lift his arms to return the embrace. R eventually pried her off of him and sat her down in the pew, where she promptly buried her head in her hands and continued to weep. Deep down, he was glad to see his sister after so many years, but he also resented her show of grief. It seemed to suggest that *her* world was over and not his. R shook Terry's hand and, in a show of sentiment not usual for the British gentry, pulled him in and patted him on the back. He spoke the usual words of condolence, but Terry didn't hear them. All he was able to do was mumble his thanks and return to his seat.

And so, the procession of mourners nearing its end, it was Terry and Amanda's turn to approach the coffin and view its contents. Amanda, supported by her parents, went first, and, as any grieving mother would, she broke down. She begged her parents, begged God, begged anyone who could hear to bring her daughter back to her. It took the combined strength of her parents, R, as well as the family doctor, the one who had said his daughter would be fine, to get his wife away from the coffin and take her upstairs to her room for some much-needed rest. Terry just stood there and did not lift a finger.

Then there was no one else. Just him alone with his little girl. He shuffled forward like a man possessed and looked down at her. There was a paleness about her that had never existed when she was alive. At that moment, he nearly broke. He just couldn't understand. *How had the pneumonia taken hold so fast, why hadn't all the drugs and wonders of modern medicine been able to save her?* He sighed, and the sound seemed to echo around the chapel. He blamed himself, of course. He was supposed to protect her like he had protected so many others, but he had failed miserably. He swore to her then, to his dead daughter, that as long as he had breath in his body, he would never fail again. He reached down into the coffin and removed the Saint Christopher medal that hung around her neck, placing it gently in his pocket; he needed something of hers to remind him of his failure and of his promise to make up for it. After pushing an errant hair away from her face, he stroked her cold lifeless cheek. "Goodbye, my darling." Reaching up, he slowly lowered the lid of the coffin, as if putting her to bed one last time, before walking out of the chapel.

Within a week of the funeral, unable to stand being in their apartment and the memories it contained, Terry was back in Cyprus, where he remained for another three months. R had said that he could take as long as he needed to be with Amanda, but he rejected the offer. Amanda had begged him to stay, but he had said there was no one else that could go, which was a lie. She had begged him to talk to her, mourn with her, cry with her, but he just couldn't. He feared that once he started, he'd never stop. By the time he returned home, his marriage was on the rocks. Amanda had grown cold. Even though his frame of mind was such that he now felt the need to talk, to be with her, the opportunity to rekindle any spark of love that had been between them had passed. Terry knew then she would never forgive him. They were divorced within the year.

17

NEW YORK CITY, 7:00 P.M. EDT

Terry set the alarm on his phone for eight o'clock p.m. but was awake by seven and watching CNN. By now the shooting on the train was national news, and it was being reported, through unnamed sources, that it was believed the shooter had been on the train. Pretty soon there would be a police sketch of him on every channel in New York, so he went to work on his appearance.

Removing the new clothes from his suitcase, he opened the electric shaver he had purchased and shaved his hair down to a number three, catching the hair in the open case. A number three cut was short enough to change his appearance but not so short that it would attract attention. The last thing he needed now was to be memorable. After taking another shower and wiping the tub clean—*no point in leaving more DNA than necessary*—he stripped the sheets and pillowcases from the bed and placed them, along with the towels he had used, in the suitcase. He got dressed in black shoes, dark pants, a slate-gray shirt, and a dark casual jacket and loaded his remaining clothes in the duffel. Just then his phone pinged with a text from K; he'd run the photos of the two dead terrorists from the boat and come up with two possible leads from Londonderry. The older of the two was definitely IRA and had been wanted for a number of bombings in the mid-1990s. The younger one was just a street thug who had aspirations to play with the big boys. Both had fallen off the map some years ago. *Bugger, a dead end.* He went back to getting his stuff together and wiping down the room, not that his prints would show up on any database, but it was best not to leave the cops any fingerprints or DNA they could have on file. He put on the New York Yankees cap he had purchased and a pair of nondescript glasses that looked prescription.

Downloading a luggage storage app on his phone, he booked a spot with a company near Grand Central Station and headed out of the hotel to drop off his suitcase. It would be found eventually, but not before he was long gone. Now he had to eat. He headed for Scotty's, an all-night diner over on Thirty-Ninth and Lexington. After wolfing down a decent steak and eggs with a double order of hash browns as well as two cups of coffee, he headed for an off-the-books safe house he maintained for just such a situation. He hadn't wanted to go there earlier, just in case it was under surveillance, and there were way too many people around during the day to spot any watchers keeping an eye on the place. A light rain began falling when he arrived in the vicinity of the safe house, which made him smile. He remembered how, throughout his regular army career, other soldiers had bitched mightily when it rained. They hated the cold, hated the way the water soaked everything and eventually chilled a person to the bone. For him, though, rain had always brought a smile to his face because if his guys were miserable, so were the enemy. This caused them to make mistakes, to be more interested in moaning and keeping warm than what was happening around them. It also made him all that much harder to be spotted. Terry didn't mind the rain; he loved it, longed for it like a distant traveler longs for their lover.

He positioned himself deep in the shadows but with a view of the building and settled down to wait for a couple of hours. He had retrieved the night-vision device from his duffle and occasionally raised it to his eye. He hoped if anyone was watching the apartment building, they would be stupid enough to sit in a car or be in some type of nondescript van, the type always used on TV shows. After a few hours, he deemed the coast to be clear and made his way to the main entrance of the building. There was an elevator, but he ignored it. Nothing worse than taking the elevator and being shot to shit when the doors opened on your floor. The stairs were much better, as they offered a chance to maneuver if it did hit the fan.

His apartment was on the top floor, the door directly opposite the entrance to the stairs. If he had to exit quickly, he had the option of the fire escape or the stairs. He opened the door of the stairwell and looked both ways down the corridor. All seemed clear. He took a deep breath and stepped across the corridor to his apartment door, opened it quickly. And entered. He cleared the apartment room by room until he was satisfied there were no surprises waiting for him, including the sort that explode.

He stripped off his now-wet clothes and retrieved a similar outfit from his closet, including a black woolen coat, and turned on the television in the bedroom. Switching the channel to the local news, he quickly dressed while waiting for the latest report on the Acela shooting. Going to the bathroom, he removed a panel along the side of the bathtub and withdrew another bag. Inside the bag, he found a couple of flashbangs—M84 stun grenades, three M18 smoke grenades, and more ammunition for his Walther. He had a feeling he was going to need it, as he had never been in a position where his entire network of Parishioners had seemed to evaporate overnight. The fact that the assailants on his boat had known where he was and knew his real name was driving him nuts, but he tried to put that out of his mind as he focused on the mission at hand. He also placed a Leatherman multi-tool in his pants pocket and a Fairbairn-Sykes fighting knife in his jacket pocket. The last items he retrieved were a block of C-4, some detonators, detcord and fuses, and two small digital timers. He transferred all this, as well as the items in his duffel, into a Bergen backpack he had stashed in the back of the closet. This allowed him to keep his hands free if anything should occur that required him to react without hesitation. He then shoved the items that were too large for him to carry back into the space alongside the tub and replaced the panel.

Proceeding to the living room / kitchen, he turned on that television and put on the kettle to make a French press coffee. He had just poured the coffee into a metal go-cup loaded with sugar when the news started talking about the shooting. After about thirty seconds, up popped a police sketch that was surprisingly accurate. He knew it was time to make a move. If anyone at the rental agency or his neighbors, who he had bumped into now and again on the stairs, were watching the broadcast, the cops would be busting in the door to his safe house within the hour. He again wiped everything down as best as possible, stuffed his wet clothes into a garbage bag for later disposal, and, without a further glance around, left his now-burned safe house as silently as he had arrived. Quickly walking down to the garage, which was one of the reasons he had chosen this place, he pulled the cover off the 2008 Cadillac Escalade he kept stashed there. Throwing the cover in the back, he placed the backpack in the passenger footwell and drove out into the rainy night. It was now time to head over to Shae's and hope that there was something in the dead drop he had set up in her apartment. This time, he knew they would be watching.

18

NEW YORK CITY, 1:00 A.M. EDT

Terry had been watching Shae's apartment building for a couple of hours and figured he had spotted four watchers. They were situated in two cars, two men in each, one across the street from the apartment and the other on the corner of the block, where they could see the service gate that led to the back of the building. There may have also been a fifth and sixth, but if the two women sitting in the window of the bar half a block away from the apartment were watchers, they knew their shit, and he just couldn't be sure. Obviously, there was no way he would be able to enter the building through the front or back without trying to take out the watchers, which was something he wanted to avoid. But what they, and Shae, couldn't know was that he had rented an apartment in the building next door. Pulling up the collar of his coat and tucking his chin down to partially obscure his face, he half ran, half walked through the rain to the building next door and hurried up the stairs. He waited on the first-floor landing, silenced Walther in hand, for five minutes to be sure they hadn't spotted him.

He entered the apartment, which was empty apart from a table and chair, a computer monitor on the table, and a TV on a wire stand.

Connected to the monitor was a long black cable that seemed to disappear into the wall. This was actually a pinhole camera that he had placed shortly after renting the space, which allowed him to see the main living area of Shae's apartment. From her side of the wall, it looked nothing more than a small nail hole on which a previous tenant had hung a painting. It wasn't as if he had been spying on her, as it was always off, but he had placed it for just such an event as this or if she had ended up in some form of hostage situation. Given what she was doing for him and that he had recruited her, he felt this was the least he could do if it came down to rescuing her. He switched it on and settled down for a few minutes, watching the monitor to see if any uninvited guests were waiting for his arrival. The picture was pretty crappy, but it was clear that the place had been unceremoniously turned over. *Now to get to work and get into her place.*

It was quite simple, really. When Shae was at her day job, shortly after first starting to work for him, he had removed a chunk of drywall about the size of a door from his side of the wall and then proceeded to take apart the dividing wall brick by brick until all that was left on her side was wood lath and plaster. It had only taken about a week, and all the removed bricks were stacked neatly in the corner of his room. He had even shored up the wall with a four-by-ten wooden header and a couple of steel jack posts, one on either side, holding it all up. After all, he'd look pretty stupid if the wall collapsed.

He went to the kitchen and took a Sawzall and extension cord out of the cabinet and set everything up in front of the hole. Turning on the TV, he found a station showing classic rock videos and turned up the volume just enough to drown out the sound of the saw. Breaking through a wall this way to gain entrance to an adjoining building was a trick the special forces used for hostage rescue or when they needed to enter a building to take the occupants by surprise. In those cases, a small amount of explosive was used to enter the adjoining building quickly. In this case, a Sawzall would do the job nicely and was a great deal quieter. Well, somewhat quieter.

Terry figured it would take ten minutes to break through to Shae's apartment; it took five. After turning off the TV and clearing away the debris, he stepped into her place, M84 in one hand, smoke grenade in his pocket, and silenced Walther at the ready. The place had been destroyed. The only things that remained intact were the windows and drywall. He checked the apartment room by room for any unwanted surprises or blood. Thankfully, there didn't seem to be any. Either they'd grabbed her without a struggle, or she was in the wind.

Clearing a path through the remnants of her bedroom, he said a silent prayer to the God of his youth: *Please, Lord, let something be here, otherwise, I'm screwed*. He knelt down in front of one of the white electrical sockets that dotted the room. Setting down the Walther and stun grenade on the hardwood floor, he took the multi-tool from his pocket and proceeded to unscrew the faceplate. He then pulled sharply on the socket. Unlike a regular electrical socket, there was no wiring connected to it. Instead, there was a plastic rectangular container. Holding his breath, as if breathing might affect the outcome of his search, he reached inside, and his fingers touched a thumb drive. *Thank you, God*.

He placed the drive in his pocket and again armed himself with the Walther and the flashbang. He was about to head out of the bedroom when he heard a slight click as a key turned in the door. *Shit!*

19

SHAE'S APARTMENT, NEW YORK CITY, 1:30 A.M. EDT

Terry turned off the light in the bedroom and crouched low on one knee, pressing his body against the bedroom wall, back from the door, looking out toward the hallway and the front door. Anyone looking in his direction would have been hard-pressed to see the barrel of the Walther that was about three inches away from the doorjamb. Considering what might be coming through the door, he was pretty relaxed; he'd been in worse situations in the past, and at least he had a decent exit back the way he'd come in. That was something they wouldn't be expecting. They also wouldn't be expecting the stun grenade from which he had already removed the pin. His breathing slowed even more as the door swung inward.

What the hell? In walked a beautiful young woman, around twenty-eight years of age, with a small, wheeled suitcase and a large shoulder bag with a light jacket tucked through the strap. Her long, dark brown hair was pulled back in a ponytail that flopped over her shoulder, partially obscuring the word "Columbia" on her gray sweatshirt. She was wearing blue jeans ripped on the right knee. To finish off the ensemble, she was wearing purple Converse high tops. He lowered his weapon slightly and replaced the pin in the stun grenade as she stopped in the doorway at the sight of all the clutter in the hallway.

"Shae?" she whispered as if in shock, then louder. "Shae, are you okay?"

At this point, a trained individual would have backed out of the doorway and gotten the hell out of there, but this lady, like most civilians, not hearing anything to be alarmed about, shut the door, dropped her bags and proceeded to investigate. Big mistake.

She yelled again, "Jesus, Shae, what the hell happened?" She walked further into the apartment. She pushed open the door opposite, the one Terry was crouched behind, and turned on the light. He heard her take a breath to call for her friend, but Terry was suddenly behind her, his left arm over her shoulder and clamping her mouth shut with his hand, pulling her back toward him in a vise-like grip. His right hand swung up behind her shoulder and pressed the barrel of the Walther into her neck just below her right ear.

"Don't make a fucking sound," he whispered.

She tried to scream but he yanked her head to the side and pushed the gun into her neck even harder.

"I fucking mean it, lady, shut the fuck up."

He felt the struggle go out of her, but he didn't relax his grip in the slightest.

"Now I want you to listen, and listen good. I don't know what the fuck has happened here, and I have no idea where Shae is. She works for me, and there are at least four bad guys outside watching this place. There's a good chance they are on their way up here right now, and if that's the case, we're both screwed. I'm going to take my hand away from your mouth, and when I do, I want you to answer two questions. Who the hell are you and what are you doing in Shae's apartment? Just so there is no misunderstanding, if you scream, I'll blow your fucking head off." He wouldn't, of course, but the threat should be enough to make her follow instructions. "Understand?" She tried to nod slightly, so he slowly released his hand from her mouth.

"My name is Kristen Burris, and I'm Shae's roommate. Please don't . . ." He clamped his hand back over her mouth.

"Shae doesn't have a roommate."

She mumbled into his hand, so he released his grip just enough for her to speak.

"I moved in six weeks ago. I work with her at NY&E Investments. I moved here from Miami after they hired me and spent three weeks in a corporate apartment. Shae and I work on the same floor, and we became friends. She knew I was looking for a place and said I could stay with her if I liked."

Fuck, fuck, fuck. What the hell had she been thinking? She must have known the danger she was putting this woman in.

She started to sob, and he was afraid she was going to lose it. He relaxed his grip a little more and moved the Walther away from her neck.

"Kristen, listen up, I need you to keep it together. I'm going to walk you over to your bag, and very slowly, and I mean slowly, I want you to empty it onto the floor. Then I want you to hand me your ID. Any sudden moves or if a weapon falls out of that bag, all bets are off, okay?"

She nodded. "Yes."

With his left hand he kept an iron grip on her left arm and pressed the gun against her kidney, and they slowly made their way back toward the front door. She leaned forward, and with her right hand, she picked up the shoulder bag and dumped the contents on the floor. Amongst all the usual clutter was a black and gray ladies' Coach wallet. She reached down, picked it up off the floor, and undid the clasp. She held it up so he could see the driver's license in the clear plastic sleeve. She was indeed Kristen Burris, and the ID was indeed from Florida. *Well, that's something, at least.* He breathed out in relief and eased his grip slightly. "Walk in front of me to the living room."

She started to ask a question, but he told her to hold off for a minute. There was one semi-intact chair left in the room, so he turned it right side up and pointed to it for her to sit. She was no longer sobbing, which was good, but now she looked angry.

"I know you must have a million questions, but first I need to know where you've been."

She looked at him as if she wanted to claw his eyes out, her eyes shifting from his face to the gun in his hand and back again. "I just spent the weekend with my parents in Indianapolis. It's where I'm originally from," she hissed. "Now what gives you the right to stick a gun in my face, huh? Who the fuck are you?" She almost spat the swear word at him.

"Like I said, I'm a friend of Shae's. She sent me a text that she was in trouble and needed my help. When I arrived, this is what the place looked like."

"Hang on, you said Shae works for you?"

"She does, but I can't get into that right now. All you need to know is that we have to get out of here and get you somewhere safe. I wasn't kidding about the four guys outside."

Kristen looked at the hole in the wall. "Who the hell did that?"

"That's down to me, I'm afraid. It was the only way I could get in without being seen. Listen, I'll explain more later. Now let's get out of here."

"Not without my carry-on, I'm not. It has all my important stuff in it, and I am going to need clothes and things."

"You've got to be kidding. You're in real danger here."

"No, I'm not kidding. I need my bag."

"Oh, for Christ's sake," he mumbled. "I'll get your damn bag. Come with me and wait in the doorway so I can keep an eye on you."

"What, you still don't trust me?" she asked.

"Not as far as I can spit, lady. Now let's go."

She stood in the doorway of the living room as he began to walk down the corridor. He was just about to pick up the carry-on when he saw the front door handle move ever so slightly.

20

SHAE'S APARTMENT, NEW YORK CITY, 1:50 A.M. EDT

Terry turned away from the door and ran toward Kristen. There was no point in being quiet now because he knew what was coming. "Get down," he yelled.

There was a loud bang as a shotgun round blew away the lock. Terry had already removed the pin from the M84 and threw it behind him as he dived into the front room. The door was kicked open. Kristen was lying on the floor screaming, and he covered her with his body, put his hands over his ears, opened his mouth, and closed his eyes. Half a second later, the flashbang did its thing.

Stun grenades are nonlethal, but they can have an astounding effect on the human body in a confined space such as a corridor, especially if you're not prepared when it goes off. The bang part of the M84 was around 180 decibels, enough to cause acute deafness, and the flash was about a million candelas, which would cause instant blindness. Terry, who had seen these devices used many times in Northern Ireland and elsewhere, was well aware of this, hence the cupping of his ears and making sure he wasn't holding his breath when the shock wave hit. Even with his eyes tightly shut and being in the next room, the flash turned the darkness into light, and he was distinctly aware of being able to see the room through his eyelids. The bang was mind-numbing and caused the entire apartment to reverberate. *Guess I'm waking up the neighbors again.* A split second later, he was on his feet and crouched in the front room doorway. There were two men down the hallway writhing and screaming in pain; another, although stunned and probably half blind, was firing indiscriminately toward him. Terry finished the shooter first with a double tap to the head and the chest and then followed up with the same to the other two. He was contemplating the silence when it occurred to him that there had been at least four of them. *Now where the hell might you be? Fire escape, dammit.* He spun on his heels to bring his weapon to bear, and his suspicion was confirmed when a bullet slammed into the doorjamb about an inch from his head. *Sometimes it sucks to be right.* He flinched to the left instinctively as the second round missed its intended target and clipped the top of his ear. *Fuck, that's going to leave a mark.* He emptied the rest of his mag through the window at the shadow that was moving to one side. There was a yell and a clatter as what he presumed to be the assailant's weapon fell onto the metal landing. He wanted to follow through and make sure the man was permanently down, but Kristen was still screaming her ass off. He walked back into the room and lifted her from the floor by her shoulders. He took her head gently between his hands and looked into her teary eyes.

"Kristen," he whispered. Then louder, as she didn't seem to be focused on him. "Kristen, we have to get out of here right now. There may be more of them, okay, and the last thing we want to do is try and explain this to the cops."

She nodded and between gasping sobs whispered, "Okay."

He picked up her purse and shoved it in his pocket before guiding her through the hole he had made in the wall. He took one last look behind him before tossing the smoke grenade back into the apartment. *If there is anyone backing them up, that will slow them down just enough.*

Picking up his rucksack and setting it on the table, he ejected the now-empty magazine from the silenced Walther and reloaded. He then put two full mags in one jacket pocket, the remaining flashbang and another smoke grenade in the other. Once they got out of the building, they had to get a block west to his SUV and he sure as hell wasn't taking any chances. Walking over to the sink, he washed the side of his face and ear before slapping on an oversized Band-Aid. It wasn't bleeding too badly, but the last thing he needed was to attract any unwanted attention.

He hurried her down the stairs, still keeping her a couple of steps in front of him. *Can't be too careful.* The Walther was still in his hand, tucked inside his jacket. When they got down to the main door, he opened it slightly and looked outside. The street was beginning to fill up with local residents who had been awakened by the noise. *Good, at least that will give us a little cover.* He grasped Kristen's hand, took a deep breath, and headed out into the street. He knew his suspicions had been confirmed when he saw the two women, now carrying large beach bags, from the bar about thirty meters away across the street, and he knew they were screwed. Unlike the rest of the onlookers, who were focused on Shae's apartment building, the women had immediately looked in their direction when they had walked out the door. *Fuck!* He quickly started walking in the opposite direction from them, half dragging the girl as he went. When they neared the end of the building, he leaned in close to Kristen.

"As soon as we get around this corner, I want you to run like hell for the next block and turn left. Halfway down the next street you'll see a black Cadillac Escalade with dark-tinted windows and Massachusetts plates. When you get there, hide by the front and watch down the street. If I'm not there within two minutes or you see anyone else come running around the corner, run like hell and find a cop. Okay?"

She nodded.

He glanced back over his shoulder and saw the two women walking quickly in his direction. The second he glanced back, they paused slightly, and he knew that they saw he'd spotted them. Then they were around the corner.

"Run," he yelled.

She seemed to pause for a second, so he pushed her slightly, and she was off like a born sprinter. He crossed the street and ran ten yards before taking cover behind the trunk of a car. He was hoping that the two women would be as useless as the others, but, unfortunately, they knew their stuff. Instead of blindly running after them around the corner, one of the women peeked around it and then what must have been a silenced MAC-10 machine pistol swung out and fired in his direction. *Fuck, she's good.* He ducked down as bullets punched holes through the trunk of the car. He ran in a squat two cars further down. He knew what she was doing, providing covering fire for her buddy to get across the street to get a firing position on him. Popping up, he returned fire in her direction, chipping the brickwork where her head had been. *Yeah, honey, I'm no amateur either. That should keep her head down for a second.* He ran down two more cars, took cover around the back of a Prius, and this time pointed his weapon down the sidewalk he'd been running along. There, a head appeared with blond hair from behind a car; he sent three rounds in her direction, shattering the rear side window. Her head ducked back behind the car just as he fired, and he hoped he had at least winged her but doubted it. The alarm on the car she was hiding behind started to emit that awful *woo woo* sound, and he prayed none of the occupants of the apartments along the street came out to investigate.

He turned his attention to the opposite side of the street and saw the other woman moving in his direction. He was about to fire when a volley of rounds from the blond slammed into the Prius. He ducked as the windshield disintegrated. *Fuck, that was close. Time to move before I get boxed in.* The alarm on the Prius started to scream. He fired back at the shooter and ran like hell as rounds shattered car windows around him from the woman across the street. More car alarms started their angry yelling into the night. Now he knew people would start heading out to investigate. He again took cover behind a car and reloaded. By now he was at the corner of the street.

"Time to get the hell out of Dodge," he said to himself.

He emptied half a magazine at the woman across the street and the rest at the woman on his side of the road, then ran like hell for the corner. They both opened up, and he dived for cover around the side of the building as the stream of bullets slammed into the brickwork.

Shit, these ladies really are good. Picking himself up, he ran down the street, figuring correctly that neither of them would be in a hurry to follow him around the corner. Finally reaching the Cadillac, he found Kristen crouched in front of it. He had already opened the doors with his key fob as he ran. He yelled at her to get in, then threw the Bergen backpack over the center console into the back and pulled out, thanking God he was parked in the opposite direction from which he'd just come. For good measure, he wound down the window and tossed the smoke grenade into the street behind him just as the rounds from one of their weapons found the back of the SUV. As he turned the next corner, he took the opportunity to glance over at Kristen. She was staring at him with eyes the size of dinner plates, obviously in shock. He smiled to try and reassure her.

"We're safe now. At least for the time being." She nodded, the numb look still in her eyes. "We need to find a place to rest up for the night and get you some food, okay?" Again, she nodded, then turned away, lowering the window and throwing up into the street.

He bought a decent laptop at the Staples on Union Square, which happened to be open twenty-four hours, then headed for the Aloft Harlem, a boutique hotel on 124th Street and Frederick Douglass Boulevard—the northern continuation of Central Park West. By the time he got there, Kristen was asleep. The second he touched her, she bolted awake in her seat and was about to scream until she saw Terry. They dropped off the Escalade with the parking valet, and Kristen waited in the lobby while he paid for a room with two queen beds. She followed him into the elevator without a word. He ordered some food to be delivered from Chocolát, a local restaurant with late hours, but she was asleep before it arrived. He decided not to wake her. He was starving, both from adrenalin and the exertions of the evening, so he ate both the meals. He was tempted to check out the thumb drive, but he was exhausted so decided to get a few hours' sleep. He set his alarm so he would get three hours' rest. *Tomorrow is going to be a busy day.* He was asleep within a minute of his head hitting the pillow.

21

MANHATTAN, 6:30 A.M. EDT

His fellow soldiers had always been amazed at the way Terry could fall asleep at the drop of a hat in the field no matter the circumstances, but now his problem wasn't falling asleep—it was staying asleep. Usually, it was only when he was in barracks or his apartment in London that he had difficulty getting a restful night. Not that he was oblivious to what was going on around him—the slightest noise caused him to spring awake. Now, though, the nightmares had returned. His mind seemed to want to exact some special form of revenge and let Terry have it full force. He was back in the bar the night Kieran Martin had been killed.

The bullets started tearing apart the windows, but there was no Ciaran Sullivan to pull him to the ground out of the line of fire. He just stood, watching the patrons crumple to the ground around him, until the only people left alive were him and Kieran Martin. Martin was standing at the bar, drinking Irish whiskey and smiling at him, smiling at all the death. Terry slowly made his way to the same metal door he had exited the night of the hit. Every step was like walking in molasses. As he walked outside into the deserted street, the same UVF letters sprayed in orange were on the wall, and there were three bodies in the exact same positions Martin and his bodyguards had been lying, except, in his nightmare, it wasn't Martin and his bodyguards.

He looked closer at the bodies. The one in the middle with her brains spilling out on the pavement and half her face missing was Ciaran. To her left was his old buddy Sergeant Major Steve "Bullet" Bailey, except his torso had been blown to pieces, and all that was left were his mangled arms and legs and a disfigured head. To Ciaran's right was his friend and minder Patrick Walsh, who had guided him through the intricacies of surviving in Belfast. Patrick's was the least damaged of the corpses, as only his lower jaw had been torn off by a British bullet. Terry wanted to scream, but his mind wasn't done with him yet. Ciaran opened her one remaining eye and looked directly at him, as if in condemnation for what he had done.

"Those fucking Protestant bastards," she wailed.

Then Patrick was looking at him, the hatred flowing like the blood from his jaw.

"I thought you were my friend," he accused.

Next it was Bailey's turn. His head fell to one side, and he just looked at him with a great sadness in his eyes.

"What the fuck went wrong?" he whispered.

Terry tried to scream, but instead, he started laughing, tears rolling down his cheeks as he doubled over. It was only when he straightened up and Ciaran was standing in front of him, her brains and blood flowing down the remains of her face, that he started to scream.

"Kiss me goodbye," she whispered, her mouth coming toward his.

He was suddenly awake, midscream and covered in sweat. It took him a second to realize he was holding the Walther as he desperately scanned the room looking for the nightmare from his past. He looked over at Kristen in the other bed, still sound asleep despite the commotion. He got up and walked over to the minibar fridge and helped himself to a couple of small, cold bottles of vodka. He didn't even pour them in a glass, just unscrewed the tops and downed them. Then he headed for the bathroom and took a very cold shower.

After ten minutes of washing away his demons, he walked into the bedroom and saw that Kristen was still asleep, so he took the laptop and headed for the bathroom once again. He wanted to see what was on the thumb drive without waking Kristen or risking her getting a glimpse of what was on it. After she had fallen asleep, he had stashed it between the box spring and the mattress just in case she had decided to see if he'd found anything at the apartment. While he waited for the new laptop to boot up, it suddenly occurred to him that they hadn't been after *him* at the apartment; they'd been after *her*. Why would they do that if she was only Shae's roommate? He and Kristen would have to have a little chat over breakfast.

It took five minutes to fire up the new computer, after which he downloaded Adobe Acrobat Reader and a few other programs. Finally, after a couple of restarts for updated programs to load, he was ready to go and inserted the drive. He was surprised there was only one file on it, dated five days ago. He opened it and stopped breathing for a second. "Fuck!" he mumbled. The first item in the file was an elaborate schematic for a bomb. It wasn't just any bomb, but a dirty bomb made with radioactive waste, and a big one at that. The next item was a photograph of an internal memo on NY&E letterhead in which the primary and secondary locations for these devices were mentioned in passing but not elaborated on. The one line that did grab his attention was that a final decision would need to be made regarding the four primary and secondary locations. The author of the memo, someone with the initials D. L., had gone onto explain that a dirty bomb with a large enough yield, and set off with the right easterly wind conditions, would have a devastating effect on the targets. Frustratingly, there was nothing about delivery method, precise locations, or the precise date of the attack. And the email was not written to a named recipient—there were just a series of numbers in the "To:" field. *How the hell had Shae managed to get her hands on this?*

The next three items were photos of a shipping container. Unfortunately, he couldn't see any of the markings on the container because its doors were open. There were five people outside the doors, four men and a woman. He enlarged the images, trying desperately to get a better look at their faces but the quality of the photos were crap, as they were taken at night. He would need a specialist to enhance them. Next, he took a closer look at the inside of the container and was stunned to see it was nearly fully loaded with weapons crates. *Sweet Jesus, the shit is really going to hit the fan.*

He heard Kristen call his name.

"One second," he shouted back.

I have to email this to K right now. After connecting to the hotspot on his phone, he wrote an email that fully described the events of the previous evening and a request to have the tech boys enhance the images as much as possible. As a mission statement, Nolan laid out that his goal, moving forward, was to find D. L. in the hopes that he could then find the location of the bombs, as well as Shae. He also requested any further information K could find on a Kristen Burris from Indianapolis. Next, he sent K a text telling him he had sent an email to his personal account and to confirm he had received it. He waited about a minute before the reply came that the email had been received. Once confirmed, he crushed the thumb drive by putting it between the toilet seat and the bowl, then flushed it down the toilet. If he did get grabbed by these bastards, at least they wouldn't know exactly how much he knew. He then broke the screen on the computer and stomped on the hard drive.

Kristen looked up at him as he exited the bathroom. Her head was cocked to one side, and she had that same sleepy expression his ex-wife and daughter would have when they had just woken up. It made him smile a little.

"What was that noise?" she asked looking at the damaged computer.

He sighed a little, thinking of his family. For some reason, that loss had been playing more and more on his mind recently. "Nothing to worry about," he replied with a shrug. "Just a spot of computer trouble."

She raised an eyebrow. "You know they have tech support for that?"

He smiled. "I know, but they just keep you on hold for so long I couldn't be bothered."

"Oh," she replied, looking at him as if he had lost his mind.

"Anyway, first up, let's get some breakfast, get showered, and then buy you some clothes. Okay?"

She nodded. "Terry, can you explain to me what's going on? I mean, those people were trying to kill us last night, and I at least deserve some sort of explanation. Let's face it—I know absolutely nothing about you or what is going on, but you want me to trust you, right?"

"Let's shower and eat first and then I'll tell you everything I can. Now, why don't you jump in the shower while I order food. I'm starving, and you must be famished."

"No kidding," she replied. "Just order me waffles and orange juice. Oh, and don't forget the coffee."

He gave her a jokey salute. "Yes, ma'am." While she headed into the bathroom, he found a menu from Sylvia's a couple of blocks over. The world-famous soul food restaurant had a great breakfast menu, and they delivered.

She had showered by the time the food arrived, and they proceeded to eat in silence—Kristen had the waffle and turkey sausage, and Terry had the country-style slab bacon with two fried eggs over medium and a side of grits and homemade biscuits. Kristen burped slightly when she finished, which made him laugh. She was about to start asking questions, but he told her to hold off until they were in his car.

The front desk was busy with guests checking in, so they just walked outside, Terry keeping his head down and away from any prying cameras, his Yankees cap pulled low over his eyes. Kristen stopped at the small shop next door to pick up some sodas and by the time she emerged, the valet was already pulling the Escalade up to the curb. Terry tipped him just enough so that it wouldn't be memorable. As they drove away, he looked over at Kristen.

"Okay, ask away."

She thought for a second. "Who were those people, and why were they trying to kill us?"

He had already thought up a cover story that would fit the events of the previous evening. He sighed as if he was reluctant to tell her anything. "I'm part of a joint task force with the FBI and New Scotland Yard. We've been investigating a group that is funding a Middle East terrorist organization, as well as others. We approached Shae a few years ago to help us find out who was involved. It seems there might be a leak in either the FBI or Special Branch, and she has been burned."

"Burned? That's horrible!"

"Not actually burned, but her work for us has been discovered by the bad guys. Sorry."

"Hang on a second, what group, and how could Shae be helping?"

"We believe that certain individuals at NY&E are funneling funds to these terrorists."

"Holy shit! So why were they trying to kill me?"

"I don't believe they were. I think they were trying to kidnap you and use you for leverage to get Shae to talk."

She fell silent for a minute. "So why aren't we heading to the FBI building or something?"

"Because I have no idea who to trust. God forbid I talk to the wrong agent."

"There must be someone you can talk to."

"There is, but you have to understand that it's not just Shae. We lost a number of other people a couple of days ago and they tried to take me out. Twice. I think the only chance of trying to find Shae is if I do this alone." *The best way to bullshit was to mix in just enough of the truth to make it seem real.* "If I can't find out something by tomorrow morning, then I'm going to the British embassy. I figure by then, whatever they are trying to get out of her they will have achieved or . . ."

"Or she'll be dead?"

He nodded. "Now it's my turn to ask the questions. You aren't just Shae's roommate, are you?"

"How do you mean?"

"You can cut the crap, Kristen. I know Shae is a lesbian, all right, and there is no way in hell she would have had you move in if you were just a roommate."

Kristen looked out the side window. When she looked back at him there were tears in her eyes. "We were trying to keep it quiet. Nobody at work knows. My parents didn't know. That's why we told everyone that I'm her roommate. Before you say anything about how being a lesbian is perfectly acceptable these days, we just weren't ready to come out yet. That's why I went back to Indianapolis. I knew it was time to tell my parents the truth. Of course, they had figured it out years ago and were really cool. Crazy, huh?"

"So why were they after you?"

"How do you know they were after me and not you?"

"Because there was no way they knew I was in the apartment. Spit it out, Kristen. What do you know? There must be something."

She looked at him angrily. "Dammit, Terry, I don't know anything. I didn't even know she was helping you till you told me."

"There must be something. Did she *give* you anything, a package or a safety deposit box key before you left?"

She looked exasperated and confused at the same time by his question. "I swear to God, Terry, she didn't give me anything. I wish I could help, honest, but I have no idea why they would be after me." She looked at him angrily. "For Christ's sake, don't you think I would tell you if I knew?"

"Okay, but if you think of anything, *anything*, maybe something she said in passing, something that seemed innocent at the time, let me know."

Kristen nodded. "So, what do we do now?"

"First, we're going to get you some fresh clothes and then I'm going to stash you somewhere safe."

"Like hell you are. If they've got Shae, I'm going to help you find her. If you won't let me help you then I'm going to try and do it myself."

He looked over at her, and her face was set in a look of determination. "You sure about this?"

"More than I've ever been sure of anything in my life."

He sighed. "Fine, it's your funeral." *Maybe I can use her to get into NY&E and then ditch her.* "There is one thing you can help me with. Who has the initials D. L. that works for NY&E or is an investor?"

"I have no idea. There must be two hundred or more people who work in the office."

"Well, it won't be some low-level person. It would have to be someone pretty high up in the food chain."

"There must be a listing of the board of directors and investors, but it's not available to people at my level. I know who the chief executive officer and the chief financial officer are, but most of the others I have no idea who they could be."

"Damn. We really need to find out who D. L. is. I haven't had a chance to check, but could this be on the company website?"

"No. It's a private company—they aren't required to make that information public. Hey, today is Saturday and the offices will be pretty much empty. I bet I could lay my hands on something."

"Not a chance, it's way too dangerous."

"It seems to me we don't have much choice. I can be in and out in fifteen minutes, thirty at the most. Just give me something to bust open the drawers of one of the executive secretaries. I guarantee you they will have that list."

Terry thought for a minute, but he really didn't have a better idea. "Fine, okay. So, what do you need from me?"

"Clothes, high-end designer label but casual, such as Tanaka jeans and makeup."

"That's it? Where do you want to go, Brooks Brothers?"

"You've got to be kidding me. Bergdorf's. And step on it."

22

NY&E OFFICES, MANHATTAN, 10:45 A.M. EDT

The plan they had come up with to get into the NY&E offices was so simple that Terry thought it might work. Of course, if the lobby security guard became a little too curious, then it would be a total nonstarter. They walked through the revolving door away from the morning chill of the city and into the warmth of the lobby—a vast cathedral of space reaching up at least six stories. Directly in front of them was a bank of ten escalators. Only two were currently running for the sparse weekend crowd. At the top of the escalators, Terry could just make out eight elevators, but he was sure there would be more, considering there were sixty-five floors in the shining glass and steel structure. In between them and the escalators were a couple of lush gardens on raised concrete beds, which provided the workers of the companies located in the building a place to sit and chat or just eat lunch. To the left was a pleasant-sounding waterfall. It was all very Zen. The lone weekend security guard sat behind a solid Carrara marble reception area to the right. *Wouldn't surprise me if the damn thing could stop an RPG.* Behind him were a bunch of monitors with live feeds of various building areas and the streets surrounding it.

There was also a monitor that was connected to cameras on the roof, every thirty seconds switching to a different view of the city.

Terry turned to Kristen and whispered, "Take a deep breath, okay, and just do it the way we rehearsed. Remember how you told me you did some acting in high school? Well, this is no different."

She looked at him and smiled. "Okay, Dad."

They were about ten steps away from the counter when the security guard looked up from whatever he had been watching in front of him. When he saw it was Kristen, he smiled broadly.

"Well, hello, Ms. Burris, I see you're back in town. How's the family doing?"

"Hi, Mike, they're fine, thanks for asking. As a matter of fact, this is my dad, Eric. He came back with me for the weekend and would really like to see where all the action happens."

"Hmmm." His mouth scrunched up. "You know the rules about guests visiting your office without an appointment."

Kristen gave him a big smile. "I know, Mike, but it's the weekend, so it's not like we're going to be bothering anyone. And the view from the office is so awesome." She gave him a sad look of disappointment.

"Oh, hell, I guess it's okay. Just be sure you guys are out of here in ten minutes, all right?"

"Do you want us to sign in?"

Mike thought about that for a couple of seconds and was about to hand them a clipboard with the sign-in sheet attached when he thought better of it and replaced it on the counter. "Better not. That may just invite questions." He handed Terry a visitor's badge. "Better wear this, though, in case you bump into any of the guys doing their rounds."

Terry clipped the badge to his jacket pocket and reached across the counter to shake the man's hand. He smiled broadly and put on his best Midwest accent. "Thanks, Mike, this really means a lot. The wife and I are very curious as to what our little girl is up to in the big city."

Mike laughed. "I have two of my own—teenagers! I don't blame you in the least. Have fun! And please make sure to return the badge on your way out."

"No problem, Mike, will do," replied Kristen. "Oh, by the way, if Shae comes in today, can you ask her to wait? She said she would join us for lunch if she can get her butt out of bed."

"Will do. Going somewhere nice?"

Kristen laughed. "I thought I'd take my dad to Katz's for a real New York pastrami sandwich."

Mike laughed. "Ah, a heart attack on rye! At least they have defibrillators there."

They were halfway up the escalator before Terry felt at ease enough to speak. "Very smooth. You handled that like a pro. You seem to have made a nice impression with only being here such a short time."

"If this can help save Shae, I am all in. As for those guys, they are really sweet. I make it a point of bringing them coffee and doughnuts at least once a week. My parents always taught me to respect the little guy. Hell, when they found out I was moving in with Shae, Mike and two of the other guards helped me move." Terry made a mental note that they may have been keeping an eye on Shae.

They arrived at the elevators. "You guys are on the top four floors, right?"

"Yup, and the offices we want are at the very top. I've only ever been up there once, which was when I met with HR and was offered the job. There's a reception desk right as you get off the elevator. I doubt there'll be anyone manning it on weekends, though."

"If there is anyone there, let me handle them, okay?"

The elevator was like a bullet on steroids. As it slowed for the sixty-fourth floor—the sixty-fifth contained the mechanics that enabled the building to function—Terry felt the g-forces pushing his feet against the floor. A soothing, electronic female voice announced their arrival. There was a soft ding as the doors began to open. They both exited. At the reception desk was a security guard wearing a suit.

Kristen smiled and walked toward the counter; this time, however, there wasn't a smile in return. He rose out of the chair, his right hand reaching slightly behind his back.

"What are you doing on this floor?" he asked testily with an obvious Irish accent.

Kristen was still smiling, seemingly oblivious to the danger. "Hi," she replied in a bubbly voice. "I hope you don't mind, but my dad is in town for a visit, and I work on the floor below. I really wanted to show him the view, but all the offices are closed, and I remembered that you can see the city from this hallway. Can we walk down to the windows at the end to get a better look?"

He shook his head. "You can't be up here. You need to leave. Now!"

Kristen was still smiling. "Oh, come on, it's no big deal. We just want a quick look." She turned to Terry. "If I'm right, Dad, you can see the new One World Trade skyscraper from that end of the building. It's . . . ."

The man started to come out from behind the reception desk. "I told you to leave, right the fuck now."

Terry chimed in, trying to defuse the situation. "Please don't use that sort of language in front of my daughter. Come on, Kristen, it's obvious we're not wanted up here. We better go." He turned slightly toward the elevator.

"But, Dad . . ."

"No buts, lady, fuck off the way you came from," the guard said.

Then he made the mistake of taking a step closer to the MI5 agent and pushing his shoulder. Terry turned and crouched, cat-like, and drove his iron-hard fingers into the guard's Adam's apple. He fell to his knees, gasping for breath. Terry was behind him in a flash and placed his hands on the guard's head, one under his chin and one just above the back of the man's neck. The guard, knowing what was about to happen, ignored how difficult it was for him to breathe and frantically clawed at the operator's hands. Terry ignored the guard's desperate struggle and, with a quick twist, broke the man's neck.

"I told you not to use that language in front of the lady, you fucking maggot," he exclaimed as he pushed the guard's lifeless body to one side.

Kristen gagged down the bile that rose in her throat and turned away hurriedly. "Jesus, Terry. Was that absolutely necessary?"

"Yes," he replied. "Best to get it over with now than have to deal with him later."

Terry grabbed the security guard and began dragging his body behind the security desk. "While I take care of this clown, you should figure out how to get the damn door open to the offices"

It took Kristen only a few seconds to find the buzzer underneath the counter that released the door lock. By then, Terry had the guard tucked away under the counter, out of sight from anyone exiting the elevator. Then they were in and searching.

"We need to move as fast as possible before his friends show up," said Terry.

Terry had bought a small pry bar at the Home Depot near Bergdorf's, and proceeded to pop open locked drawers of desks and the file cabinets behind them, allowing his accomplice to quickly search for the directory they needed. He knew they needed to get the hell out of there as quickly as possible; he was sure the guard wasn't working alone. He was popping open the drawers on his seventh file cabinet when Kristen yelled that she'd found something.

"Is that it?" he asked, pointing to the blue file folder she was holding.

"Seems to be. It is the main directory for the board and investors. Now I just have to find D. L."

"Just take it with us, we have to get out of here."

"We can't, Terry, without being asked a ton of questions from Mike. They even check our bags when we leave from downstairs."

"Shit! Okay. Step aside." He took out his cell phone and snapped photos of the pages, emailed them to himself at a secure server, and then deleted the emails from his folder and the photos from his phone's memory. "Got it."

He was about to run toward the elevators, but Kristen took the time to put the directory back where she had found it. "Despite all the broken file cabinets, no point in giving anyone the heads-up about what we were looking for."

"Good thinking. Now, let's go."

They were about to exit the glass doors leading to the elevators when the steel door to the fire stairs opened and two men wearing suits walked out. They looked through the glass at Terry and Kristen and then at the empty reception desk. Terry pushed Kristen to one side as both men went for their weapons. "Get down!" he screamed.

All three men had armed themselves at the same time, but Terry managed to dive to one side and roll away as they all fired. The glass shattered around them. Terry's first two rounds from the Walther caught the first man in the throat and mouth; the back of his head exploded all over the door as he crumpled to the floor. He was about to turn his attention to the second guard when he felt a sharp burning pain in his left calf. *Fuck!* He rolled again as more rounds hit the floor where he had been lying. He fired two rounds at the second guard, both of which hit him in the chest. The man was thrown back against the wall and was stunned for a second but raised his weapon to fire again. *Shit, body armor.* He fired two more rounds, this time aiming at the man's head. Both connected, and the brief firefight was over as quickly as it started.

He slowly got to his feet, his calf screaming in protest. "Motherfucker," he exclaimed, more in disgust at his bad luck than the pain. He limped to the nearest chair and half collapsed into it before pulling up his trouser leg to check on the damage. Kristen was kneeling in front of him in a flash.

"Oh my God, Terry, are you okay?" she said looking at the bloody wound.

"I will be. It's a through and through and doesn't seem to have hit bone or a major blood vessel, but it has done some damage to the muscle. Rip me off a piece of one of their shirts and bring it over. I need to tie this fucker off until I can take care of it properly."

She looked over at the two mangled corpses and hesitated for a second at the thought of getting any closer to them. *Jesus, what have I got myself caught up in? If this is what we are up against, Shae is most likely being tortured right now, or worse.* Then, shaking off her revulsion, she ran through the remnants of the door and tore off a large piece of the first guard's shirt. Seconds later she was back and bandaging his leg tight enough to stop the bleeding.

"Thanks. Now all we have to do is get past your buddy downstairs and we're home free."

They walked over to the elevators, and within seconds, one arrived. Kristen entered but Terry held back a second. "Hold the door, I'll be right there."

Terry walked back behind the security desk and searched the guard's pockets. He found the man's wallet and flipped it open. Nothing apart from a couple of hundred dollars, which he pocketed before returning to the elevator.

"Let's go," he ordered.

She was silent for a few seconds, but he knew there was more she wanted to say.

"You're not a nice man, are you, Terry?" The look he gave her sent a chill down her spine.

"No, Kristen, I'm not."

"You wouldn't do that to me, would you?" There was a slight quiver to her voice as if she feared his answer.

"Unlike the garbage I'm hunting, I don't kill civilians," he replied.

She tried to put a brave face on his answer but couldn't quite manage it. "Good, I'm glad to hear it. I'm not going to end up being charged as an accessory to murder, am I?"

Terry laughed. "For helping to take out a terrorist organization, I shouldn't think so."

In less than a couple of minutes, they were at the bottom of the escalator and walking toward the main reception. Terry did his best not to limp or let the bullet hole and bloodstain on his pants show. Mike was focused on a TV and looked up when they approached.

"So, what do you think?" he asked

"Very impressive, indeed," replied Terry. "I'm so very proud of my little girl." He smiled at Kristen.

"As you should be," replied Mike. "She's a great kid."

Terry handed him the badge. The security guard seemed to take a closer look at the Band-Aid covering Terry's ear.

"What happened there? Looks painful."

Terry reached up and touched his ear. "Oh, that. My own stupidity, really. I was working on a drill press at work with the guard up and the bit broke. Nearly took my damn head off." He laughed. "Kristen and the wife gave me a right talking to."

Mike laughed. "As they should, my friend. Anyway, a pleasure to meet you, Mr. Burris. No sign of Shae, but enjoy Katz's. I'll let her know you're heading over there." He winked at Kristen.

"Thanks, we will," she replied with a wink back. Both of them laughed, and Mike was still chuckling as they headed for the revolving door.

Once back in the Cadillac, Terry took out his cell phone and accessed the secure server. He and Kristen looked at what she'd found.

"It seems our mysterious D. L. is Daniel Lander," she said. "He's on the board of directors and owns a chemical company called Exconn Gasses, Inc., in Danbury, Connecticut."

"Danbury, that's what, about an hour from here?"

"I have no idea. I've never set foot in Connecticut, but I have a feeling we're heading there now." She had a grim look on her face.

He smiled broadly, happy to be in the chase. "Damn straight. What's the matter? I hear Connecticut is beautiful this time of year."

She laughed. "I'm a city girl, Terry. I hate the fucking countryside. And I was hoping we actually would go for lunch at Katz's!"

He was laughing hard now despite the throbbing pain in his leg. It felt good to laugh again. He tried to remember the last time it had happened and realized it was when his daughter had still been alive. *What was it about this girl that made him feel so at ease?* Also, he really did want to save Shae. What had started off as something to ease his own conscience had now morphed into something much more. Part of him knew she was most assuredly dead, but he still had to try for his and Kristen's sake. He dropped the SUV into gear and pulled out into the busy New York traffic.

23

DANBURY, CONNECTICUT, 1:00 P.M. EDT

Traffic out of the city had none of the madness of a weekday, so they made good time. On the way to the George Washington Bridge, they stopped at the opulent CVS pharmacy on Fourteenth Street and Eighth Avenue. Terry sent in Kristen with a list of first aid supplies to take care of his leg wound, which had started bleeding again. He also asked her to pick up three large bottles of Gatorade, as he was desperately in need of electrolytes due to the blood loss, and a couple of cans of Red Bull. He really needed to eat, but that would have to wait for now. While he waited for her, parked in a bus stop with his hazard lights flashing, he took the opportunity to text K on the developments of the day and where he was headed. He also requested floorplans for both the Exconn plant and Daniel Lander's house and stressed that they get a move on with the photo enhancement of the group at the storage container. A simple "Will do" was the reply.

When Kristen returned, he got out and climbed in the back seat. "You drive for now. I have to take care of this bloody leg."

"That's insane, you need a hospital. What am I supposed to do if you bleed to death? What about Shae?"

"Calm down, I'll be fine. It's just a simple through and through, and I've had much worse. Just focus on driving and, for Christ's sake, don't get pulled over. As for Shae, let's worry about saving her when the time comes."

She looked at him like he had lost his mind. She opened her mouth to argue but closed it when he looked at her. She turned back and put the car into drive. *What am I supposed to say to him, no? He is the best chance I have of getting Shae back and the last thing I want to do is piss him off so much he turfs me out of the car.*

As she pulled away from the curb, heading for the West Side Highway, he took off his pants so he could get a better look at the damage. There was a three-inch gap between the entry wound and the exit wound. After wiping away the blood, he had to admit to himself that he had been damn lucky. A couple more inches over, and he likely would have bled to death.

"Hey, Kristen. How did you and Shae meet anyway?" he asked. Not that he cared for backstory, but he had found in the past that talking helped distract from the pain he was about to inflict on himself. There was another reason: he wanted to see how naturally she answered his questions without having to think about them. Not that he thought she was lying about her relationship with Shae, but after carrying out hundreds of interrogations over the years, he had become extremely adept at recognizing when a subject was lying.

Now came the fun part. The bullet had carved a lovely round piece of his pants off, and it was likely that a small piece of material was stuck in the wound. If it stayed where it was, he would probably develop one hell of an infection, so every bit of cloth had to come out.

"At work, initially," replied Kristen. "We went for lunch a few times as friends, then I took the chance and asked her out on a date."

He opened the CVS bag and pulled on a pair of blue nitrile surgical gloves from the box she had bought. He ripped open one of the four-inch-long povidone-iodine-soaked cotton swabs. It would do the job nicely. Taking a deep breath, he pushed the swab into the wound until it appeared on the other side. He moaned loudly as the nerves in his leg protested at this interference.

"Oh, where did you go?" he gasped.

He pulled it through. No fabric. So, taking another deep breath he did it again, and this time he was rewarded as a small piece of pants material was stuck to the end as he pulled it out the other side. The wound was bleeding pretty freely now, and he was sweating like a pig, but he kept going.

"I asked her to the Coney Island Mermaid Parade. We had a blast, and Shae really got into it. She even dressed up. Anyway, it was when we were walking in the parade that I kissed her, and that was that. We have been a couple ever since."

Opening the bottle of iodine Kristen had picked up, he poured it liberally over the entry and exit wounds before soaking some non-stick dressing pads and pushing them roughly into each of the holes. He almost passed out but gritted his teeth to avoid screaming.

"Sounds like you two really hit it off?" he gasped as he spoke.

In the front seat, Kristen smiled to herself. "We sure did, Terry. I fell head over heels in love with her walking in a crazy-ass parade dressed as a mermaid."

Next, he busted out his secret weapon, two ultra-absorbent sanitary pads. Covering both holes with these, he taped everything up with surgical tape and then applied the bandage.

"Good for you, Kristen. You both deserve a chance at a future together, and I'll do my best to try and make that happen."

"Thanks, Terry. I appreciate that more than you can know."

Sitting back, he looked over his handiwork and was satisfied at the result. After putting his pants back on, he downed one of the Gatorades and quickly drank half of the second one. He was tempted to ask Kristen to pull over for food but decided they would wait till they got to Connecticut.

Within the hour, they crossed the state line and turned onto I-84 heading east. His phone pinged with a text message from K. "Call me ASAP." Terry spotted a rest area and asked Kristen to pull over. While she went to the restroom, he opened a Red Bull and stepped out of the SUV into a surprisingly warm day. *Crazy how warm it is for April. I bet it's raining cats and dogs back home.* He called K, who answered immediately.

"Terry, how are you doing, son?"

"Well, apart from a nasty little through and through in my leg, I can't complain. You have those blueprints for me?"

"Just about to send them. Listen, lad, you've really stirred up a hornet's nest over here. I briefed the prime minister personally, and she was all set to call the president but I managed to persuade her to hold off for now."

"Good. God forbid the FBI gets involved with this, because if they pick up Lander, he's just going to lawyer up and then we are totally screwed. Best to let me see how far I can get before involving the Yanks."

"My thoughts exactly. We do have some help on the way, however. A team of our Special Air Service chaps should be arriving in New York in about three hours and will await instructions at the consulate."

"The Americans aren't going to be pleased about that, sir."

"Fuck 'em. They don't have at least four dirty bombs heading in their direction."

"They could have already arrived. That's what we need to clarify, and quickly."

"Precisely. We've been doing some digging into Lander. It seems he's a bloody billionaire and has his fingers in a lot of pies. A subsidiary of Exconn deals with nuclear waste disposal."

"Oh shit."

"My feelings exactly. It's also estimated he has about one hundred million invested in NY&E."

"Does that make him the money man?"

"Oh, I would say he's more than that. He has been very vocal for years about Britain pulling out of Northern Ireland and returning the six counties to the South."

"I'm sure Dublin would love that. The Protestants in the North would lose their fucking minds. There'd be bombs going off in Dublin within a month."

"I hate to admit it, but you are most probably right. Here's the catch. He has some pretty well-connected friends in Congress. You have to try and tread carefully."

"I'll try, sir, but I can't promise anything. I guess it depends on how forthcoming he is with the information we need. Any news with the photograph?"

"You can forget getting anything about the woman—her face is turned away just enough that we can't run facial recognition. As for the others, we're putting them through the system now."

"Okay, good. What have you found out about the girl?"

"Kristen Burris was raised in Indianapolis, as she's said. Her parents have an Irish connection, but that appears to be her great-grandparents on her father's side, who came to the States during the famine. Other than that, we're still looking. We are also sending one of our consular people to talk to Shae's parents to find out if this relationship story holds water."

"Thanks."

"So, what are you going to do with her?"

"How do you mean, sir?"

"You can't keep her with you."

"Why not?"

"What the hell do you mean, why not?" said K, his voice starting to rise. "She's a bloody civilian, a liability for Christ's sake."

"It's not like I can just ditch her, sir. She's already said that if I do, she is going to try and find Shae herself. If she goes to the police and tells them what's been going on, we'd be screwed, sir."

"But Terry . . ."

"Anyway, sir. For some reason these bastards are after her; it wasn't me they were trying to grab at Shae's apartment. It isn't going to be long before the cops put two and two together and plaster her face all over the television, asking for the public's help in trying to find her. Sir, if that happens, she wouldn't last five minutes on her own and you know it."

"I know that, Terry, but think about the risk to the mission."

"The mission is a hell of a lot safer if she stays with me. At least I know ways to hide her in plain sight. You never know, she may prove to be useful. There is also the problem we've discussed in the past. After what happened to me on the boat and all the others, I'd feel a hell of a lot better about her safety if she remains with me. I'll tell you one thing, sir, this girl's got balls." He neglected to mention that, even though all the points he had made were valid, he was enjoying just having her around. Plus, she was, as the Americans like to say, a bit of a smart ass, and right now he needed someone who made him smile.

K sighed. "Okay, I'll let this thing play out, for now, but if she proves to be trouble, you are to dump her in some out-of-the-way hotel. Maintain operational security around her. Keep in mind this is bigger than any one person, including you."

"I know that, sir. That's why I'm talking to you right now. She's in the bathroom at a rest area along the highway."

"Fine, just make sure you keep your head out of your ass."

"Yes, sir."

"Oh, and if you are planning on going after Lander at Exconn, forget it. The place is buttoned up as tight as a drum. Not only do they have private security but they also have Connecticut State Police permanently patrolling the perimeter. Something to do with hazardous chemicals and gasses make the place a prime target for our Arab friends. Also, the perimeter is permanently floodlit and covered by numerous CCTV cameras."

"Bloody marvelous. So, I guess that leaves the house?"

"Yes. That's going to prove interesting as well. It's situated on a peninsula on the Candlewood Lake reservoir. Has a wall around three sides. I made some calls to a couple of British businessmen who have had dealings with Lander, and it turns out one of them spent the Fourth of July there with his family and a bunch of other guests. Lander also has a round-the-clock private security team. So . . ."

"A wall on three sides, you say. Good, then I have my way in."

"If you say so, old chap. When are you going to make a move?"

"Not until dark. Until then, I'm going to get some food and look for an out-of-the-way hotel."

"One thing to remember, Terry. They get the New York news channels up in Connecticut, and right now you are hot news as a person of interest in the Acela shooting; your face is running on all the local stations."

"Nice to know. Better make it a motel, then. I'll have Kristen check us in. I'll get back to you when I have more news. Have to go, she's on her way back to the car."

"Good luck, old man." And with that, K was gone.

He got into the driver's seat of the Cadillac and adjusted it to his liking. "All better?" he asked Kristen.

"Yes, thanks. Now what?"

"Well, I happen to know of this diner off Exit Ten that does this amazing Thanksgiving turkey sandwich with all the trimmings—mashed potato, gravy, cranberry sauce straight from the can. I presume you're hungry?"

"Hungry isn't a strong enough word. Famished is more like it."

"Yeah, I know the feeling. Buckle up, I'd sure hate for us to get pulled over for not wearing a seatbelt."

24

MI5 HEADQUARTERS, THAMES HOUSE, LONDON, 4:12 P.M. GMT

K hung up the phone and looked around the large glass conference table at the other men and women who had been intently listening in to their conversation. It was just after four in the afternoon, Greenwich Mean Time, a time at which most civilian office workers were watching the clock and biding their time until they could scurry away from their daily drudge. There was none of that here. There was a solemness of those gathered in the bowels of Thames House in a sensitive compartmented information facility, or SCIF, room. This one was particularly unusual due to its large size, but it still performed the function it had been designed for. They had brought in a criminal psychologist, who also worked as a hostage negotiator with New Scotland Yard for the phone call. K turned to her first.

"Well?" he asked.

She was still scribbling her thoughts down on a notepad. She stopped and looked up at him, pushing her glasses further up the bridge of her nose. "He's tired and in some pain . . ."

"I could have told you that, for God's sake. Let's forget all the psychobabble and get to what's important, shall we?"

She nervously looked down at her notes and looked up again, returning her glasses to their previous location. "I can say with near absolute certainty that he has not been compromised in any way. Like I said, he's stressed, but given his history and the amount of time in the field, I don't see it becoming a problem. However, the events surrounding his daughter's death and divorce and the fact that he seems to be latching onto the girl could prove . . ."

"Yes, yes, we've heard all that from you before." He neglected to add it had been on his mind ever since Shae's disappearance. Knowing how protective Nolan was of her didn't make things any easier. "As for the girl," he looked down at his notes, "Kristen Burris. He knows what he's doing, and he does have a point. If she were to go to the police, there would be hell to pay and our chances of stopping these NIRA bastards would be less than zero. Just tell me, us, can he see this through to the end, no matter the consequences?"

"Most certainly, sir."

"Good, now if you wouldn't mind leaving us, I'll call you back if and when we need you."

"Yes, sir. Absolutely, sir." She got up and headed for the door.

"One other thing, Rachel. If you breathe a word of what you have heard in this room to anyone, even your kids, ever, I will end you. Understand? No trial, no cozy prison cell. You'll just be gone."

She looked nervously at the other faces around the room, but none of their looks offered her any solace. "Absolutely, sir. I won't breathe a word." She scurried quickly out of the door, and it closed behind her with a pressurized hiss.

"By the way, per the prime minister, that goes for the rest of you, including me. We are not going to have a repeat of that *Spycatcher* bullshit." Everyone looked around the table at each other and nodded their understanding.

K flicked a switch in front of him, and there was a slight buzzing sound as the electronic countermeasures that prevented anyone from monitoring conversations in the room, as well as preventing telephones from making or receiving calls, came back to life. He took a sip from the coffee cup in front of him and let out a brief sigh. He hated lying to Nolan about who knew about the current operation, but this was now much bigger than the life of his agent, or Shae for that matter. Shae was already dead, no doubt.

"So, next moves, people?"

The secretary of state for Northern Ireland was the first to speak. "Obviously, we have to alert the rest of the Security Services and our counter-terrorism branch at the Yard. We also need to put our SAS chaps on standby so they can move at a moment's notice." A number of heads around the table nodded in agreement. K, as the head of the Security Service, or MI5, which usually focused on threats within the United Kingdom, and an individual known as C, the head of the Secret Intelligence Service, or MI6, weren't among them.

"No," replied C. "If we do that and these bastards get wind of it, they will go to ground. Then we have real problems because they could just pop up when we're not checking our radar. Right now, they don't know what we know, and we can use that to our advantage. This is probably the reason Terry is still alive: they're trying to figure out what information Shae passed along to him."

"I completely agree," replied K.

"One thing I will say," continued C, "is that we need to have some of our MI6 people briefed and ready to go in case your man falls off our radar for good." He saw that K was about to disagree and held up his hand to signal that he wasn't finished. "I know our MI5 friends might disagree with this, Northern Ireland being their backyard after all, but this operation has now spread way beyond their purview. Sorry, K, but that's just the way I see things."

"I must admit, K, this seems a hell of a risk, trusting the safety of the nation to just one man. What makes him so special anyway?" said the deputy prime minister.

"Before I answer your question, sir, I would like the others to know that for the purpose of these meetings I have been instructed that you, Sir Alec, will be acting as the prime minister's de facto deputy."

Sir Alec nodded in acknowledgment.

K smiled a little. "Sorry, sir, but if you knew Terry like I do, that question wouldn't even have crossed your lips. I have personally known Terry for thirty years. I met him right after Kieran Martin was removed."

"*He* was responsible for that?" asked the secretary of state for Northern Ireland. "But I thought that was down to the UVF."

K smiled and nodded. "That's what you were meant to think. He spent nearly a year undercover and very nearly was killed for his troubles at the extraction. What I am about to tell you doesn't leave this room." He looked at each of the attendees to reinforce the point before continuing. "Terry is one of the best, if not the best, agent working for MI5. He has been personally responsible for the elimination of a number of terrorist cells that were planning attacks against this country. He primarily achieved this by working undercover at great personal risk. These are operations, I might add, that none of you in this room are cleared to know about. Not only is he highly skilled with a variety of weapons as well as his bare hands, he is one of the most intelligent operatives to ever work for us."

"But how come we've never heard of this man before?" asked the deputy prime minister. "I mean, if he's as good as you say he is."

"Oh, he is," replied K. "As for not hearing about him, his real identity was scrubbed years ago and the identities he operates under are only known to a select few. His connection to an operation was once brought up by our last prime minister, and I offered to give him a full briefing about Terry, but he decided against it lest he ever let something slip. His cover is such that he operates strictly off the books and communicates directly through me unless there is an utmost need for him to contact MI5. In that case, he is code word protected. Put it this way, ladies and gentlemen: I trust Terry with my life and know he will do everything in his power and more to protect the citizens of this country or die trying."

C was the first to speak. "You have my support."

Others around the table nodded in agreement.

"Good. Now, if we can continue with the problem at hand," said K.

The First Sea Lord, Admiral Frasier, decided to add his thoughts to the discussion. "We also have to alert the Royal Navy about the current threat."

"Not a chance," replied K angrily.

"I'm sorry, K, but we most certainly have to. Not of the precise nature of the threat, but they must start monitoring all merchant ships in the North Atlantic. That includes all submarines we have on station at present. We should also have our Special Boat Squadron units report to all our submarines and surface ships in port and sail immediately. If your man finds out that these damn bombs are at sea, we need to be ready to intercept them."

"But security is what will make this operation a success and needs to be maintained at all costs," replied K.

"I've been thinking about that," replied the First Sea Lord. "The wonderful thing about our ships at sea is we can shut down all unauthorized communication at will. We can also give our captains and their seconds-in-command the heads-up with a for-their-eyes-only communication. The only person I would need to be read in on this fully is the Fleet Commander."

C looked at K and nodded his approval. "Seems reasonable, old man. We really can't risk these damn things getting through."

K sighed in resignation. They were right, of course, but it still pained him to disseminate any of this information. He had even had a heated argument with the PM about bringing in this group of people until she had put her foot down. "Fine. But the one thing you are forgetting, ladies and gentlemen, is that they may already be here."

"In which case, we are in trouble," replied the secretary of state for defense.

"Not necessarily," replied the Deputy Commissioner of the Metropolitan Police. "What the public doesn't know is that our CCTV cameras have the ability to detect the gamma rays emitted by radioactive materials. We can also have the cameras on our drone fleet and our helicopters do the same. I'm not saying it will be easy, by any means, given the amount of radioactive material that is used in hospitals, et cetera, but they tend to be stationary, so we can plot those locations. But it can be done."

"We can also do the same at our ports," replied the Permanent Secretary of HM Revenue and Customs.

"True," replied K. "Unless, of course, the weapons are shielded. Then it's going to be down to good old intelligence and police work."

"We still have to bloody well try," replied the Deputy Commissioner.

"I understand that, ma'am," replied K. "It's just that we have to be realistic of our chances if they get through."

"Has anyone thought of a possible date for this attack?" asked C. "After all, these lunatics tend to want to make a statement when they carry out these actions."

"Two dates immediately spring to mind," replied K. "And unfortunately, they are both this month."

"Jesus," muttered the Deputy Commissioner for the Metropolitan Police.

"The first," continued K, a little testily after being interrupted, "is the tenth of April. This is the date of the Good Friday Agreement. A number of our New Irish Republican Army friends look upon that as a sellout. If this is the date, then the devices are most certainly already here."

"Bloody hell, but that's days away," interrupted the secretary of state for Northern Ireland.

"And the other?" asked C.

"April twenty-fourth. That would be my best guess, if I was pushed, as it's the anniversary of the Easter Rebellion in 1916. As I said, if they want to send a message, this is the date they would use."

"I have to concur," replied C.

"What about potential targets?" asked the deputy prime minister.

"I would have to say London and, of course, Manchester, the second largest city in the country, are at the top of the list," replied C. "As for the others?" He shrugged his shoulders.

"The other thing we have to be aware of is there may be demands," said K. "If it was me running this op, I would detonate one of the devices in a smaller city and issue demands."

"Such as what?" asked the deputy prime minister.

"Well, obviously that Britain would relinquish any claim to Northern Ireland as part of Great Britain."

"That will never happen," replied the deputy prime minister. "Britain does not negotiate with terrorists."

"I'm sorry to say," replied C, "but in this case we may have to. Given the amount of radioactive waste described in the plans, the casualties alone from such devices would be catastrophic and the damage to the economy would bring the country to its knees."

A number of people mumbled their agreement.

"May I suggest we brief the prime minister on where we're at so far and meet back here around six in the morning? Do you think your man will be checking in by then?" asked C.

K nodded. As everyone got up, there were no handshakes, just looks of worry on all their faces. K sat, watching them leave, and took a drink of his now-cold coffee. He stretched and yawned slightly. It had been a long few days, and he needed sleep, but that would have to wait. He looked down at his phone. "Godspeed, Nolan. You're going to need it, old friend."

25

BLUE COLONY DINER, NEWTOWN, CONNECTICUT,
2:45 P.M. EDT

They had both opted for the Thanksgiving sandwich, which was basically a full Thanksgiving dinner, minus the green bean casserole and pumpkin pie, piled high between two thick slices of country white bread. Conversation during the meal had been nonexistent, as Nolan had been looking over the floor plan of Lander's property. When he was satisfied with his plan, he returned the phone to his pocket.

"Can I ask you something?" said Kristen as she pushed the remnants of her meal to one side.

"I guess."

"Are you married?" She was looking at the wedding ring he still wore.

"I was, but it ended a long time ago."

"What happened?"

"All my fault, really. We had a daughter. She died and I couldn't deal with it, so I buried myself in the job. The marriage didn't survive."

"I'm sorry," said Kristen. "To lose a child must be terrible."

Terry shrugged. "People die," he replied nonchalantly.

"But losing a child. I don't know if I could live with that."

He looked at her and she saw she had touched a nerve. *Maybe he isn't living with it and is just going through the motions?*

"You find there isn't much choice, Kristen. You just keep putting one foot in front of the other, and eventually you find a way not to want to scream every minute of every day."

Kristen could see the pain it caused him, no matter how much he tried to hide it. She quickly changed the subject. "So, what now?" she asked.

"First, we find a motel and you get some rest. I, in the meantime, have some shopping I need to do."

"But I want to stay with you."

"It's important that you try and get some sleep. Tonight is going to be very busy, and we may have to leave town quickly. In which case, you're driving. Plus, if anything should go wrong, I need you to get to the British Consulate in New York and let them know. They'll protect you until all this is over."

"By something going wrong, what you're actually saying is if you get killed?"

"Yes," he replied bluntly.

"Can't we just call the police or the FBI? You shouldn't have to do this on your own."

"Unfortunately, no. As I told you, it's partly a trust issue. The other problem with involving law enforcement is that we have no hard evidence of anything. The people involved in this would just get away scot-free."

"There must be something they can do?"

"Maybe after tonight, but for right now, no. If you're done, we need to get moving."

She nodded, so they headed out into the bright sunlight. As they got into the car, Kristen turned to Terry and kissed him on the cheek. There was a sadness in her voice as she spoke. "I lied, I really do love it up here."

He smiled back at her, reached over and gave her hand a squeeze. Without another word, they drove away to whatever fate awaited them.

26

BROOKFIELD, CONNECTICUT, 10:00 P.M. EDT

Nolan returned to the motel just before five and immediately hit the hay for some well-deserved rest. His shopping trip, although exhausting due to his injury, had been productive, but he'd left the gear he had purchased in the back of the SUV so as not to attract any unwanted attention. Kristen woke him up just after eight. He was surprised that he had slept through his alarm. *Must be more tired than I thought.* He rubbed his hand across the stubble on his cheeks. *What I really need is a shower and a shave and about ten hours' sleep.* After he splashed some water on his face and downed a large Red Bull, they headed out to Frank Pepe's pizzeria, a New Haven-style pizza place he'd heard good things about. The conversation as they devoured a white clam pizza pie washed down with the weirdly toothpasty Foxon Park White Birch Beer was lacking, apart from when Kristen dropped her napkin under the table. After retrieving it, she leaned across and whispered to Terry that his leg was bleeding again. Looking down, he saw three drops of blood on the floor, which he wiped away with the sole of his shoe.

"We better get out of here before this gets noticeable."

When they returned to the motel, he took a quick shower, and she helped him rebandage his leg. It was absolute murder, but he gritted his teeth and let her get on with it. He was worried he was developing an infection. For now, there was nothing much he could do. Now that it was after dark, he headed out to their vehicle and started to carry in the items that he had bought.

"What's all that for?" she asked.

He grimaced from the pain in his leg and held up the item she was looking at. "That, my dear, is a dry suit. The only way I have any chance of getting into Lander's compound is to swim across the lake. It's way too cold for a wetsuit, so I had to buy one of these. I also bought all the other equipment I would need—booties, gloves, tank, and a mask."

"Where on earth did you find it all?"

"I figured there is no way a lake this size doesn't have a nearby diving club with equipment for sale, and I was right. Of course, before they'd sell me the gear, I had to sign up for a whole bunch of lessons because I didn't have my diving certification with me."

"But you know what you're doing, right? I mean, that has got to be hard enough without a hole in your leg, and now?"

He angled his head to her and pursed his lips.

"Okay, sorry. Of course you do." She looked over at the other items in the corner of the room. "Is that what I think it is?"

"Sure is."

"A crossbow? You're not going all Rambo on me, are you?"

He laughed loudly. "No, but remember, the guys at your offices were wearing bulletproof vests."

"Right."

"A handgun isn't likely to penetrate body armor, but a crossbow bolt sure as hell will. If there are any guards on the lakefront, this will take them out and do it silently. I'll switch to a handgun once I get ashore."

"You're nuts. You know that, right?"

He gave her a goofy smile with crazy eyes. "Comes with the territory, I'm afraid."

She laughed. "So, what's the plan?"

"I plan to find Lander and question him till I find out who the others are that are involved."

"Don't forget about Shae."

"And I'll find out what's happened to Shae."

"That's it?"

"Yep. There's a great saying: KISS. Keep it simple, stupid. In other words, the more complicated you make an op, the more it's likely to go to shit pretty quickly."

"What's going to happen to Lander?"

He looked at Kristen as if he was going to answer but remained silent.

"Oh."

"Come on, help me get this gear ready."

"What do you want me to do while you're off making like Stallone?"

"I need you to wait on this side of the lake and make sure no cops turn up. I bought a couple of walkie-talkies—they're in the car. If anything goes wrong, do not get involved and try and rescue me or anything. I want you to call the preprogrammed number on my phone and ask for a man called K. He's my boss."

"By going wrong, you still mean if you're killed?" She looked horrified at the thought of him dying.

"Yes. Now this is important. If for some reason you can't reach him, go directly to the British Consulate in New York and ask for the trade secretary, no one else. Tell him what's happened and that I asked him to send the team he has there to go after Lander. It will most probably be too late to get him, but it will be worth a try. Tell him also to contact K or, if he can, reach out to C. Got that?"

"I've got it, but please do stay alive." She walked over and hugged him. "That's for luck."

Nolan was a little shocked but smiled and hugged her back. "Good, and I promise I will try my hardest not to die."

"Okay. So, what time are we doing this?"

"One in the morning. By then, most people will be asleep, so we shouldn't run into any nosy neighbors. We'll leave here at midnight, which will give us time to check out the area. Anything else?"

"Yes, but I get the feeling there's no point in asking. I did tell you this is nuts, right?"

"That's what makes life interesting."

27

MI5 HEADQUARTERS, THAMES HOUSE, LONDON,
4.45 A.M. GMT

K was back in the SCIF after having briefed the prime minister and joined C at their mutual private club for dinner. The briefing, which had been to the full cabinet—at the prime minister's insistence—had gone about as well as expected. Some of the members had wanted to throw rocks at the Security Services, but the prime minister had slammed her hand on the table and quickly quietened these voices by reminding them that if wasn't for MI5, a vast swath of the country would have ended up uninhabitable, and none of them would have been the wiser before the weapons were detonated. At the end of the briefing, she had asked for percentages in regards to stopping the attack. K had replied seventy-thirty. Many of the people present had commented that those odds seemed pretty good until he finished the statement by saying that it was seventy-thirty in the terrorists' favor of successfully mounting an attack. The room had fallen silent with the realization of the gravity of the situation.

The prime minister had sighed and looked at K. "Thank you for your honesty, K. Others wouldn't have been so blunt, but I fear a situation like this demands it."

K nodded. "Thank you, Prime Minister. Please be assured I have our best person on the job."

C brought up the possibility of preempting the attack by announcing that Northern Ireland was to be given its independence. This was quickly dismissed as unreasonable, as they hadn't explored every avenue yet. Besides, the Protestants in the North would reject such an offer out of hand. The meeting had culminated with the prime minister telling K that she intended to call the president of the United States as soon as K heard from his agent, good or bad. K stressed that, when they did talk, she had to impress on him that this was information for his ears only. He did, however, request that the investigation into the Acela shooting be reined in; the last thing they needed was their man being shot by one of New York's Finest.

Over dinner, K and C had decided to put whatever assets MI6 had available in the United States into play. Unfortunately, those assets were pretty thin on the ground; the United States being an ally, spying on them was frowned upon. By now, every possible air asset that could be brought to bear was conducting aerial reconnaissance for radioactivity over every major city in the United Kingdom. Most of the Royal Naval fleet would be sailing by morning; all their submarines had already sailed, and all Special Air Service and Special Boat Service personnel had been recalled to their bases until further notice. They even had the Royal Air Force reconnaissance squadrons plotting shipping in the Atlantic as well as the waters around the country. The problem, of course, was that it just wasn't enough. Though the Dover sole was no doubt exquisite, K doubted either of them had tasted one bit of it. After dinner, C had returned to Vauxhall Cross, headquarters of MI6, with the understanding that he would be back at Thames House, with his number two, by six in the morning.

K let out a long yawn and looked at his watch. Four forty-five a.m., another night without sleep. He took a drink of the room-temperature black coffee that sat in front of him. He would have to get some sleep soon, but he would wait until he heard back from Nolan. His phone was sitting in front of him, and he looked at it impatiently, willing it to ring. *Sod it.* He rose stiffly and stretched, then headed over to the coffeemaker on the small table to help himself to a fresh cup of the vile brew. *Why is it that government coffee always tastes like rubbish?* He had just filled a fresh cup when one of his intelligence personnel came running into the room carrying a laptop.

"Sir, the Zephyr reconnaissance drone you requested from the Canadians is about to arrive on station."

"About bloody time. What was the holdup, Eddie?"

"It seems our American cousins took a little persuading to allow it into their airspace. They eventually relented with the assurance that it was just an endurance test flight."

"Fucking Americans can be a royal pain in the rear sometimes."

The officer was taken aback briefly; it was the first time he'd ever heard K curse. "Yes, sir."

"Well, come on lad, pull up the bloody image, will you."

It took about two minutes before they were able to see what the drone was seeing. Which was nothing. The screen was black.

"Have you got their operator on the phone, Eddie?"

"Yes, sir." The intelligence officer held up his cell phone.

"Tell him to get his finger out and switch it over to thermal, as we can't see a damn thing."

The drone pilot on the other end of the phone must have heard him, as the image switched to thermal without Eddie having to say a word. Suddenly the image took on a reddish hue, and they could see the white heat blooms from streetlights and houses.

"Better. Zoom in on Lander's location."

In about thirty seconds, the compound filled the screen. Five more seconds and the thermal image had been fine tuned.

"Oh, shit," said the officer.

"Get me a secure line to the British Consulate in New York right now, Eddie." K looked at his watch as the officer ran for the door. It was five past midnight, Nolan's time. K grabbed his phone and hit his agent's number when it came up on the screen. It went straight to voicemail. "Goddamn it!" he yelled.

His intelligence officer ran back in the room carrying what looked like a large iPhone, except it had a short antenna and was thicker. "I have them on the phone now, sir."

"Yes, this is K." He motioned the officer to be quiet for a second, then gave the person on the end of the phone a seven-digit code. "I need you to put me through to the team commander." He then waved the officer back in as a *click click* could be heard on the phone. "Captain Huntington?"

K listened for a second.

"Yes, sir," replied the captain

"Do you have a helicopter handy?"

"I can have one on the roof in ten minutes, sir."

"I hope it's a fast one, son."

"One of the fastest, sir. An Airbus H155."

"What about the pilot? Can he be trusted?"

"Ex-British Army sir. Flew in Iraq and Afghanistan. Has his own company here but is exclusively used by the consulate in New York, and every now and again by the embassy in Washington, D.C."

"Good. Get it there in five. I need a couple of your operators to head up to Connecticut right now, and make sure they are the best snipers you have." He heard Huntington start yelling at his men.

"Heading up to the roof now, sir. Where exactly in Connecticut?"

"Good chap. Danbury. Oh, and make sure you have a medic with you and all his gear. There's a good chance he may be needed."

"Already done, sir. May I ask what's going on, sir?" asked Huntington.

"I'll fill you in when you're in the air. Call me back on this number as soon as you take off. And for God's sake, make sure it's a secure line. The last thing we need is someone listening in."

"Absolutely, sir."

K ended the call. His intelligence officer was looking at him wide-eyed. "Sir, you can't put men on the ground without the direct authorization of the prime minister."

He looked at the young man and smiled thinly. "Who said anything about them landing?"

28

BROOKFIELD, CONNECTICUT, 1:00 A.M. EDT

They had spent thirty minutes keeping watch in the neighborhood on the Brookfield side of Candlewood Lake before finally coming to the conclusion that everyone in the area was bedded down for the evening. There was a wooded park opposite Lander's property, so Terry had Kristen slowly pull into the trees with the headlights off. After five minutes, they were in a position where he could observe the opposite shore without being easily seen. Once in position, he began to change into the dry suit, no easy task in the pitch blackness and with a bullet hole in his leg. It was excruciating, but after ten minutes, he was geared up and ready to go. Using the driver's side mirror, he applied the camouflage cream he had picked up at the same store he had purchased the crossbow from, then did one last radio check with Kristen. He gave her his cell phone, then put the walkie-talkie in the small dry bag that also contained his silenced Walther. Picking up his flippers, he was about to walk away when Kristen wound down the window.

"Are you really sure about this, Terry?" she whispered. "Because I have a bad feeling that I can't seem to shake."

He looked at her and smiled, gave her a thumbs up, and proceeded to walk clumsily down to the water's edge. Once there, he squatted down next to a tree and took one last look across the lake using his night-vision device. He'd spotted one of the guards earlier when the guard had taken a moment to light a cigarette. *Fucking amateur.* The other had been harder to spot, but eventually he'd seen the guy move. *So, I have two at the rear of the house.* Terry figured the most he was going to have to deal with was four individuals on the outside and one in the house. He slipped the night-vision device in the dry bag, did a final check of his air, and slowly slid into the water.

The water was freezing cold, and the parts of his body not covered by the suit grew numb quickly. He swam slowly but steadily about five feet under the surface of the lake. He slowed every so often to check the compass on the diver's watch he had purchased, always heading toward the side of the beach where the non-smoking guard was situated. *Best to take out the smart one first.* Being an experienced diver, it took him less than fifteen minutes to make it across, even with regular pauses to stick his head slightly above water to check he wasn't drifting too far off course. By now, his leg was killing him with the effort required during the swim; the cold water brought him no relief, as the dry suit kept him warm. But, like so many other special forces operators, he had learned to pack it away in that special part of his brain where he boxed away the pain and pushed on with the mission. When he was twenty feet offshore, his fingertips grazed the bottom of the lake; he stopped swimming but remained underwater. He removed his flippers and clipped them to his utility belt. The crossbow and bolts were attached to the same belt. Unlatching the crossbow from its carabiner, he pulled one of the bolts from the hard case they were stored in. Cocking the crossbow by feel alone proved less difficult than he thought; loading the bolt would wait till he was finished with his other tasks. Removing his air tank, he took one last breath and spat out the mouthpiece. Slowly, very slowly, he raised his head above the water. Now came the tricky part.

Pulling the tank up the sandy bottom about two feet with his left hand, he let go of the shoulder strap and planted his left foot on it to prevent it rolling away into the depths. His eyes never left his target as he slid the bolt into place. Barely breathing, he raised the bow just enough out of the water to clear the lapping waves and took aim. The man was sitting on a boulder around fifteen feet from the water's edge and kept looking out over the water and then back toward his comrade in arms at the other end of the beach. Nolan took a half breath, held it, and fired. There was a slight click as the bolt left the weapon, and he worried that it had missed its mark until he noticed the man was no longer moving. He wondered where he had hit him, but it really didn't matter. Terry slowly backed away from the shore. After clipping the crossbow back on his belt, he put the tank back on and headed underwater to repeat the procedure on the other guard. A few minutes later, he was pulling his gear up onto the beach next to the second dead guard. He noticed the man was armed with a silenced Heckler & Koch MP5 submachine gun, so he left the crossbow and bolts with the rest of his gear and armed himself with the weapon as well as the spare thirty-round magazine that was stuffed in the man's belt. *Now for the others around the front of the house.*

Using the cover of some boulders and a firepit, he found that he was still about eighty feet from the main house. It was a two-story modern affair, all aluminum and windows, and the lights inside were off. Lying down next to the brick firepit, he took out his night-vision sight and spent a few minutes observing the property and the grounds. Nothing stirred. *It's now or never, Terry, old son.* In a crouch, he started to make his way toward the building and was about halfway there when the grounds were suddenly lit by floodlights mounted on the main house. *Fuck!* He raised his MP5 to shoot out the lights and a hail of bullets landed around his feet. He wanted to fire at his assailants, but the sudden light was blinding, and they remained in the shadows. *For some reason, I'm not dead yet.* He slowly lowered himself onto both knees, laid the weapon down beside him, and interlocked his fingers behind his head. It was only then that the eight dark-clothed figures emerged from where they had been hiding. They positioned themselves in a semi-circle around him facing the lake. He looked up at their faces; they were all cold and hard. One of them nearer the end spoke out to the others.

"The fucker killed James and Michael." The accent was pure Belfast.

Terry grinned a big shit-eating grin. "Good evening, gentlemen, how's your night going? Water's a little cold, so I wouldn't advise taking a dip."

The speaker took a couple of steps forward and kicked Nolan in the balls. "Fuck you, you British shit."

Terry doubled over in pain and curled up in a ball, moaning. While in the fetal position, he armed himself with the one thing that might offer him a chance to at least kill some of these shitheads before they finished him off. He heard one of the sliding doors open at the house.

"Now, now, Simon, please be nice to our guest." The accent was American, from somewhere out west, but with a hint of something else.

"Yes, Mr. Lander."

"Now, please apologize to Mr. Nolan for your rudeness."

"You've got to be joking, Mr. Lander, he fucking killed . . ."

Terry heard the click of a handgun being cocked. "If you lot want to go ahead and shoot each other, how about some ice for my balls and a nice mug of tea first?" he mumbled.

"Shut the fuck up, Nolan, before I shoot you myself," replied Lander.

"That's not exactly a nice way to treat a guest now is it, Lander?" mumbled Terry.

Lander looked down at his captive, shook his head, and refocused back on his man. "I said apologize. Now, Simon." Lander's voice had become stern, commanding.

"Yes, sir. I'm sorry I kicked you in the balls, Mr. Nolan."

Terry, still rocking slightly in the fetal position and moaning softly, nodded in acknowledgment.

"You see, Simon? He accepts your apology. Now we're all friends again."

This guy is fucking nuts. Nolan opened his eyes slightly to try and get a better look at where the men were standing. *Somehow, I have to take back the initiative before I'm restrained.* He started counting down from ten.

"Now, gentlemen, how about we help Mr. Nolan to his feet and show him into the house."

The first man had just touched him when Nolan heard a *wop, wop, wop* in the distance heading toward them. *Who the hell could* that *be?*

Suddenly, the men seemed to forget all about him and trained their weapons out over the lake.

29

MI5 HEADQUARTERS, THAMES HOUSE, LONDON,
6:23 A.M. GMT

Most of the others had started to arrive when K's secure phone rang. He snatched it off the desk and answered, leaving the room to be out of earshot of the others.

"Yes?"

"Sir, it's Captain Huntington. We're about to be over the target. We have nine men standing in a semi-circle around a man lying in the fetal position. I need your verbal permission to engage, sir."

"You have it, laddie. Be sure not to hit the man on the ground. He's one of ours."

"Will do, sir. Engaging now." The line went dead.

K looked back into the SCIF. What he had just ordered would probably cost him his career, but he didn't care. *Hopefully, Nolan is still alive, so it will have been worth it.* He walked back into the room, calmly helped himself to a fresh cup of miserable coffee, and resumed his seat.

30

CANDLEWOOD LAKE PARK, BROOKFIELD, CONNECTICUT,
1:18 A.M. EDT

Kristen was struggling to stay awake as she looked out over the pitch-black waters of the lake into the moonless darkness of the night. She caught herself nodding off again and snapped her eyes open. "Screw this! All this waiting is ridiculous. I should have driven around the lake to the house," she mumbled and stepped out of the SUV into the cold night air.

If anyone had been watching her, they would have wondered what the crazy lady was doing jogging in place and spinning her arms around like propellers in the middle of the night.

She walked down toward the shoreline, enjoying the calmness of the still air. As far as she could tell, all was quiet at the Lander house. Squatting down almost in the same location where Terry had entered the water, she dipped her hands into the blackness for a second, then wiped her face with the cold water

Standing up, she was about to walk back toward the Cadillac when floodlights sprang to life on the property on the other side of the water. To her horror, she could clearly see Nolan kneel and lay down a weapon by his side before putting his hands behind his head. *Oh my God.*

Watching the events unfold, she desperately wished there was something, anything she could do, but she was completely helpless. She was frozen with fear. She wanted to yell or scream but was afraid they would start shooting at her. Then the helicopter turned up.

She could feel the wash from the rotors as it flew in low over the trees. The shadow of the helicopter rose up higher, about halfway over the lake. She found her voice as the shooting started and began to yell "Terry!" over and over, but her voice was drowned out by the noise. Suddenly, there was a bright flash that, even at this distance, caused her to see spots and then an enormous bang. She ducked instinctively, then ran back to the car.

It was about a twenty-minute drive to reach the Lander house, but she knew he would need her, so she intended to make it in fifteen. Reaching behind the driver's seat, she dug around in the backpack until she found one of his other handguns. She'd never fired a weapon in her life, but that didn't matter. She knew it was loaded and that's all she cared about; she'd figure out the rest when she got over there. *I have to try and save him because he's my only hope of rescuing Shae.* All thoughts of her own safety left her mind as the wheels of the Cadillac dug into the gravel of the path she was parked on and threatened to spin her out; she corrected like a champ and sped off into the night.

31

LANDER'S HOUSE, DANBURY, CONNECTICUT, 1:25 A.M. EDT

The first rounds from the helicopter cut down the two men that were standing directly above him. There were no loud bangs, just the crack of the rounds as they impacted their targets. As the other men started returning fire into the night sky, Terry tossed the stun grenade he had removed from his belt while curled up in a ball toward them. The effects of the flashbang were not nearly as devastating as they were in an enclosed space, but it still gave him a few seconds to grab the MP5 and run toward the side of the yard. He had nearly made it when he felt a sharp burning pain on the side of his ribs. *Fuck! I've been hit. Again!* Diving to one side, more rounds hit the ground around him. He rolled so that he was facing the house and emptied the magazine, spraying the grounds. He saw one man go down but didn't have time to gloat, got to his feet, and made a dash for the side of the house.

The helicopter was still out there putting down covering fire. There were seven men down, one of whom was crawling toward the property until more rounds hit him from above and he lay still. Terry had no clue who was doing the shooting, but he didn't care. They weren't shooting at him, so all was good.

He looked up in the direction of the chopper and pointed at the floodlights; shots rang out again, and his world was plunged back into darkness. He started to make his way toward the open sliding door. Seven down, two to go. Running in a slight crouch, he had almost reached the opening when shots rang out, smashing the glass. Swinging the barrel of the MP5 to his left, he let fly, emptying half a magazine into the room, then dived through the open door and rolled for cover behind a large, overstuffed leather chair. He was waiting for more bullets to come in his direction, but none came.

Moving from behind the chair, he sprinted and dived behind a couch. Still nothing. Slowly rising to his feet, he made his way through the darkness further into the house, feeling along the wall for a light switch. Still no rounds came in his direction. Finally, his fingers touched a switch plate, and he turned on the main overhead light. The shooter, the kid named Simon who had kicked him in the nuts, lay crumpled in front of a large, marble-covered island. Walking over to the body, he checked the man's pulse in his neck for any sign of life. Nothing. *What a fucking waste.* He started to move from room to room looking for Lander, but the first floor was clear. *Where the hell are you, Lander?* He ran up the stairs and checked the bedrooms, closets, and bathrooms, still finding nothing, so he made his way down to the basement. It had struck him as odd while reviewing the blueprints that the house had a basement this close to the lake until he realized that the property sat on a slope high above the water. The water table had to be at least twenty feet below the house.

The door to the basement stairs was locked, but a couple of well-placed rounds opened it without a problem. He was sweating slightly from his exertions while wearing the dry suit as he made his way down the stairs. Reaching the bottom, he was about to start searching the various rooms when he heard a car engine start and a garage door open. Terry ran at the door he guessed led to the garage with his shoulder down and bounced off it back into the room. He felt like he had practically broken his shoulder. *Fucking steel door, dammit.* He lay on the ground for a second, the gunshot wound to his ribcage screaming, the gunshot wound to his calf throbbing, and now his aching shoulder protesting the abuse he had inflicted on it. "Yep, you've definitely got some broken ribs there, old chap," he mumbled to himself. He wondered why it had taken Lander so long to make a break for it until he saw the open gun safe in the corner of the room.

Heaving himself to his feet, Terry ran up the stairs three at a time in the hopes of making it to the driveway before his quarry escaped. He burst through the front door and ran as fast as he could across the lawn, but the black Audi R8—basically a street-legal race car—was already speeding toward the opening gates. He emptied the rest of the magazine at the sports car to no avail. He was hoping the helicopter was still around, but the night was silent apart from the roar of the engine. *Fucking son of a bitch.* He was about to give up when his Cadillac pulled to a stop in front of the gates.

He was running toward the Audi when he heard shots ring out from the car, shattering the side window on the SUV. "Kristen," he yelled, "get the hell out of there."

The driver's door of the Cadillac swung open, and he saw her rest her arms on the hood, then she started shooting. He heard glass shatter on the Audi as it spun off the driveway and impacted the brick column that supported the gate with a sickening crunch. "Fucking hell," he mumbled. Ten seconds later, he was running up to the Audi. He glanced into the side window; the windshield was gone, and Lander lay crumpled over the deflated airbag, dead. He kept running toward the far side of the SUV and found Kristen with her back against the side of the car, shaking. He took the SIG Sauer from her hand and placed it to one side. He knelt down in front of her.

"Are you okay?" he asked.

She looked at him and seemed to come out of her daze and shook her head, then she threw her arms around his neck and started to cry. He held her tightly and whispered in her ear.

"It's okay," he said. "It's okay."

"I thought you were dead," she sobbed. "I saw them catch you."

He tried to make light of it. "Don't you know by now, I'm like a cat, impossible to kill."

"But cats get run over," she replied as she started to calm down a little.

"Yeah, but none of them were driving cars."

She laughed a little, and he helped her to her feet. "Lander? What happened to Lander?"

He looked over at the car.

"He's dead?" she asked. A look of horror crossed her face as it occurred to her what that meant. "Oh God, Terry, what are we going to do? He was the only lead we had to find Shae." She started to sob a little.

"Hey, it's okay, I think we may have something better than trying to get information out of that bastard."

"Okay," she replied.

"We have to get out of here," he said softly. "If the cops weren't already on the way, they sure as hell are now after you were blasting away with that cannon."

He helped her into the passenger seat after clearing away the broken glass. "I'll be right back, okay?"

She grabbed his hand as if afraid to let him go. He pried her hand off his. "Seriously, it's okay, I have to get something from Lander's car."

"Okay," she whispered, and he ran toward the wreck.

When he had looked into the car's interior, he'd spotted a hard-sided black attaché case lying in the footwell. *That's why you didn't get the hell out of there sooner.* He tried the door, but it was still locked, so he shot out the side window with his silenced Walther and snatched the case off the floor. He was back in the Caddy in seconds. No sooner had he started to speed away than he heard sirens in the distance. He needed to get the hell away from there and get out of the damn dry suit as soon as possible so he could take care of his ribs, but first they really needed to ditch the car and find some other wheels.

As he finally headed out of Danbury, the heater going full blast to counter the cold air whistling in through the broken window, Kristen was already falling asleep from the shock and exertions of the evening. He was tempted to wake her up but decided to let her rest. Reaching into his drybag, he pulled out his phone. It rang immediately when he turned it on. He answered.

"Where the hell have you been?" yelled K.

32

MI5 HEADQUARTERS, THAMES HOUSE, LONDON,
6:57 A.M. GMT

"Sorry sir, I've been a little busy," replied Nolan. As he drove, he was holding on of the sanitary napkins against his side. It was bleeding as badly as his leg, but the last thing he needed was to pass out behind the wheel from blood loss.

"Yes, son, we all saw."

"You saw?"

"I had the Canadians put a Zephyr up earlier. I tried to warn you about the welcoming committee, but your phone was off."

"Sorry about that, sir, but it tends to put a damper on things if the phone goes off at an inappropriate time."

A new voice appeared over Nolan's phone. "Good evening, Terrance. Very well done. So, what is the news about Lander?"

"Who exactly is this?" asked the agent.

"This happens to be the deputy prime minister," the man replied, a little miffed.

Nolan paused before answering. "If you don't mind, sir, it's Terry. My mother only ever called me Terrance when she was mad at me."

There was laughter in the room, which made the agent a little pissed off. *What the hell is this, pizza and a movie night at MI5?* "As for Lander, he's dead, the girl killed him."

"Oh, how unfortunate. I thought the purpose of this evening's little jaunt was to find out what Lander knew. Pity it's been an abject failure."

He was growing red in the face. *Jaunt, fucking jaunt. I'll give this asshole a fucking jaunt.* Terry was about to explode when he heard K's voice.

"Maybe I should take this off speaker for a second."

Terry waited thirty seconds, his blood still boiling. Then K was back on the phone.

"Sorry about that, laddie."

"You can tell that pompous son of a bitch I said to shove his little jaunt up his miserable ass. Why the hell are all those people there? This was supposed to be off the radar."

"Thank you, Nolan, I'll take that under advisement. As for why they are here, the prime minister wants them involved, so if you have an issue with that, I suggest you take it up with her. Now tell me, what happened?"

"You know what happened, you were watching. It was a bloody set up. They were expecting me."

"How can you be sure they were expecting you? They could have just been lucky."

"I'd usually agree, sir, apart from one little detail."

"And what was that?"

"Lander, sir. He knew my bloody name, my real name. No doubt, no question, he knew it was me the second he walked out of the house."

"Oh, hell!"

"You can say that again, sir. We have a traitor in our midst."

"Could the girl have warned them?"

"One hundred percent no, sir. Those weren't fake bullets Lander was firing at her and she took him out like a champ."

"She trained?"

"I doubt that very much, sir. More luck than skill, I'd say. Plus, she could have taken me out or had a weapon on me numerous times. Sorry, sir, but she's as solid as they come."

"She could be playing the long game. We've done the same. Hell, son, you've done it in the past."

"Never killed one of our own though, have we? Anyway, I'd stake my life on her being on the up and up, and if it turns out I'm wrong and she is working for the other side, I'll eliminate her myself."

"You already are, Nolan. Just be aware of that. As for her working for the other side, I expect you to clean up your mess."

"Yes, sir."

"So, in your opinion, it has to be somebody on our side of the pond. Shit! That's not good."

"I'd say not, sir, and it doesn't help that every Tom, Dick, and Harry seems to know what's going on over here."

"This is now bigger than you and Shae, Terry, even the girl. We are talking a national crisis. Unfortunately, that means others need to be involved. Anyway, you'll do what you're told and leave the other stuff to me to sort out," snapped K.

"Totally understand, sir."

"Right. Was the deputy prime minister correct? The op was a total wash?"

"I think not, sir. Lander was delayed trying to make a run for it retrieving a case from his gun safe. I have it with me now. Seems to me there must be something important in it."

"Well, what the hell is it?"

"Sorry, sir, but I haven't had a chance to look in it yet. Kind of been more concerned about getting out of Dodge first, sir."

"Yes, of course."

"If you don't mind, sir, can we keep the information about the briefcase under wraps for now?"

"I'll make sure it stays between me, the prime minister, and C."

"Thank you, sir, I appreciate that. One other thing."

"What's that, lad?"

"Somehow, we have to keep tonight's events quiet. We need at least twelve hours, twenty-four would be better."

"Not asking a lot, are you, Nolan? I'll give the PM a call as soon as we finish. I guess she's going to have to give the president a bell after all. Can't promise anything, but we'll try."

"Thanks, sir. Oh, and can you have C's boys do a deeper dive on Lander? I can't put my finger on it, but there was something about him. Don't ask me what, but there was just something."

"Okay, Nolan, I'll get them right on it. Anything else?"

"No, sir."

"Are you okay? Physically?"

"Apart from being grazed by a bullet and a couple of broken ribs, I seem to be doing wonderfully, sir."

"Jesus, Nolan, you should have said. I have an SAS medic on that chopper. I'll have them back for you both in no time."

"Thanks. Most appreciated. Thanks for the help at the house, sir."

K smiled. "You are most welcome. Now let's figure out a place for them to give you a lift."

33

RIDGEFIELD, CONNECTICUT, 2:45 A.M. EDT

They had settled on the football field at Ridgefield High School for the pickup. Although there were civilian houses close by, it was far enough from the nearest police station that it would take the local police at least five minutes to get there. By then, they would be long gone. Terry had told K they would be at the field in forty minutes, as he had to take care of the car first. As soon as he got off the phone, he started to wake Kristen, but she was dead to the world. *Sod it, I'll give her another few minutes.*

He found the small, wooded area K had suggested for the disposal of the car less than ten minutes' walk from the football field. He was driving along the dirt road into the center of the wood when the bouncing around woke Kristen.

"What's going on?" she asked.

He grinned. "We're getting out of here in style."

She smiled back. "That will be nice. What do you mean?"

He tapped the side of his nose. "All in good time, all in good time."

Pulling the Caddy over and throwing it in park, he jumped in the back. "Now, if you don't mind giving me a little privacy while I get out of this damn dry suit, I'm sweating like a pig."

After a few minutes of grunting and struggling, he was finally free of his misery and wearing pants and shoes. His ribs were another matter. There was a nasty gash that was still bleeding. Looking down at the wound, he realized how lucky he had been. Another inch over and he could have been dealing with a collapsed lung, or worse, a bloody great exit wound where the bullet would have taken out a bunch of his ribs, causing him to bleed to death. He asked Kristen for a little help, and she obliged with another sanitary pad and a ton of surgical tape.

When they were done, he had her stand about twenty feet from the car while he rigged a small amount of C-4 to the gas tank and some more around the VIN on the driver's side dashboard near the windshield as well as the VINs on the door frame and engine block. No point in making it too easy to identify the car. He hooked all that up to a timer set to go in seven minutes, by which time, with a painful little jog, they should be at the field awaiting their ride.

They had just started running when he stopped. "Something's wrong," he said to Kristen.

"Like what?"

"I don't know." He started checking his bag. *Nope, that isn't it.*

"Terry, the explosives."

"I know, I know," he replied. He started checking his pockets, but they were fine. He was about to leave when his hand went to where the Saint Christopher medal should have been hanging from the chain around his neck . . . nothing. "Oh, shit," he mumbled.

"Wait here," he said to Kristen and started running back to the SUV. He quickly stopped the timers, none too soon as they were down to just over two minutes. He desperately started searching the car where he had been sitting, still nothing. A horrible thought crossed his mind that he could have lost it at Lander's house, but he seemed to remember it still being around his neck. *Where is it, dammit?* He ran to the back of the SUV and started running his hands over the ground. It was then that Kristen joined him.

"What is it, Terry?"

"Dammit, Kristen, I thought I told you to stay back."

She ignored that. "How can I help?"

"It's Miranda's Saint Christopher medal. I can't find it."

"Oh, hell. Where do you want me to look?"

"I don't know," he replied still searching the ground. "Maybe try the back of the Caddy."

"Terry, we really need to get out of here."

"Don't you think I know that?" he snapped, continuing to search.

Kristen nodded and hit the auto open button on the tailgate, which proceeded to beep as it went up. Both of them stopped what they were doing; the beeping sounded like screams in the night. Nolan continued his frantic search but was still coming up empty.

All that was in the back of the SUV were the different parts of the dry suit. Kristen shook the booties and the hood, nothing there. She grabbed hold of the full body suit and pulled it out of the back. There was nothing on the carpet lining of the vehicle, so she grabbed the dry suit by the legs and shook it. Like a shooting star, the medal flew out of the neck opening in the direction of the bag that Nolan had searched, and, as if by some supernatural intervention, covered the twenty or so feet and landed on top of it.

Terry watched it land on his bag. "Well, I'll be damned," he whispered.

"No kidding," replied Kristen, who stood shaking her head in disbelief.

Terry slipped it over his head and kissed it gently. His elevated heart rate began to slow. "We need to get moving. Start heading down that trail. I'll be with you in a minute."

Not wanting to delay the destruction of the Cadillac any longer, Nolan restarted the timers without changing the time left on them and began to sprint as best he could to catch up with Kristen. As he passed the spot where the medal had landed, he touched it and smiled. "Thanks, Miranda," he whispered.

Just as K had promised, they saw the helicopter come swooping in over the stands of the high school football field as they heard a faint *whump* in the distance when the Cadillac exploded.

34

MI5 HEADQUARTERS, THAMES HOUSE, LONDON,
8:00 A.M. GMT

Before heading back into the SCIF, K took the time to call the prime minister on her private line to give her a heads-up on the evening's events and to pass on his agent's request for a news blackout. She assured him it would be taken care of. He also told her that he was sure there was a mole working with the NIRA and that this would prove to be a bigger issue. She agreed and gave him the I'm-sure-you're-up-to-taking-care-of-the-situation speech. He thanked her, but if he had to be honest, he wasn't so sure.

Walking back into the SCIF, he helped himself to a fresh coffee, sat down, and turned on the electronic countermeasures. Looking around at the faces in the room, he wanted to explode but kept his tongue, as losing his temper right now might not prove fruitful.

"I just got off the phone with the PM and gave her an update on this evening's events."

"I hope you informed her what a complete shambles this operation has . . ." The deputy PM grew silent as K fixed him with an ugly stare.

"We have a mole working with the NIRA."

"Surely not," said the Deputy Commissioner of the Metropolitan Police.

"I'm sorry, ma'am, but we most certainly do." He sighed loudly and took a drink of the vile brew, wishing it was a twenty-five-year-old Macallan. "I want a list of everyone you people have told about this operation and the degree that they know what we know."

"Now hold on, old chap. Surely you can't think one of us could have spilled the beans?" said the secretary of state for Northern Ireland.

K started to lose it a little. "I'll tell you what I do know. My agent walked into a bloody ambush this evening, and if it wasn't for the help I had managed to provide, he would be dead, or worse."

"Worse?"

"An MI5 operative being tortured by the NIRA is worse than death."

He looked up at C, who nodded his approval. *Go on*, he mouthed.

"If you think I'm speculating about this, you should know that Lander called my agent by his name, his real name, and that, my friends, hasn't been common knowledge for a number of years, not even in the walls of MI5."

"Jesus," replied C.

"Precisely," said K. "Oh, and one other thing. If any of you hold back a name, and I don't care if it's your damn dog, you'll be spending time getting intimate knowledge of what is on offer for dinner from Her Majesty's prison system before the day is out. That isn't from me, by the way—that's a direct quote from the PM."

There was a look of real consternation on the faces around the table. Sir Alec, the deputy prime minister, and the secretary of state for defense looked like they were going to kick up a stink until C picked up his pen and proceeded to write down three names, his own being the first, on the pad in front of him. He tore off the sheet of paper and slid it across to K.

"That's it?" asked K.

"That's it," replied C. "I did warn them not to discuss this with anyone else, but if I were you, I'd have your inquisitors drag them in and slap a lie detector on them."

"Thank you, C, we will."

The other high-ranking individuals in the SCIF were not used to being called out in such a fashion but acquiesced to K's demand and started writing down names and what they had revealed. The only one of them who only wrote their own name and no one else was the secretary of state for Northern Ireland. Even discounting the men and women at sea, the list was still too long for comfort; there were over forty names. K rubbed the stubble on his face. *Christ, this is going to take weeks, and God knows who these people may have told.* K fixed each of them with a stare and asked if there was anyone else who may have been in a position to listen in or may have seen something in writing. That produced another thirteen names. *Goddammit!*

He wanted to ask them more, but suddenly the lack of sleep overwhelmed him. He took his leave of the group, asking them to reconvene in five hours, and headed up to his private oak-lined office and retired to the single bed that was kept made up in a small room at the back. He lay down and called his private secretary to tell her to wake him in four hours. He also told his number two to arrange for all the offices of every cabinet member, the prime minister, and all those attending the meetings in the SCIF to be swept for listening devices.

"If any of them protest," he growled, "have them take it up with the prime minister, then ask them politely to pack up their desks and start looking for another job."

His number two said he would, but K knew he wouldn't use the job-hunting line. K then told him to secure warrants for phone records of the names he had given him and for all the names of the people listed on the paperwork in his desk drawer. "I also want wiretaps on all their phones, aside from those in the cabinet and the PM."

He was assured that would also happen as quickly as possible. Finally, he got to switch off the light and close his eyes. *Three and a half hours isn't enough, but it's just going to have to . . .*

He was asleep before he had finished his thought.

35

HELICOPTER HEADING FOR NEW YORK STATE. 3:10 A.M. EDT

They had started running for their ride even before its wheels had touched down. The door slid open and a man wearing baggy cargo pants and a loose T-shirt waved them forward. Kristen slowed slightly when she noticed the semi-automatic handgun in his other hand, but Nolan, who was behind her, pushed her on. He wanted to tell her it was okay, but the downdraft from the rotors made hearing impossible. Kristen was having trouble making it through the rotor wash, and Terry was having a little difficulty himself, what with the weight of the Bergen backpack, the attaché case, his broken ribs, and the gunshot wound in his leg. The soldier gestured to one of the other men, who leapt out the door and unceremoniously picked up the woman and tossed her on board. He turned to help the MI5 agent, but Terry waved him away, threw his rucksack and case through the door and then, exhausted from the pain, crawled on board himself. The soldier in the doorway dragged him further in, then slid the door shut. The immediate reduction in noise was wonderful as the helicopter smoothly lifted skyward.

Terry looked up at the men, who were grinning back at him, as he pulled himself up and flopped into one of the plush leather seats. He nodded and turned his attention to Kristen, who was sitting in a similar style captain's chair. Between them was a minibar in place of what would have been a third seat. He grabbed a couple of glasses and emptied an airplane bottle-sized Grey Goose Vodka into each, handing one to Kristen, who took it with a grateful smile. He then downed the whole thing before opening another mini-bottle and pouring himself another.

"I hear you've had an interesting night, sir."

Terry laughed then winced from the pain. "You can say that again, mate."

One of the other men pulled out a gym bag that was between the seats. "Hello, sir, my name is Paul." He pointed to the other two. "This is Eric, and the boss over there is Captain Rupert Huntington." All three of them shook his and Kristen's hands.

"Thanks for the ride, gents. I'm Terry and the young lady is Kristen. You cannot imagine how much your help saved my ass."

"Oh, I think we can, sir." All of them laughed, and Terry joined in until his ribs caused him to groan in pain.

"Sir, why don't you take off that shirt so I can have a look at you," said Paul as he opened his bag of medical tricks. In a matter of minutes, Terry had an IV sticking in his arm, the bag hanging from a pop-out jacket hook above the door. After being injected with pain meds around the wound, he began to feel a welcome numbness. There was a blue pad spread under his side and over his lap, more to protect the interior of the helicopter than his clothes. The medic had cleaned up the gash over his ribs as best he could and was now applying some very neat stitches.

"I presume you've had a lot of practice at this," said Terry, groggily.

"Unfortunately, sir, too much."

Terry could see the wear and tear on the soldier's face—he had to still be in his twenties—from too many combat missions. "Sorry to hear that, son," he replied.

Paul smiled slightly. "Comes with the territory, sir." He looked at the scar on Terry's abdomen. "I presume you already know that."

Terry and the medic shared a brief look of understanding and then the stitching was finished. Paul applied a sterile field dressing and wrapped

Terry's torso in a gauze bandage. "Sorry, sir, can't do anything for the ribs." Paul handed the agent five more field dressings and an equal number of bandages. "Change it every day, and for God's sake, keep it dry. If you have to shower, stick a rubbish bin liner over your head like a jumper."

Terry nodded. "Thanks." He put the bandages in his Bergen. "While you're at it, can you take a look at my leg? I picked up a round earlier and it keeps bleeding like a stuck pig."

The medic frowned as he raised his pants leg. "Sir, that is pretty nasty. Are you telling me you swam that lake with your leg like this?"

Nolan nodded and winced as the medic started cleaning the wound.

"Another twenty-four hours and you would have been in deep shit from this, sir. Forty-eight and you would have lost a good portion of the muscle." He pulled out a syringe and proceeded to inject the agent with a large dose of antibiotics.

"Thanks again," said Nolan.

"What you really need is to rest up for a week to give those ribs and your leg a chance to start to heal, but I have the feeling that isn't going to happen."

Terry gave him a knowing look, and Paul shook his head.

As Terry was getting dressed, the medic handed him a bottle of antibiotics and one of codeine. Terry tried to refuse the codeine, but Paul insisted. "You'll thank me later, believe me."

While they had been taking care of his wounds, the helicopter had flown out over Long Island Sound. Huntington, who had been having a conversation with the pilot over his headgear, turned to Terry.

"Sir, the pilot would like to know if you would like us to take you to the consulate or drop you off somewhere else."

Terry thought for a second. "Can he take us to Westchester Airport? I need to rent a car and find a place to get a few hours' kip."

"And the girl, sir?"

"For now, she stays with me." There was no way he could risk putting her in the hands of the consulate because of the traitor in their midst. "I'm also going to need one of your communication sets and a rifle and ammunition."

Eric broke down his rifle and helped the agent pack it away in his Bergen, along with three full magazines of ammunition. He then removed his comms gear and packed it away as well.

"Thanks, lad. So how do I get ahold of you if I need you?"

Huntington handed him a satellite phone with his number already plugged in. "You'll also find your boss's number in there as well."

They were ten minutes from landing when the pilot radioed back to Huntington again.

"It seems our pilot has taken the liberty to order you a Lexus GX on his company account; all they'll need is a driver's license when we arrive. He has also booked you an executive suite with a connecting room at the Ritz-Carlton in White Plains for a couple of nights. Everything is paid for, and they have been told that you are a VIP who doesn't like to be disturbed."

Terry asked the captain to thank the pilot. Huntington spoke over the headset for a minute and grinned.

"He says it's all part of the service, sir, and good luck."

36

RITZ-CARLTON, WESTCHESTER COUNTY, NEW YORK,
10:00 A.M. EDT

Kristen was enjoying the luxury of the king-size bed as she slowly awoke. Suddenly, she remembered the events of the previous night and sat bolt upright in bed. It took her a second to remember exactly where she was as she looked around the room. She immediately felt incredibly guilty, having spent a night in comfort while Shae was probably going through hell; that is, if she was still even alive. Kristen had thought about insisting that they keep looking for her the night before but had been so exhausted, from both lack of sleep and coming down from her adrenaline rush, that she had been unable to keep her eyes open. She wondered how Terry was doing; he had told her about the impromptu medical care he had received on the helicopter as they drove over to the hotel. Getting up, she put on the fluffy hotel robe that lay draped over the end of the bed. Having no nightclothes or clean underwear, she had slept naked. After taking care of her morning ablutions, she walked over to the connecting door and lightly knocked. Nothing. She opened it and saw that Terry was still sleeping and was tempted to wake him up, but she decided that he needed the rest. She wrote him a note at the desk in his room. She remembered seeing a Macy's across Main Street in the Galleria mall when they checked in, so she helped herself to a couple of the thousand-dollar wraps of bills from his backpack. *Time for some fresh clothes for us both, I think.* After dressing in the clothes she'd worn yesterday, she headed down to the lobby of the hotel and nipped across to the store.

She was quite pleased with herself upon her return, having purchased outfits for both of them. Most important: fresh undergarments. She had guessed at Terry's size and hoped that what she had bought him would fit. When she entered her room, she heard the television on in his room and knocked before she walked in. He was sitting up in bed, alternately drinking coffee and fiddling with the locks on the attaché case.

"Good morning, Terry," she said happily, placing the bags on the foot of the bed. "I hope you don't mind but I took the liberty of doing a little shopping for us both."

One of the locks popped open. He looked up and smiled. "Thanks, I was kind of dreading wearing that gear from yesterday." He set the case aside. "So, what did you buy?"

She pulled out a couple of pairs of black Tommy Bahama faded jeans, as well as dark blue golf shirts of the same brand. She then produced a couple of quarter zip Tommy Bahama sweaters as well as Calvin Klein boxer briefs and dress socks.

"I hope you like them."

Terry felt a tinge of sadness when it occurred to him that Kristen was the first woman since his divorce who had bought him clothes. "Very much so," he replied. *Am I doing the right thing keeping her with me and exposing her to so much of my world?* He pushed the thought aside when he saw the spark of happiness in her eyes.

The big grin that spread across her face reminded him of his daughter when she would give him a Christmas or birthday present. He suddenly got a little choked up thinking about Miranda. He shook it off as she proceeded to show him everything that she had purchased for herself.

"And last but not least," she said joyfully as she pulled out a fairly small bikini. "If it's okay with you, I saw that they have a pool on the roof, so I thought I'd go for a swim while you do whatever it is you do." She pointed at the case.

He laughed. "Enjoy. I should be done with this in about half an hour. How about we grab lunch at the restaurant downstairs? And then you need to put in a call to your parents over the satellite phone. Don't worry, no one will be able to track it."

"Thanks, I'll do that. Hang on. I thought you had to stay a little incognito because of the news?"

He flicked between each of the twenty-four-hour news channels on the TV. The only one that mentioned anything about the Acela shooting was CNN, and they reported that a suspect was in custody. There was nothing at all about the events of the previous evening.

She whistled. "Wow, I guess you have some pull after all."

"Yeah, I guess so. Now bugger off for a bit while I see what was so important to Lander."

She laughed and gave him a mock salute. "Yes, sir," she said and ran for the door as he threw his socks at her.

He waited until he heard her leave her room for the pool before opening the second lock. After it sprung open, he left the lid closed, got up, closed the blinds, and turned off the light. In near total darkness, he lifted the lid slightly and slid his fingers in the gap and gingerly felt around for any wires. He was sweating slightly as he opened the case a little more and felt around inside. All he could feel were papers. Taking a deep breath, he fully opened the lid. Nothing. *It didn't go bang, that's a good sign.* He removed the papers from the case and, as a final precaution, placed the case on the floor at the side of the bed furthest from the door and the main light switch. Walking over to the closet, he took out the ironing board and held it in front of him as he flicked the switch. He cringed slightly as the room was suddenly bathed in light and breathed out loudly when nothing happened. *Thank fuck for that.*

After opening the curtains, he took the papers over to the desk and started to read. "Holy shit!" he mumbled.

37

MI5 HEADQUARTERS, THAMES HOUSE, LONDON,
4:00 P.M. GMT

K felt like total crap when he woke up but resisted the urge to slam down the phone that had brought his tired bones back to the living and go back to sleep. After shaving, which was something he usually took great pleasure in—to the point that he even used a shaving brush and single-blade safety razor—he showered, finishing it off with the water bitter cold, as was his way. He put on a fresh suit from the small selection he kept in his office and donned the regimental tie of the Coldstream Guards, of which he'd been a member in his youth. Anyone looking for his service records would find themselves dismayed, though; they had been sanitized of any mention of him years earlier—the records of his time at Sandhurst, the Royal Military Academy, gone with the wind.

Deciding he could no longer stomach the coffee at the SCIF, he sent one of his people off for a large café Americano with milk and sugar. *My wife would crucify me if she knew I was having sugar with my coffee, but right now, I need the energy.*

Within a few minutes, he was heading down to the basement in an empty lift when his secure phone rang. It was Nolan.

"Good morning, lad. How are you feeling today?"

"Much better, sir, thank you. The medic did a great job stitching me up."

"Glad to hear it. Now, what news, if any, do you have for me? I presume there was something interesting in that case?"

"How about a primary and secondary target list, for one."

"Really? Do go on."

"The primary targets are the City of London—"

"Well, that was a given," interrupted K.

"Yes sir. The others are Manchester, Birmingham, and Glasgow."

"Bloody hell! These bastards aren't messing around. I guess that rules out holding us hostage with only one detonation. They must know if they attack a major city, we could never negotiate."

"I guess not, sir, but that's above my pay grade."

"I have a feeling it's above mine as well, Nolan. Anyway, I digress, do go on."

"Yes, sir. The secondaries are Windsor, Sheffield, Liverpool, and Edinburgh."

"Hmm, Windsor . . . why Windsor, I wonder."

"I have it right here, sir. It has to do with wind direction. If it's a westerly wind, then London still gets hit."

"Of course, it would. Still, if the wind wasn't blowing that strongly, it could spare a major portion of the city. I don't suppose it mentions how they will be delivered to the targets?"

"I'm afraid not, sir, but I do have a shipping receipt."

"Bloody marvelous. I know I don't tell you this enough, my boy, but you are doing one hell of a job."

"Thank you, sir, that means a lot. It seems that the items were shipped on four separate containers, but it doesn't list the contents. The shipping company, Appella Freight Services, is based out of the Port of New York."

"How long ago, Nolan?"

"Sorry, sir, all it says is that the shipping was finalized and paid for two weeks ago." Terry heard K ask how long it took to ship a container from the United States to the UK, then the line went silent for a few seconds.

"Dammit! It seems it can take anywhere from ten days to two weeks to ship a container from the United States to Europe. What else?"

"One thing it does specify is that they had to pay more because all the containers were shipped separately."

"Now there's something. We may be able to locate the containers at sea if we move quickly. I'll get on the phone to the Admiralty as soon as we're done and have them check on cargo ships sailing from the Port of New York. So, I presume your next move is to pay a visit to this company?"

"Yes, sir. Tonight. One other thing. Any news on that facial recognition for the photograph I sent over? The reason I ask is that this paperwork also mentions some names."

"Run them by me and I'll kick the analysts in the bloody rear, as they should have something by now."

"One name I have in a copy of an email that might prove interesting is Congressman Nathan Brennan."

"Oh shit, a sitting United States congressman. Now, that does put things into a different light."

"Totally, sir. The other is a businessman out of New Jersey, a Kevin Stratton, and you'll never guess what his company does."

"Enlighten me, Nolan, and stop pissing about."

"Sorry, sir. I did some research online. It seems his company buys used medical equipment such as MRIs and X-ray machines, reconditions it, and then sells it on to other countries. His bio on the company's website also mentions that he is of Irish descent and that his great-great-grandparents came over during the famine after the rest of the family died."

"Damn! Well, that's one hell of a motive in a twisted sort of way. What's the name of this company?"

"Global Medical Logistics."

"And this is a legit business?"

"Yes, sir."

"I'll get the researchers on this right away. Maybe these morons are in the photograph, then we might have something to take to the FBI."

"Bugger the FBI, sir. All they'll do is slow us down."

"Sorry, Nolan. But it appears the president was just a little ticked off by last night's antics. I understand he settled down somewhat when he was advised of our situation."

"Shit, sir, that's just great. Now half the bloody press corps will have their hands on the story by this afternoon."

"I don't know, Nolan. It seems the PM was pretty adamant that it not get out."

"I do know. Remember what my cover is, sir? I actually did the job of a journo, so I know what I'm talking about."

"Maybe that's why you're such a pain in the ass. Never met a journalist who wasn't." K started laughing.

"Thanks very much, sir. Anything else on Lander?"

"No, nothing . . . Hang on a second, Nolan, one of my people just handed me something. Oh, hell."

"What is it, sir?"

"Hold on, Terry, I need to make sure this has been double checked."

The line was silent for a good minute.

"Nolan, I've got some extremely bad news."

"What is it, sir?"

"I'm sorry, Nolan. It's your ex-father-in-law."

"What? What happened?"

"It seems they made a play for your ex-wife last night at the family home. She's okay. However, it appears that your father-in-law was fatally wounded in the attack. Luckily, he had a firearm on the premises and took out two of the assailants. Two others managed to escape."

Terry was stunned. "There has to be some mistake, sir. I mean, there has to be."

"I'm afraid not, Nolan. We have your ex and her mother in protective custody."

"But why? Why would they? It just doesn't make sense."

"When did it ever have to make sense, son?"

38

THE PLAZA, NEW YORK CITY, 8:00 P.M. EDT

Something had changed in Nolan when Kristen got back to the room. Gone was the earlier jovial attitude; it had been replaced with a coldness she hadn't yet seen. She had tried asking him if everything was all right, but he just grunted in reply, so she'd left it at that. *I wonder what put him in such a bad mood? I'll leave it be for now and try and find out later.* The hotel had a steak house on the premises—BLT Steak, and they both ate like there was no tomorrow. Terry loaded up on protein, starting with a jumbo shrimp cocktail and a bowl of superb lobster bisque, then moving on to a sixteen-ounce NY strip, medium rare, with a side of hen-of-the-wood mushrooms and truffle mashed potatoes that he shared with Kristen. She went with the crab meat ceviche, wedge salad, and ten-ounce filet mignon, medium. For dessert, they split a crème brûlée with fresh berries. By the time the last bit of crème brûlée was gone, they were both ready to pass out in a food coma.

They headed back up to their rooms to rest before heading into the city. Kristen had fallen asleep and only woke up when Terry shook her awake at five. After packing their stuff, they had headed back down to the restaurant and dined well again—albeit with smaller portions—before driving out to the city.

It was past dark when they arrived in Manhattan; the rain was falling again, which perfectly matched the mood in the Lexus. The offices they were looking for were near the Red Hook Container Terminal in Brooklyn, and Kristen had thought they would head over there right away, but Terry insisted on checking into a hotel first. She was astonished when he pulled up in front of the Plaza. He smiled a little. "Might as well live a little, right?"

"I guess. Won't your boss be pissed off when he sees the bill?"

He looked over at her and grinned, broadly this time. "Totally, but fuck 'im. Anyway, it's not like you can take it with you. C'mon, let's go."

For a brief second, she hesitated, but then stepped out of the Lexus and headed into the hotel. Her eyebrows raised at check-in when she found out the room, or suite, to be more precise, was over $2,000 a night, and he'd booked it for three nights. She grabbed his forearm as they headed for the ornate elevators.

"Wow, Terry, have you lost your mind or something?"

"Could be the 'or something,'" he laughed. "Seriously, don't worry about it. Tell you what, how about we order the dessert cart after we arrive in the room? I haven't had a cigarette in days, and I could sure use some decadence right now."

She laughed with him. "I think you've gone nuts, but sure, what the hell."

They were shown to the Vanderbilt Fifth Avenue two-bedroom suite, which was indeed luxurious. Terry tipped their tour guide (which is what the bellhop felt like to him after showing them around) with a hundred-dollar bill, and the bellhop left with a smile. Terry was about to go into his bedroom when Kristen stood in front of his door, preventing his entry.

"Terry, you need to tell me what's going on. You've been acting a little off since I got back from my swim this morning, and I need to know why. I *deserve* to know why."

He looked down at the floor. "Tell you what, I have to hit an electronics store before they close. How about you order a bunch of desserts and a big pot of coffee, and when I get back, we'll talk, okay?"

"You promise?"

"I promise." He held up three fingers in the Boy Scout salute.

She moved to one side. "Like I said, off."

She took a bath while he was gone, which was well needed. The bruises from her night's adventure were really coming into bloom, the one on her right thigh being particularly painful to the touch; the bath seemed to drain away all her aches and pains. She needed her partner in crime—that was how she was beginning to think of him—to open up to her more and not be the stoic macho man of old movies. *Hell, I deserve that much from him after what we've been through together.* She planned to break that particular barrier over dessert.

Kristen was in her hotel robe with an embroidered Plaza *P* above the left breast, brushing her wet hair when Terry returned from the store. She had already ordered half a dozen desserts and two pots of coffee. He took the two shopping bags—one from Best Buy and one from Home Depot—into his room and told her he would shower. He appeared a minute later in his underwear with a large black garbage bag over his head. She laughed loudly. "Is this what all the fashionable secret agents are wearing this season?"

He spun around like a fashion model. "You don't like my new look?"

"On you, it looks good."

He sniggered like a kid and disappeared back into his room. By the time he emerged wearing a Plaza robe, their evening snack had arrived. He sat down across the table from her, poured himself a large coffee, and helped himself to a piece of New York cheesecake with a raspberry compote. After taking a bite and reveling in its silken luxury, he finally spoke.

"So, what do you want to know?"

She thought for a second before replying. "What happened this morning?"

He sighed loudly, then began to tell her everything. He didn't stop at that day's events but came clean—100 percent. When he finished, she sat in total silence, stunned by what she had heard.

"Should you be telling me all this?"

"Well, you asked," he said nonchalantly. "And what the hell, the chances are we'll both be dead before this is all over. Unless, of course, you'd like to knock your involvement on the head right now and we can call it a day?"

"Is that why you told me all of this, to get rid of me?" She felt hurt thinking he wanted her gone, and if she was brutally honest with herself, part of her wanted to run for the hills, but she couldn't do that, or could she? Kristen shook her head, no. *I'd never be able to look at myself in a mirror again.*

"Maybe, maybe not. I just thought it was time you found out how much shit we and Shae are really in. There is no shame in you heading home for a while until all this blows over once and for all."

She thought about that for a few minutes while she ate a particularly tasty piece of black currant cheesecake. "No, you won't get rid of me that easily, I'm in for the long-haul."

"Okay, it's your funeral, as they say. At least you can't accuse me of misleading you. At least, not anymore."

She was silent again for a minute. "You are sure this isn't some crazy hoax? I mean, nukes, for Christ's sake," she replied. "They are going to set off nukes."

"Not exactly. Dirty bombs. Conventional explosives to spew radiation. If they do succeed, then much of Great Britain will be toxic for many years, and a lot of people will die."

"And you're saying it's basically just you working on this, no FBI, no task force, nothing?"

"Yeah. Until the other day in Shae's apartment, we had no idea of what they were planning."

"Holy crap! But what about Shae, do you think she's still alive?"

"Honestly, it's doubtful, but you never know, we may get lucky." He smiled. "And we're the good guys remember, so . . ." He trailed off as she looked at him. "No, I'm afraid she's not still alive."

Tears welled up in her eyes, and she wiped them away. She wanted to scream and just break down in a corner somewhere but managed to keep it together. "Jesus," she replied. "We have to inform the FBI or somebody."

"It's already been done, at least that's what I've been told. Which is partly why there's been no news coverage of what happened at Lander's place. I think the reason they're letting me run with it for now is that I don't have to secure things like warrants, and not everything we have has to directly tie together. Remember, we don't have weeks or months to investigate this. Also, none of the information I've been able to gather has come into my possession legally. Now, I'm no lawyer, but I guarantee you that none of this would ever make it into a courtroom."

Again, she sat silently eating a large piece of Brooklyn Blackout cake, taking it all in. "So, you weren't just being flippant when you said you can't take it with you?"

He shrugged. "I guess not."

"Okay. Like I said, I'm in."

"Now hang on a second! Before you make a decision you'll regret. After tonight, I really was thinking of giving you enough cash to hang out here for a week and take it easy before sending you home to Indianapolis for a while."

"Nothing doing," she replied angrily. "You just said they've probably killed Shae. Terry, I can't ever feel safe until these bastards are taken out. I'd be looking over my shoulder for the rest of my life. Hell, they killed your father-in-law in cold blood. What's to say they wouldn't come after my family?"

"That's not very likely."

"Not very likely doesn't mean never. I'm in until we see this through. That's *we*, you and me. Anyway, you owe me for taking out Lander."

He smiled and held up his hands in surrender. "Okay, okay, you're in it till we win it." They both laughed, but it was gallows humor. He stood and started walking toward his room. "Come on, then, we've got some offices to rob." He was about to enter his room and stopped. "You know, I didn't want to mention this before, but you remind me of someone."

"Who?"

She saw the tears well up in his eyes. "My daughter," he replied. "She was a firebrand as a kid and crazy beautiful as well."

He shut the door to his room and leaned back against the door, rubbed his hand through his short hair, and took some deep breaths. *Nolan, you're getting too old for this shit.* It wasn't that he was beginning to feel overwhelmed, it was that he was beginning to feel conflicted between his need to protect Kristen and hopefully save Shae and the overall mission. It didn't help that the more he was around Kristen, his grief for what might have been with Miranda and his wife reared its ugly head with increasing frequency. What he really needed to do was talk to Amanda; she had been his rock since they had met in the islands until his daughter's death. But she had her own grief to deal with right now. He walked to the bathroom and splashed his face with cold water. Leaning on the sink, he looked at his tired reflection in the mirror.

"Just keep it together till this is over, dammit. You owe it to Shae, Kristen, and K."

He held out his hands and noticed a slight tremor. He shook them in front of him and held them out again; the tremor was gone. He smiled. It had taken a few minutes, but he was finally satisfied he had buried his pain back where it belonged, and he could keep moving forward.

39

APPELLA FREIGHT SERVICES, PORT OF NEW YORK,
NEW YORK CITY, 11:45 P.M. EDT

The rain was still steadily falling, causing the streetlights to glow with halos. Terry and Kristen had been sitting, parked on a side street, watching the freight company building for about fifteen minutes. Conversation was nonexistent as they both stared intently at Terry's target.

"What do you think?" she asked.

"Piece of cake," he replied.

The building was a two-story stand-alone red brick affair with fire escapes at both ends. They knew from the address the offices would be on the second floor, but unfortunately, K had been unable to find a floor plan online, so in that respect, they were blind.

"Are you going in from the fire escape?"

"Nope. Right through the front door. If there's an alarm, it will be in their offices, and seeing as other companies use the building, no one will be surprised to see someone going into the building this late at night. Now, if I was to be spotted on the fire escape lurking around, you can bet your ass the cops would be called."

"Good point," she replied. "I'll remember that next time I plan on breaking into a building."

They both started to giggle, and then they were laughing hard. It felt good to relieve the tension. They finally got it together, and Nolan handed her his night-vision device.

"Keep an eye out with that. If you see anything, get on the walkie-talkie."

He opened the door and was about to slip out into the night when she threw her arms around him and hugged him tightly. She held him there, not wanting to let him go. She really had begun to love this crazy British man. Sure, he was incredibly dangerous, but there was a gentleness in him, and she understood how his wife and daughter must have loved him very much. She could also see why the loss of his daughter was still affecting him so deeply after all these years. The thought of anything happening to him was almost more than she could bear. He touched her cheek with his hand and wiped away a tear running down her face.

"I'll be back," he said in his best Arnold Schwarzenegger impression as he released himself. "Always wanted to say that." They both started to giggle again and then he was gone, his head tucked into his shoulders, the raised collar of his coat protecting his neck from the cold rain while also hiding his face from any security cameras in the area.

As he walked away, she suddenly felt so alone in the world it was almost unbearable. She had come to accept that Shae was certainly dead, and now she was watching him walk away into God only knew what danger awaited him. She wanted to run and stop him, but knew that she couldn't, and it nearly broke her. *Take a breath, Kristen, he knows what he's doing. Just keep it together and do your job.*

The lock on the main door took a few seconds to disable with the battery powered Dremel he had purchased earlier at Home Depot. After the door shut behind him, he took out a small wooden wedge and shoved it between the door and the frame where the lock had been. Anyone checking that the building was secure would have to use their shoulder on the door for it to open. He ran up the stairs and took out the red-light flashlight he had purchased, shining it on the names on the doors until he found the Appella Service's offices. He opened the door with the Dremel, and he was in. He stood for a second as the alarm started to beep its warning, then walked toward the keypad and was relieved to see it was an older model. He set down the small backpack he was carrying and pulled out the alligator clips that were attached to a battery pack that he would need disable it. Hooking them up to the appropriate wires, he then ran another wire from his phone to the keypad and started a program that had been loaded onto the phone by MI5 for just such an occasion. It took all of five seconds for the beeping to stop. Keeping the alligator clips attached, he disabled the alarm wires and keypad permanently while maintaining the circuit. He sighed with relief that the program had worked—it was known to be a little temperamental at times. *Now where are those shipping manifests?*

There were a number of locked metal file cabinets, and he proceeded to pop them open one by one. Luckily, they were in alphabetical order, but he came up empty. *Where the hell are they?* He saw a glass-fronted door with the company president's name and title underneath it. This one wasn't locked, so he walked in and looked around. Still nothing. There were several pictures of ships on the walls, and he started to look behind them. There he found what he was looking for, a wall safe. *Bingo.*

It had always amused him how movies depicted blowing a safe as just slapping some plastic explosive on the door, and voila, it popped open with ease. In reality, to blow a safe door that way would require so much plastic explosive that either all the contents would burn to a crisp or the entire room would be taken out, and the safe would have remained closed. As he had learned, the problem with explosions is they take the path of least resistance, which, in the case of a safe, was out into the room, barely leaving a dent in the steel. What was actually needed was something with weight to put over the explosive and create a shaped charge to force the explosion inward. In this case, that was achieved with a garbage bag full of water hanging over the C-4, pressing it against the door. This plan also had the added benefit of requiring a smaller shot and putting out any potential fire. Additionally, it deadened the sound of the explosion quite dramatically.

It took him five minutes and then he was ready. He walked into the other room, took the radio out of his pocket, and keyed the mic.

"Is everything clear out there?"

"One second," replied Kristen. "Why, what's up?"

"There's a wall safe I have to blow. Keep an eye out in case it attracts any attention."

"Will do."

He hit the electric detonator, and there was a muffled bang and a flash of light from the other room. The door of the safe was twisted open and the room covered in water. There was smoke from the explosion, but nothing was on fire. Opening the safe door fully, he was surprised to see a great deal of cash on hand, at least $30,000. He quickly shoved it in his pockets and the small backpack and then started checking the papers in the safe. He smiled. There it was: a manila envelope with the name Global Medical Logistics.

Folding the envelope, he stuffed it down the back of his pants and then proceeded to toss files and paperwork all over the offices. He hoped to make it so hard to find what specifically was missing they'd put it down to a straight robbery for a few days. He removed the silenced Walther from his bag, slid it in his coat pocket, and took one more look around the office before slipping out the door. When he got to the entrance, he radioed Kristen to make sure the explosion hadn't attracted any undue attention, which it hadn't, so he walked confidently and slowly back to the Lexus.

"Got it?" she asked when he climbed back into the Lexus. She was grinning like the Cheshire Cat with relief at his safe return and reached over to grip his hand.

"Yup," he replied. "I told you I would be fine. Now, I don't know about you, but I sure would fancy a bottle of port with the rest of those cakes."

"Couldn't have put it any better myself."

40

MI5 HEADQUARTERS, THAMES HOUSE, LONDON,
6:15 A.M. GMT

It was 6:15 in the morning, and the heads of the various departments of the British government that had been at the previous meeting were already in attendance. Outside the SCIF, tables had been set up for a decent breakfast buffet; the British love their breakfasts to be quite filling. K settled down at the conference table with a nice British fry-up, right down to the fried bread that his wife would have never allowed to be served at their house. He had been reduced to oatmeal, a boiled egg, and wheat toast since his minor heart attack nine years earlier. Not that he could complain, really, as the strict diet and exercise routine his wife and doctors had forced on him had made him feel healthier than he had in years. The thing was, every now and again, he liked to splurge a little and pay for the consequences with an extra fifteen minutes on the treadmill.

He tucked into a rasher of bacon and took a sip of coffee; he'd finally sent his assistant out to buy some good stuff from Harrods the day before. Things were beginning to look a little less bleak after the phone conversation yesterday, and there were actually some smiles shared between the various members in attendance, this time around. All they needed now were the names of those bloody ships and the identification numbers for the containers. He had finished his breakfast and was helping himself to another coffee while chatting with C when his secure phone began to chirp. He pulled it from his suit pocket and gave a quick thumbs up to C before answering. It was Nolan.

"Good morning, son. I presume all is well with you and the girl?"

"Good evening, sir," responded the agent. "Yes, all is well with us. Everything went without drama, for a change, sir."

K chuckled. "Nice to hear it. So, what do you have for us? Hold on a second while I put this on speaker." They both heard a clicking sound. "Okay, go ahead, Terry."

"Yes, sir. The items we're interested in shipped out ten days ago. Two from Red Hook Container Terminal in Brooklyn and two from the Conley Container Terminal in Boston. All the containers were shipped separately. The two vessels out of Boston are the *Aegean Commander*, which is headed for Hartlepool, and the *Hamburg Dawn*, which is headed for Felixstowe. The two ships out of Brooklyn are the *Yankee Flyer*, which is headed for Liverpool, and the *Inge Nord*, with London as a final destination. I also have the container numbers." He quickly reeled them off.

"Absolutely fantastic, Nolan. Bloody good work. Give me one second."

K turned to his assistant and ordered, "I need someone to find those damn ships, now."

K started talking to his operative again. "Anything else for us?"

"No, sir. Anything for me?"

"Now that you mention it, I do. We have some information as to the identities of the men in the photograph. Three of the individuals are Daniel Lander, Kevin Stratton, and our friendly congressman, Nathan Brennan. Now the fourth one is most interesting. His name is Patrick O'Keith, a real nasty piece of work. He was an up-and-comer in the Irish National Liberation Army back in the day. Disappeared right before the Good Friday Agreement was signed. It was thought maybe someone in the PIRA had taken him out, as he was totally against the agreement and had made threats against Martin McGuinness, called him a sellout and a British stooge. You get my drift."

"Yes, sir, and I've heard of him. He was suspected in the death of two members of the Royal Ulster Constabulary and a number of other assassinations, if memory serves. Liked to get up close and personal."

"That's the one. He was also an expert at making bombs, although that isn't so widely known. Acquired that skill in Gaddhafi's training camps. I'm told he showed a real flair for it."

"Shit, that's just great. So, you think the INLA might be behind this? I mean, let's face it, there was no love lost between those animals and the IRA."

"Maybe, Terry. Or it could just be a bunch of radicals from both organizations who are dissatisfied with the peace and came together as part of the NIRA. If so, they certainly sent a loud message with the suicide attacks at the army bases the other day. What's strange is that there have been no claims by who did it to the press, and that's unusual."

"What about the woman?"

"Sorry, Terry, no joy there at all. There is one little piece of information that might be of interest to you. Kevin Stratton has a bloody big mansion in the Hamptons out on the eastern tip of Long Island. Playground of the rich and famous. What we can see from satellite imagery is that Stratton's compound is very secluded. From inquiries that we have made, we found out there is a private road leading to the property that is permanently guarded by armed security. C had one of his guys and another agent from the consulate do the we're-lost-can-you-give-us-directions thing, and apparently the gentlemen on the gate were not too happy, and they happened to have Northern Irish accents."

"So, you think that's where they could be holding Shae?"

"Maybe, but that is secondary to the mission at hand, and don't you forget it. If she is alive, the mission comes first before saving her, understand?"

"Yes, sir."

"We are sending up a Zephyr in a few hours to take a closer look.

We would put one up sooner, but it's going to take a while to get a flight plan cleared with the Yanks. Just another training flight as far as they are concerned, but they tend to get a little testy if they think we're spying on them." K laughed. "So, what are your plans for next steps? Coming home to roost yet?"

"Not yet, sir. If you don't mind, Kristen and I are going to have a couple of beers and get some sleep."

"Sleep. Yes, good idea. Just out of curiosity, where are you staying?"

"Oh, just a regular old hotel, sir. Anyway, after that I think I may pay a quick visit to Long Island and take a peek at what Stratton is up to."

"Fine. I'll let our chaps at the consulate know to be ready to gear up this evening."

"Thank you, sir. They may prove very useful."

41

HMS SUTHERLAND, NORTH ATLANTIC, 5:35 LOCAL TIME

The sun had just started to rise above the horizon. The weather in the North Atlantic had decided to kick up a few hours earlier, but it was nothing the Type 23 frigate couldn't handle. At five feet, eleven inches, Commander Joselyn Lee was a formidable woman. A former rugby player at Dartmouth, the Royal Naval College, she had also played for the Royal Navy women's team and could, if she had wished, have played for England. Instead, she had dedicated her career to becoming the master of her own ship, and now she had her. She truly did love *HMS Sutherland* and her crew and made sure that both were well looked after.

The order to set sail within eight hours had come as a surprise, as they had just returned from a long deployment in the Pacific. Her crew were tired and looking forward to spending some well-earned leave with their families, as was she. But when duty called, you rolled up your sleeves and got on with it, no complaining. They had sailed after just six hours.

Sealed orders marked top secret had been delivered by courier with instructions that they were not to be viewed by her or her lieutenant until out at sea. Just after leaving port, they had met in her cabin and looked them over.

They were to make full speed to an area three hundred nautical miles west of the northern coast of Ireland and monitor all shipping in the grid they were assigned. It was a large area but not something they couldn't handle. It was when they read the part about dirty bombs that eyebrows were raised.

"Make sure all the crew is fully issued with chemical, biological, radiological, and nuclear gear. I want the crew, as well as officers, drilled day and night until putting on CBRN gear is second nature."

"Yes, ma'am. They've been trained, ma'am, so they should be well-versed in its use already."

"I understand that, John, but if we do happen upon one of these things and it should go off, I want to make sure all of our people walk away from this. Understand?"

"Yes, ma'am."

"Also, let's review the drill for decontaminating the ship while at sea. No need to get into why we're doing it, let's just say, if asked, that it's on orders from the Admiralty."

"Yes, ma'am."

"Oh, and one other thing. Make sure our guests are taken care of. They are all invited to dine with me this evening, regardless of rank. Before that, have their officer in charge meet me in the wardroom. I want to know how much he knows and what he needs from us if we happen to find one of these abominable weapons."

"Right away, ma'am."

That had been two days ago, and she was pleased that her crew was now able to be fully dressed in their CBRN gear and at their stations in record time. Tonight, she would let them sleep. She had left the bridge and was in the operations room enjoying a well-needed cup of Earl Grey. She was looking at the plot her people were constantly updating of ships in her patrol area when she was notified of flash traffic from one of the ship's radio operators. She headed to the communications center, where one of them was decoding the message. When the decoder was done, he handed it to her like it was red hot. Joselyn headed up to the bridge.

"All ahead full," she ordered. The *Sutherland* was like a well-tuned

McLaren when she was let off the leash. The CODLAG (combined diesel-electric and gas) propulsion system drove the ship to her maximum speed of thirty-four knots. She looked over the radar plot and found her quarry. "Helmsman, make your heading zero four nine degrees."

"Zero four nine degrees, aye," replied the helmsman.

"Number two, have all officers, including our Lynx pilot and our guests, report to the wardroom immediately. We have been cleared to brief the officers and crew. Our target is the CSCL *Hamburg Dawn* container vessel." She pointed it out on the plot, approximately seventy-five nautical miles from their current location. "Lieutenant, stay here and man the bridge. If I'm not back in twenty minutes, bring the crew to action stations, MOPP level two for now. Also have the hanger crew get the Lynx ready to deploy."

"Yes, ma'am."

The briefing ended up taking thirty minutes; after precisely twenty, they heard the Klaxon sounding the crew to action stations. At the end of the meeting, the captain summarized everything that had been discussed to make sure everyone was on the same page.

"Ladies and gentlemen, to finish. It was decided that the Lynx HMA.8 would fly on the port side of *Hamburg Dawn*, just in case she refuses to stop or there is a threat to set off the device. Remember, we are under orders to sink her only if absolutely necessary. The *Sutherland* will come alongside the container ship on its starboard side. The seas should be calmer on that side of the vessel for boarding operations. This will be done after launching the Special Boat Squadron's Arctic 28 Rigid Hull Inflatable Boat a quarter of a mile out. We will also maintain a distance of one hundred meters between the two ships. This way we can have sailors with general-purpose machine guns mounted on the rails of the ship provide covering fire if needed. At this point all crew are to be at MOPP Level Two, no exceptions. Is that understood?"

"Yes, ma'am," replied the naval officers, the SBS officers, and others present.

"Once *Hamburg Dawn* is stopped, the crew will be taken into custody, hopefully voluntarily. We will continue with the operation until the specific container is found. Now remember, people, she is a big bugger, 187,541 gross tonnage, four hundred meters long, and a fifty-nine meter beam. It should also be noted that CSCL *Hamburg Dawn* has a capacity to carry nineteen thousand containers. I hope the container locations are computerized, which I am sure they are unless someone decides to disable the system. If the system is functioning, I have been assured by our SBS guests and the other two gentlemen from Royal Logistics Corps that they should be able to disarm the device fairly easily. Once that is done, we will allow the crew to continue to port while under watch from our men.

"I have just been informed by the Admiralty that, if the device has been armed, we are to evacuate most of their crew. Arrangements will be made to get a crew out to us from the Royal Fleet Auxiliary. Once they arrive, we will proceed to an as-yet-to-be-specified location in the Shetland Islands, where the disarming of the device will be carried out. That is all, ladies and gentlemen."

The meeting broke up, and they all headed to their respective stations. After changing into her Noddy suit, as the CBRN suits were affectionately known because they resembled the pointy-hatted children's book character, Joselyn entered the operations room to find out their exact location and how long it would take them to intercept their target. Forty more minutes left. She did a quick tour of the decks and stopped to speak with the SBS detachment who were readying their gear before heading back to the bridge.

They were ten minutes out now and rapidly catching up with *Hamburg Dawn*. Using her binoculars, she could clearly see the behemoth. At a quarter mile out, her second-in-command gave the order for all slow, and she watched as the RIB was lowered into the water with her special forces crew inside. A lifeboat was also being lowered and would hold station out of any line of fire, just in case the SBS men ran into difficulty and had to be fished from the ocean. The RIB would hold station off *Sutherland*'s aft until she closed with the container ship and ordered her to stop all engines and prepare to be boarded. That was when things might get a little . . . interesting.

Sutherland powered up again, and Commander Lee picked up her radio handset and called *Hamburg Dawn*.

"Captain, this is Her Majesty's Ship *Sutherland* of the Royal Navy. I am ordering you to stop your engines immediately and lower a ladder for boarding." Nothing.

She tried again, this time adding, "If you fail to comply, you will be fired upon."

This bought the desired response. "Sorry, this is Captain Aagesen. I was away from the bridge for a few moments. We are complying with your request." The ship began to slow noticeably.

All seemed to be progressing smoothly. As the RIB began to pull alongside the massive vessel, a large watertight door opened in the ship's hull about twenty-five feet above the waterline, and two crew members started to lower wooden and rope ladders so they could be easily boarded. Then Lee heard shots coming from the bridge. Suddenly, she saw two armed men running along the deck by the rail. One of them, realizing what was going on below, aimed his weapon over the side of the rail and was about to shoot at the SBS men when Commander Lee got on the radio.

"Take them," she ordered. Her men manning the two general-purpose machine guns had all seen what was about to happen and began firing just as she gave the order. Unfortunately, both guns fired at the same man who was about to open fire, shredding him instantly but allowing the other to disappear from view amongst the containers. *Hamburg Dawn* now began to speed up noticeably.

"Shit," mumbled the commander. She looked down to see the RIB pulling away from the ship while the last of the soldiers scrambled up the ladder into the bowels of the ship.

"Godspeed, gentlemen."

All she could do now was wait.

42

CSCL HAMBURG DAWN, NORTH ATLANTIC

"Andrew, Matt, with me," yelled the Special Boat Service captain. "We're heading for the bridge. Tom—you, Vic, and Tony take our two disposal guys up to the main deck and start looking for that container, but heads up, I just heard from the *Sutherland* that we have shots fired on the bridge. And some armed bastard is running around the deck, most probably heading for the container, so watch your backs, and please try and keep our friends from the Royal Logistics Corp alive. They may prove useful."

The two bomb disposal officers gave each other a quick look as if to say, Who the hell does he think he is? but decided against voicing their opinions.

"Now, let's move," ordered the captain.

Although they had been able to study a deck plan of the *Hamburg Dawn*, they still had to practice some caution as they reached each deck since they couldn't be sure of how many men aboard the ship were hostile. As they cleared each deck, they came upon a few occupants who were just hanging out in their cabins or sleeping. Each of the civilians, in turn, were confronted by two armed men and roughly searched before being ordered down below. The going was slow, and the SBS officer, Captain George Erickson, was tempted to split up the team before they got to the main deck, but that would be inviting trouble. Standard operating procedure demanded that they clear each of the lower decks before splitting, otherwise they could be opening themselves up to an ambush from the rear.

The container ship was really moving by the time they reached the main deck, and both teams went their separate ways.

Captain Erickson led his team up to the bridge, and the three men headed for the port side watertight door. Erickson took a quick look through the window in the door and ducked back down. There were two armed men. One of them had his weapon trained on the helmsman while the other had taken up a position covering the rest of the bridge crew closer to the starboard door. The captain lay bleeding profusely from a stomach wound and was propped up against the main console that ran the width of the bridge. The only way in would be to blow both of the doors with C-4 placed against the hinges.

Erickson ordered one of his men over to starboard and told him to blow the door on his "Go," and then he would blow the port door a second later and throw in a stun grenade. Hopefully, the first door being blown would distract the two men long enough for him and Matt to make a breach and take out the two men. There was no point in trying to fire through the windows, as they were thick enough to protect the bridge from Atlantic storms. Their L119A2 C8CQB assault rifles would take so long to smash the glass that the bridge crew would probably be dead by the time they were done.

Five minutes later, the special forces operator on the starboard side radioed that he was ready to go. Erickson and the other SBS soldier backed away from the door.

"Go," said the captain.

There was an explosion from the starboard side as the door was blown open, and a splitsecond later, Erickson blew his door and tossed in the stun grenade.

"One, two," he counted. The stun grenade exploded and both men entered the bridge, Erickson high, Matt low. The crew members were all lying around the bridge, obviously disorientated from the grenade. The plan had worked excellently, as both the terrorists had been focused on the starboard side door and were only just trying to reorient themselves to the threat behind them. The stun grenade had worked its magic, the terrorists barely able to see and firing blind. Within a second, both of the terrorists were dead—double tapped, one in the chest and one in the head.

"All clear," yelled Erickson as his other operator came through the door. "Andrew, take care of the captain and get some of these guys to take him down to the RIB. He's in a bad way, and we have to get him across to the sick bay on the *Sutherland*. Matt, check over the other crew members, I'm heading down to the main deck." He radioed across to the *Sutherland* to explain their situation and ran down the stairs to his other men.

Minutes later, Erickson opened a watertight door onto the main deck area and bright sunlight. He stopped for a second, the vastness of what lay before him causing him to pause. "Bloody Hell," he mumbled. Triggering his mic, he radioed the other team.

"Ozzy, where the hell are you guys?" he said to Sgt. Tom Osbourne, his number two.

"About halfway along the deck, sir, on the starboard side. I saw one of the fuckers as he ducked around a container, but I didn't have a shot. He's definitely making for the bomb, sir."

Erickson was running like hell along the deck when he heard shots ring out and then a sustained burst from a C8. His earpiece sprang to life.

"Got the bastard, sir."

By the time the captain caught up with the rest of his team, the ship had slowed down again and was nearly at a stop. He rounded the corner of one of the large containers and was greeted by the sight of his men and the bomb disposal experts standing around a body that was half in and half out of a container.

"Cut that one a bit close, sir," said Ozzy. "Another few seconds and we might all of been glowing in the dark."

"Nice work, Oz. Tony, can you go help the others with Captain Aagesen. He's in a bad way."

"Yes, boss," replied the man, and he was off, running for the bridge.

Erickson's radio crackled in his ear. "Yes, ma'am, everything's good." He listened for a second. "Yes, ma'am, they're all dead. There were four of them and we have located the container in question." He listened again. "Absolutely, ma'am." He laughed a little. "As soon as we are done over here, I'm sure the men will be glad to join you in the wardroom for a pint."

Smiles passed amongst the men who were listening.

"God bless the Royal Navy," said the captain, raising a pretend glass.

"And all who sail in her, cheers," replied Ozzy, doing the same, which really set them off laughing.

43

MI5 HEADQUARTERS, THAMES HOUSE, LONDON, 9:20 A.M. GMT

The main phone rang, and the deputy prime minister answered. K was just returning from a trip to the bathroom.

"It's for you," he said, handing K the phone.

K was silent for most of the call, intent on listening to the report he was receiving. After a quick thank you, he hung up.

All the room was waiting as he sighed before taking a deep breath.

"Per the Admiralty, HMS *Sutherland* intercepted the *Hamburg Dawn* just over an hour ago. There were four terrorists on board, apparently posing as paying passengers. There was a gun battle between these men and our Special Boat Service soldiers. All four terrorists have been killed. I was informed that one of them was mere feet from the device but didn't have the opportunity to arm it." There were smiles on the faces of everyone around the table. "The only casualty was the captain of *Hamburg Dawn*, who unfortunately died of blood loss. His wounds, I might add, were inflicted by one of the terrorists when he attempted to slow the ship so our men could board her. As for the device, our disposal team has disarmed it without incident."

"Well done, old chap," said the deputy prime minister, and he reached over the table and vigorously shook K's hand.

"Bloody good show," said the secretary of state for Northern Ireland.

While all the congratulations were being voiced around the table, K and C both looked at each other and remained silent. Eventually C held up his hands and the room slowly became silent.

"Do you know why she wasn't in port yet?" asked the leader of MI6.

"According to the crew," answered K, "it seems she had a problem with one of her turbines, which held them up for a few days departing Boston."

"So we got lucky," responded C.

The head of MI5 sighed. "Yes."

"What about the other ships?" asked the Deputy Commissioner for the Metropolitan Police.

All eyes turned to the First Sea Lord. "Unfortunately, ladies and gentlemen, it appears all the other vessels are now in port and unloading."

"Jesus," muttered the deputy prime minister.

"Arrangements are already underway to deal with this," said K. "Our friends from the Special Air Service have been tasked with intercepting the other devices."

"When is that supposed to happen, and why weren't we briefed earlier?" asked the secretary of state for Northern Ireland, somewhat testily. His frustration was turning to panic.

"You weren't briefed earlier because last time we tried that someone almost got Terry killed. As for our men going in . . ." K looked at his watch. ". . . well, actually, right about now."

44

AEGEAN COMMANDER, HARTLEPOOL DOCKS, NORTH WEST ENGLAND, 9:40 A.M. GMT

The captain of the *Aegean Commander* was having a frustrating day, and he was trying not to take it out on his bridge crew. They had arrived in port at four in the morning the day before, where they were promptly told by the harbor master that the crane operators were on a twenty-four-hour strike. Now that he was finally docked and unloading, it seemed as if those same operators were pulling a go-slow, as everything seemed to be taking twice as long as it should. "Friggin' English," he mumbled. By rights he should have been well on his way to Rotterdam by now to unload the rest of his cargo, but that wasn't likely to happen until well into the night.

The problem, as usual, was the upper management who owned his ship. They didn't care about a strike or a go-slow; all they cared about was the schedule and the money the delay was costing. Given the need for them to take their frustrations out on someone, he was the natural target, and his ass was getting sore from being chewed off every hour on the hour. He watched as another container made its glacial progress out of his hold toward the waiting transport. *Fucking unions.* What also didn't help were the four rough-looking men who'd made the journey across the Atlantic with them. They were ostensibly there to escort a container of medical equipment and were now far below him, pacing the main deck and cursing at anyone that would listen. Every so often, one of them would make his way to the bridge and give him a mouthful, but all he could do was shrug his shoulders and point at the cranes. He swore that the next time one of them came up to the bridge, he was going to punch him squarely in the nose. Finally, he saw one of them point at a container as it was being hoisted high up into the air. He slapped another on the back, and they all ran off the deck headed for shore and the eighteen-wheeler that was waiting for its load. He smiled. Well, at least that was one problem that was finally out of his hair. He took a large swallow of coffee and headed to the bathroom in his quarters to relieve his aching bladder.

45

HARTLEPOOL DOCKS, NORTH WEST ENGLAND, 9:40 A.M. GMT

Capt. Mathew "Taffy" Jones had been serving with the Twenty-Second Special Air Service Regiment for the past two and a half years, and he was due to rotate out to his parent unit, the Welsh Guards, before the end of the year. After he had received his briefing barely two hours earlier, it had crossed his mind that he may not be alive that long. The nine men he had with him on the mission, the seven from the SAS and two Royal Logistics bomb disposal experts, had seemed nonchalant, but professional, about the whole thing after he'd briefed them on the tarmac as they waited for the two 658 Squadron Dauphin 2 helicopters to arrive. He wondered if secretly they'd been thinking the same thing he was. *If this thing goes tits up, we're royally screwed.* It was too late to worry about it now, as they were already deploying to assault the ship.

The problem, as Taffy saw it, was that the container terminals had large open spaces between the ships, the gantry cranes, and the containers stacked to one side. Running across an open space of thirty meters in full view of everyone was not conducive to one's health. On the flight there, Taffy and his number two had been patched in to the SBS assault commander who had taken out the *Hamburg Dawn*, so he knew their objective had most certainly been accompanied by at least four individuals. The only way to achieve their goal would be to go in dressed as dock workers or ship's crew. After reviewing the few aerial photographs that they had found on the internet and the helicopter flight directly over the ship, a plan began to formulate itself in his mind.

Taffy was going to deploy two of his men, one fore, the other aft of the ship on top of the stacks of containers, armed with Heckler & Koch HK417 sniper rifles. Not only would they be able to remove any potential threats but they could also radio his men on any movement on the ship. Two of his men would commandeer one of the trucks used to move the containers to get as close to the ship as possible, and the others would casually walk toward the ship carrying their weapons in large shoulder bags as if they were crew. It was a risky move, but if anyone aboard the ship produced a weapon, they would regret it instantly. Taffy had personally spoken to the harbor controller after they had landed and given him a brief rundown of what was going on and his needs. It turned out the harbor controller was ex-merchant navy and was more than willing to provide them with every assistance. Within minutes he'd informed the crane operators that a military exercise was being held and to ignore the men on top of the containers. He'd also secured a vehicle for them to use. Looking over their clothing, the harbor master shook his head and proclaimed they looked way too neat and ran downstairs; five minutes later he reappeared carrying some scruffy coats, and he smiled in satisfaction as they put them on.

"Now you look like seamen," he exclaimed.

One of the nice things about the coats was that they were so large and baggy that the men could forgo the shoulder bags and sling their weapons underneath them.

That had been twenty minutes earlier, and Taffy's two men performing overwatch were in position and radioing back everything they were seeing, especially the four individuals roaming around the deck of the *Aegean Commander*. It had also been decided to wait until the container was being off-loaded from the ship and the terrorists were on the dock before engaging them. So, here he was with three of his men positioned approximately fifty meters from the objective, out of sight behind a container. Now it was all a matter of timing.

"Boss, we have movement on the deck," radioed one of his men.

"Right, lads, let's go." The four men walked out from behind the container and started slowly walking toward the ship's gangway. "Move in now. Out," Taffy radioed back.

His other two men on the truck would be driving toward the ship from the opposite direction.

When they were twenty-five meters away, their quarry began walking down the gangplank. They were all carrying shoulder bags with their hands inside them, obviously holding weapons. Taffy saw the truck he had commandeered pull up behind the truck that was waiting to receive its container of death.

"Twenty-five meters," Taffy radioed. His right hand was a little sweaty and he wiped it on the outside of the coat. "Twenty meters," he radioed again.

One of the four men stopped walking and pointed in their direction. The others shrugged him off and continued walking toward the waiting eighteen-wheeler. But the man seemed unsure and continued looking.

"Fifteen meters."

The truck driver was out of the cab, watching the container as it was lowered the last two feet onto the bed.

The terrorist who had stopped walking started pulling a weapon out of his bag.

"Go, go, go!" yelled Taffy.

The other men began to react as his men moved into a line abreast and pulled out their weapons. "Too late, you fucking muppets," he muttered as the men struggled to get their weapons out of their shoulder bags.

A shot rang out from behind them as one of the snipers took out the man who had reacted first. There was a slight puff of blood from the headshot; he hadn't stood a chance.

The driver, seeing the first man fall to the ground and the other three producing weapons, dived under his rig and crawled toward the other side.

One of the terrorists crumpled to the ground, taken out by Taffy's men in the truck behind them. The other two terrorists attempted to follow the truck driver to safety. Taffy and the two men with him opened fire. The terrorists fell to the ground, barely making it a couple of feet.

Taffy's men in the truck jumped out and were screaming at the truck driver of the target vehicle to stay on the ground but come out from under the truck.

It had taken seconds to neutralize their targets and secure the load. *Textbook.*

Capt. Taffy Jones got on the radio to the two bomb disposal experts. "All clear. Now let's finish this up and get home for lunch."

46

MI5 HEADQUARTERS, THAMES HOUSE, LONDON,
10:10 A.M. GMT

This time there was no phone call, just an aide who entered with a printout. K read it and handed it to C.

"Well, what is it?" asked the deputy prime minister.

"One second, sir. If you don't mind, K and myself are going to step outside for a few minutes," replied C.

There was some mumbling between the others around the conference table as both men left and closed the door behind them.

"I guess they only got one of the devices," said K. "That's disappointing, to say the least." He looked at the sheet of paper again. "It makes no mention of what happened in London or Liverpool."

"Does it really matter if we missed them? They could be anywhere."

"Let's go check with Operations. I would like to know by how much."

A quick elevator ride and they were in the heart of the communications center of MI5. K motioned for his department heads to join him and C in a conference room.

"What happened with the other two targets?" he asked.

"Liverpool was a complete wash, sir," replied one of his personnel. "The

Inge Nord had nearly finished loading all of her containers and was due to leave port within the hour. Our men conducted a search, just to be sure, but the container had been unloaded hours earlier. They even called in a number of police officers, and they are currently checking all the containers in the port, which is going to take hours, but I suspect it's long gone."

"And London?" asked C.

"Two hours, sir. We missed them by two hours," responded a security officer.

"Damn," said K.

"The police are also conducting a similar search, sir," she continued. "We do, however, have closed-circuit television from both locations, and our SAS teams are reviewing these to hopefully be able to track the vehicles on other CCTV cameras and intercept them."

"I want copies of those videos here as quickly as possible, and I want you to coordinate with the Metropolitan Police, the Merseyside Police, and the Greater Manchester Police in reviewing every CCTV camera on every route possible leading from the ports. These bastards haven't just disappeared into the ether."

"Yes, sir," they all replied and filed out of the room.

"London and Manchester are still in play, then," said C.

"Sure seems like it."

"There is the question of the royal family. I understand Her Majesty is currently at Buckingham Palace."

"Yes, she is, but you know her, there is no way she will just up and leave. Not if the city is in danger," replied K.

C smiled. "I know. Maybe the PM can have a word."

"With what's going on with this Brexit rubbish, I don't get the impression that the prime minister is the flavor of the month at the Palace right now."

C burst out laughing and K joined in. "You could be right, there," C replied, wiping his eyes. "So, what's next?"

"Now it's down to our wonderful officers in blue, their magic cameras, and boots on the ground."

"And Terry. You can't forget your man, Terry."

K sighed. "How could I ever forget about him?"

47

THE PLAZA, NEW YORK CITY, 6:00 A.M. EDT

Terry's phone was ringing, and he was trying desperately to ignore it, but it would not leave him alone. He had two choices, answer it or smash it . . . and he just didn't have the energy to do the latter. He reached over to the nightstand and picked up the instrument of his anguish.

"What?" He thought it would come out like a shout, which would have been quite satisfying. Instead all that emanated was a horse whisper. *Way too many cigarettes last night.* He cleared his throat. "What?"

He heard his master's voice and sat up in bed. "Sorry, sir." His head began to throb, so he lay back down. *Hungover after half a bottle of wine, what the hell?* He sat up again, more slowly this time. As K told him of the night's events, he made his way to the bathroom. "One second, sir." He muted the phone while he went to the bathroom and walked barefoot through the suite and headed for the minibar to get a Coke. He opened it, drank half the can, and unmuted the phone. "Sorry about that, sir. Now what is it you were saying about the *Aegean Commander*?"

After K finished, Nolan was silent for a minute.

"Terry, are you there?"

"Yes, sir. Sorry, sir. Only two? To be honest, I was hoping we would get more."

"And you don't think we were?" shouted K incredulously. It wasn't that his job was most assuredly on the line if he failed to prevent the attacks or that he would be hung out to dry by his political masters in the press. In this day and age, that was to be expected. It was the thought of letting his fellow countrymen down, and being a patriot, that would be more than he could bear.

"Sorry, sir, of course you were." He wanted to change the subject. "What do you need from me, sir?"

"I'd like to know where you are, for starters."

"The hotel, sir."

"Very funny, Nolan. What hotel?"

"Perhaps you've heard of it. It's called The . . . um . . . Plaza," Terry said, as if he had to look it up on the hotel's stationery.

"The Plaza?!" screamed K. "What were you thinking, getting rooms at the Plaza?"

K sounded like he was going to have a stroke, but Terry didn't care. He'd been shot twice and was nursing broken ribs. "Actually, sir, I didn't book two rooms. It's a suite, I booked a two-bedroom suite."

He could hear K start to lose it. A noise that sounded like someone placing a particularly grumpy cat in a blender emanated from the phone. Then it went silent. Finally, there was a long sigh. "You know what, son? Fuck it."

"Pardon, sir?"

"You heard me. I said, 'fuck it.' You've had a hell of a week and pretty much saved us from two dirty bombs. If anyone tries to give you a hard time over your expenses, I'll deal with it. Personally."

"Thank you, sir."

"What are your plans for the Stratton house?"

"Haven't really thought about it yet, sir. I was planning on taking a look-see later on today and getting the lay of the land, then making a go of it tonight."

"The powers that be want me to ask you if there is any chance of going in during the day."

Nolan had been sitting back on the couch in the main area of the suite. He sat bolt upright.

"Sir, you're joking . . . right?"

K sighed again. "No, Nolan, I'm not."

"Not a chance, sir. For one, it would be bloody suicide, and for another, from what I have been able to see from aerial photographs I pulled up on Google Earth, the house may be secluded somewhat, but there are a lot of civilian properties on the main approach roads. Also, given the weather we've been having, there are sure to be a number of boats swanning around in the area. Not only would it be a massacre but there is a good chance that civilians would get caught up in the crossfire."

"I understand, lad. That's precisely what I told them, but they insisted that I ask."

"Yeah, I bet they did, especially as it's not their asses on the line, sir."

"You have a point there, Nolan. So, what do you need?"

"For one, have that SAS guy, Rupert . . ."

"Rupert?"

"You know, the officer in charge."

"Oh, him. Okay."

"Yeah, have him and his medic come over here." Nolan gave K the suite number. "Tell them I'm going to need some gear and clothing." He gave K a list of things he would need. "Also, have you got the Zephyr up yet?"

"Should be on station in about two hours, and it can stay there until the job is done."

"Good. I need to be patched into the live feed, so have them bring a secure laptop."

"That shouldn't be a problem. What else?"

"Can you have that same helicopter on standby; we're going to need it."

"Done."

"Good. I'm going to need those SAS boys tonight, so give them a heads-up. When Rupert gets here, we'll put together a plan for the assault on the property."

"Right. There is one thing you should know. You're going to have some American company tonight."

"Americans?"

"Apparently, the president wants his people involved from now on, so you're going to have six off-the-books operators with you to 'give you a hand.' That is directly from the president."

Hmm, either CIA or Navy SEALs. "Well, as long as they know their shit, sir, why the hell not?"

"I'm assured they are 100 percent reliable."

SEALs. Nolan grinned. *Those fuckers at Stratton's house won't know what hit them.*

48

MONTAUK AIRPORT, LONG ISLAND, NEW YORK,
10:00 P.M. EDT

Nolan, along with Huntington, Kristen, and a presumed Navy SEAL who only gave his name as Josh, had taken a ride out to Long Island to take a look at their objective at eleven that morning. They had driven around the town to see exactly the approaches to the property they could take advantage of later in the evening. Kristen and Josh had even done the lost tourist bit, while Nolan and Huntington waited at an outdoor table at Bostwick's Chowder House, a local seafood restaurant. It was a pleasant sixty-four degrees, so most of the customers were inside.

They had eaten a fabulous lunch, starting with tasty bowls of clam chowder—two New England and two Manhattan. Then everyone ordered the "Clambake," a lobster (size of your choice) served with steamed clams (white wine, butter, and lemon), mussels, potatoes, and corn on the cob. Slices of key lime pie were brought out for dessert. It was a pretty pricey lunch. "Order whatever you want," Nolan had stage-whispered to Kristen and Huntington. "After all, Uncle Sam is paying." That had brought on a well-needed bout of laughter.

One of the nice things they had discovered from their reconnaissance was that the property was surrounded by wetlands on three landward sides; the house backed up on the ocean. They should be able to approach the house most of the way unseen, the cold water of the wetlands lowering their body temperatures, making them much harder to spot on thermal sights. The downside, of course, was that they would be bloody cold and miserable. That was a fair trade-off. Cold and miserable was much more preferable than dead.

After lunch, Josh called the rest of his team and made arrangements to meet at a secure location for a briefing. It was decided the SEALs would come ashore using scuba gear just as Terry and his SAS men were starting their assault from the land side of the property. It was hoped that the diversion of the frontal assault would enable them to gain easier access to the house and catch their quarry in a crossfire.

Of the utmost importance: they needed Stratton, Congressman Brennan, or O'Keith alive for interrogation purposes. There were still two bombs to find. The president himself had told Josh via telephone that he wanted Brennan alive so he could personally lock the door of the supermax prison when Brennan was found guilty of everything the Justice Department could come up with. Josh had assured his commander in chief that he would make that happen if at all possible. When he briefed his team, he advised them that the president wanted Brennan taken alive but had not instructed that he be in perfect condition. That had brought smiles to his fellow operators' faces, all of whom had worked with their counterparts in the British military and were livid that Americans were involved in a plot of such magnitude.

"What about Stratton?" asked one of his men.

"What about him?" asked Josh.

"Any particular instructions about keeping his ass alive?"

"Nothing at all. Does that answer your question?"

His fellow SEAL smiled. "Absolutely, boss."

So here they were, standing around the H155 helicopter in a deserted corner of Montauk Airport. The airport personnel and air traffic controllers had been advised to keep all vehicles and aircraft away from the area. Airport personnel had even turned off the lights in their location so there was little danger of prying eyes. The pilot of the H155 had removed a row of seats so five of the SEALs could fit on board with all their gear. He was going to drop them off in the ocean a mile out, then quickly return for one of the SEALs and a member of the SAS, who would provide cover fire with their sniper rifles. As Terry had said, it had worked well at the Lander house. The rest of the team and Kristen would drive near to the property in the Lexus, where Kristen would then wait with the vehicle while the others advanced on the property. They had tried persuading her that she should stay away from the house as the shit hit the fan, but she was adamant that she was coming even if she had to stay with the vehicle.

"If Shae is alive," she argued, "she's more likely to talk to you if I'm there." The doubt of her ability to be a member of the operation she was about to take part in started to eat away at her self confidence. *I must be insane to want to be part of this, but I have to see it through. If there is even a remote chance she is still alive, I owe it to her to be there.*

Terry knew this was total bollocks, but he had to give it to the lady: she had persistence.

It was time. Hands shaken, "good lucks" uttered, the rotor blades started to turn. All of them were quiet, determined, as a last-minute comms check was carried out. Those left on the ground watched the machine swiftly rise in the air and head out as low as possible over the surrounding houses on its way out to sea.

"Let's go," said Huntington.

Nolan finished the cigarette he'd been sharing with two of the SAS men, ground it into the tarmac, and climbed into the Lexus.

49

STRATTON PROPERTY, LONG ISLAND, NEW YORK,
11:00 P.M. EDT

They had been watching the live thermal feed from the Zephyr when Terry noticed that two of the guards at the main entrance had returned to the house, leaving only two men guarding that approach.

"I think a change of plan is called for," he said to Huntington. "How about four of you go through with the original plan of approaching through the wetland, and Paul and myself take a leisurely drive up to the gate and take out the two guards when they stop the car? We can stop the Lexus halfway down the driveway and come in on the east side of the property. That way we can block the exit with the vehicle and take them from three sides."

"What about Kristen?" asked Huntington.

"She can climb in the back, and once we stop the car, she can move about fifty-meters away from the vehicle and hole up till we're done."

"I don't know, Nolan. That could prove awfully risky. I'd prefer it if we left her behind."

"Like hell," said Kristen. "I can look after myself, just ask Nolan."

"I'm sorry, Kristen, but he's right," Terry said. "It's way too dangerous for you to stay in the car. I'll leave you one of the radios and call you when we're done." He gave her the spare key to the vehicle. "We'll leave the Lexus just past the gate and that way you can drive up once I give you the all clear." He felt bad for Kristen, but she really didn't understand how risky the operation they were about to undertake was. Even if their plan went off without a hitch, he didn't expect them all to make it through unscathed. *If this goes to shit, none of us may make it out of this one alive, and I can't put her through that after everything else she has been through.* He could tell Kristen was pissed, but Huntington was right, this was no place for her. Plus, if anything happened to her, he'd never forgive himself.

That had been thirty-five minutes earlier. After dropping off the four SAS men, Terry, Paul, and Kristen had driven to a side street about one hundred meters from the main entrance and waited, engine running with the lights off. Terry's headset crackled to life.

"In position." That was Huntington.

He was just about to answer when one of the SEALs got on the air. "In position here. Over."

"Let's get this show on the road," said Terry to the other two occupants of the car.

Kristen got out of the back seat and watched as the headlights on the Lexus sprang to life and pulled out onto the side street, heading for the property. She was pissed about being left behind, but on reflection, she had to agree that having her come along, given that she had no training at all, was a bad idea. All she could do was hope that Shae was there and would survive what was about to happen. Other than that, she was just a spare cog that could end up getting herself or others killed. The last thing Terry needed was to be worried about her safety while he was trying to do his job. She walked up to the corner of the house at the entrance to the property and watched as the SUV drove slowly down the driveway. "Good luck, old man," she whispered as the rear lights got smaller and smaller. Then they brightened as Paul applied the brakes. "Here goes," she mumbled to herself.

They had both the front windows down and the radio turned up full blast as they drove down the driveway. Paul was purposely weaving the SUV slightly as they headed for the main gate. Both men were singing along at the top of their lungs to "Dead or Alive" by Bon Jovi as they came to a stop in front of the two men. *Nothing to see here, boys, just a couple of drunks headed back to their hotel.*

One of the guards shook his head to the other one and made a drinking gesture with his hand. Both of them laughed as one guard headed for the driver's side of the car, the other to the passenger side. Big mistake. The guard on the driver's side yelled something, but it was unintelligible over the blaring music.

"What?" yelled Paul in his best impression of an American accent.

The guard made a gesture to turn the music down.

Oh, mouthed Paul. He used the controls on the steering wheel to lower the music while keeping his right hand on the silenced 9mm SIG Sauer he had on his lap. Nolan in the passenger seat held the silenced Walther in his lap.

"I said," yelled the guard, "you can't come down here, it's a private road."

"Whaddaya mean private road?" yelled back the soldier, again doing his American accent, which sounded like a bad impression of J. R. Ewing. "This is the way to the Holiday Inn, isn't it?"

Both guards took a couple more steps toward the Lexus.

"Sorry, son," he replied with a broad Northern Irish accent. "It's back that . . ."

Both of the guards were double tapped before he could finish the sentence.

There was a spike strip across the road preventing them from proceeding forward; Nolan jumped out and pulled it out of the way. After the SUV had pulled forward far enough, Terry dragged it back across the road, then grabbed one of the guards and dragged his lifeless body out of view of the driveway in case someone else decided to drive down to the gate from the street. Paul took care of the other guard. They drove fifty meters down the driveway with their lights off and pulled the vehicle over at an angle blocking the road. Nolan got on the radio.

"Moving in now. Out." He was answered by double clicks in his earpiece from Huntington and then from the SEALs. Ten minutes later, after crawling through the freezing water of the wetland, they were in position.

The exterior lights of the building were on, and Terry could clearly see six men on guard.

"Rupert, I see six to my front. Paul and I will take the two on the right, you guys take the other four on my call, over."

Two more clicks in his ear. *They must be pretty close to the house if they aren't talking over the radio.*

The medic, who was carrying a HK417 sniper rifle as well as an L119A2 C8 CQB personal weapon, leaned over and whispered in Nolan's ear.

"I have the man on the right, who is further away in my sights."

Nolan whispered back, "Roger that," and settled the sights of his C8 CQB on the other man. He took a breath and whispered into his mic. "Engage."

All six of the men guarding the house dropped to the ground with barely a sound.

"All six down," he whispered. "Move in."

He heard a "Roger that" from Huntington and the SEALs. On the other side of the driveway, all five of the SAS men rose with him and started to make their way in that typical operator short-step movement that had been adopted by many SWAT teams around the world. They were about thirty yards from the main building when the main doors burst open, and all hell broke loose. They began receiving fire from five men who had rushed out of the door as well as at least two men on the roof. Nolan hit the ground and rolled before propping himself up on his elbows so he could see above the scrub grass that made up the wetland. He sent a burst flying at one of the men taking cover behind the planter at the top of the steps and was satisfied to hear a groan from him as he fell back onto the stone patio. He looked over at his wingman. "Shit," he mumbled. The SAS man was trying to administer aid to himself for a stomach wound. Nolan was about to crawl over to see if he could help, but Paul waved him away and gave him a thumbs up.

The fire from the building was withering, and they were about to be cut to pieces if help didn't arrive soon. He keyed his mic.

"I need that chopper over the front of the house now or we're fucked." He fired again at another man but missed, the man moving to another position just as he fired. *Shit!* He saw another of the defenders drop to the ground, taken out by one of the other SAS men. He hoped the SEALs were having an easier time.

"Where's that fucking chopper?" he screamed.

Just then, he saw it swing sideways over the roof and the shooting ceased from up there. The snipers on the helicopter were doing their job well.

"Sorry, Army, our Navy friends ran into a little bother. All good now," radioed the pilot.

As the helicopter swung further away from the building, he saw another terrorist fall to the ground, taken out by one of the snipers. He was about to shoot at one of the two men left on the expansive front patio when he saw something protrude from the open doorway; it was a short tube with a kind of metal grating on the side. He let fly with a full mag as he toggled the mic.

"Stinger!" he screamed. The man in the doorway pitched forward, dead, but it was too late. There was a puff of smoke as the deadly missile left the tube, then a sheet of flame burst out of the back. He rolled over, hoping that it hadn't time to lock onto the helicopter, but he knew it was gone. The explosion lit up the night sky and the surrounding grounds.

50

OUTSIDE THE STRATTON PROPERTY, LONG ISLAND,
NEW YORK, 11:25 P.M. EDT

Kristen had been listening to Terry on the radio after he and the soldier had taken out the two guards at the entrance. She was still a little pissed at being left behind and was determined to keep up with what was going on.

When she heard Terry yelling for the helicopter, she could no longer stand being a spectator and started running down the driveway toward the Lexus. She saw the spike strip and pulled it off the road, and as she turned to head toward the house she heard the MI5 agent scream over the radio. There was a trail of flame coming away from the house, and then a massive explosion in the night sky. She stopped, mesmerized, as she watched the flaming remains of the helicopter fall to the ground. "Jesus," she whispered to herself, knowing that three brave men had just been killed.

She started running again and keyed the radio. "Terry, Terry!" she screamed. "Are you okay?"

Nothing.

She was nearly at the Lexus when she heard his voice. "Going in the front door now, Navy."

51

STRATTON HOUSE, LONG ISLAND, NEW YORK,
11:35 P.M. EDT

There were only three of them left standing by the time the other two men on the patio had been neutralized. Nolan ran over and checked on Paul—he seemed to be hanging in there. The medic was in agony from his wound but had managed to staunch the flow of blood. Terry reached into his pocket and pulled out one of the morphine syrettes Paul had given him. Terry removed the cap, then injected it into Paul's thigh before writing an M on his forehead in blood, to indicate morphine had been administered. He squeezed the soldier's upper arm before running for the main door. He saw Huntington and another soldier running from his left. They stopped on either side of the doorway.

"Paul?" asked Huntington.

"Stomach wound, but he should make it. Your other guy?"

Huntington shook his head.

Nolan keyed the radio. "Going in the front door now, Navy."

"Making entry in the back, one down, four coming in," replied the SEAL team leader.

Huntington threw in a stun grenade and waited. There were three explosions, the men at the rear following the same entry tactic. Nolan went through the door from the right, Huntington and the other soldier from the left. They heard muffled shots from the rear of the house, then silence.

"One neutralized," crackled his earpiece.

They started clearing the downstairs room by room without finding anyone. Yet, when they cleared the master suite on the ground floor, Nolan noticed something odd. There was an enormous floor-to-ceiling mirror against one of the walls, which seemed a little out of place, even in a house like this. Then he noticed the smoke detector in the corner of the room above the mirror. He signaled for the two SAS men to follow him of the room.

"I think there's a panic room in there," he whispered. "Behind that big-ass mirror."

"I was thinking the same thing," replied Huntington.

"Got any breaching charges with you?"

"Sorry, no, but our SEAL friends might."

Nolan keyed the radio again. "Where are you guys?" he asked.

"Just finished clearing the upstairs and about to move onto the roof. Why? What's up?"

"Do you have any breaching charges with you? I think we have a panic room down here."

"Sure do. Will be down in a minute. Out."

"We need to take out that camera in the smoke detector in the corner of the room just in case they have a way of shooting at us through a firing port or something."

"I can help with that, sir," replied the SAS soldier. Digging in his top pocket, he pulled out a flashlight and smiled. "High powered, sir. I'll blind it while you shoot the thing. They'll be blind before they know it."

Nolan took out his silenced Walther. "Go," he said.

The SAS man swung his arm around the corner of the door and aimed the beam of light at the smoke detector. Instantly, the left side of the mirror shattered as whoever was in the panic room opened fire blindly. Nolan rolled into the room, easily avoiding the shooter, got to one knee, and fired two rounds. The smoke detector disintegrated, and the firing stopped.

He stepped back out into the corridor. "The problem with panic rooms, gentlemen, is once you are in there, you can't get out without opening the door."

While he waited, he got on the radio to Kristen. "Bring up the Lexus. We have at least one wounded man who needs to go to the hospital."

"I'm already outside, and he's in the back of the car. Are there any more?"

"Thanks, Kristen. I don't know about the Americans, but I will let you know. Keep pressure on his wound, and I will get a medic over there right away." He had to admit she really did have guts. "One second, Kristen" he said as the SEALs walked toward them. "Is your guy okay?" he asked.

"Yeah, just a leg wound," replied Josh, the SEAL team leader. "Should be up and running in a couple of weeks. Yours?"

"One dead, one wounded in the stomach," replied Huntington.

"Nasty," he replied. "We may be able to help you there." He changed the channel on his radio and put a call into the local Coast Guard station, requesting a medevac helicopter. When he was done, he looked at Nolan. "Ten minutes at the most." He turned to two of his men. "Eddie, help Jerry around to the front of the house. Phil, go and see what you can do for their guy, okay? Make sure you take real good care of him. We've already lost too many tonight." Phil was off and running before he'd even finished. "Phil's our doc and he's . . . bloody good." Terry smiled. "Now, what's this nut you want us to crack?"

Terry radioed back to Kristen to hold for the medevac helicopter rather than driving Paul to the hospital.

They heard the Coast Guard helicopter arrive and leave before they were done setting the charge on the panic room door. First, they had to demolish the mirror frame in order to set the charges. Only once had the occupants tried to shoot at them again through a sliding metal gun port, but that had ended when one of the SEALs had returned fire at the opening.

Kristen came running in. "There are a shitload of cops heading down the driveway," she said, out of breath.

"That's just great," replied Nolan.

"I'll deal with them," replied Josh. "You guys keep working on that charge." He returned a few minutes later, smiling broadly.

"How did it go?" asked Huntington.

"Oh, just peachy. Had them patched through to the secretary of the Navy. Never heard him telling a cop to shut the fuck up before. The cops are waiting outside till we're done, so I guess they got the message. How's it going?"

Two minutes later, they were done placing the explosives.

Terry admired their handiwork. "Let's blow this fucker."

52

STRATTON HOUSE, LONG ISLAND, NEW YORK, 12:25 A.M. EDT

The SEALs used a strip-shaped charge that they had run on both sides of the hidden door to take out the hinges and any locks that were on the other side. The explosion tore into the steel just enough to pop the door off its frame and swing open. No one locked in the room was killed, but the explosion was powerful enough to cause some serious damage to their faculties. The two SAS men and the MI5 agent stormed into the bedroom and pulled the door wide open. What greeted them caused them to stop in their tracks.

"Put the weapon down," yelled Huntington.

"Fuck you, you British fuck," replied the voice inside.

Kristen, who was waiting in the corridor, couldn't understand why they weren't shooting. She stuck her head around the door and gasped in shock.

"Shae!" she yelled and tried to force her way into the bedroom. One of the SEALs grabbed her and pushed her back into the corridor. She started to cry and kick at him.

"Let me go. I have to see her," she screamed.

The SEAL placed a gloved hand over her mouth and whispered in her ear. "Listen up, lady. If I let you in that room, she's dead and so are you, understand? You need to stay away, or she's dead. Now take a breath and let the professionals deal with this because this is what we are trained for. Nod if you understand?"

Kristen, whose nostrils were filled with the smell of gunpowder and oil off of his glove, looked at him with wide eyes and began to calm down. She nodded and he slowly released his grip.

In the corner of the panic room, furthest away from the door, sat Shae, duct-taped to a chair, the only Parishioner on this assignment Terry had personally recruited as Vicar. Her mouth was duct-taped shut. Behind her stood a man with a gun in one hand and what looked like a detonation device with a wire leading down to Shae in the other. In the other corner, another man was sitting with his knees tucked up to his chest and his face buried in them. He was gently rocking himself back and forth and seemed to be weeping.

"It's over, Stratton, give it up," said Terry.

"Fuck off, Brit. I want an American in here now. Understand? Or we all blow," screamed Stratton.

The SEAL team leader stepped into the room, his gloved hands open, palms out at his side. "You want an American? Here I am. What do you want?"

"I want a goddamn chopper, that's what I want. Then I want a fully fueled Lear to take me to the country of my choice."

The SEAL looked down at the man curled up in a ball. "What about him?"

"Fuck him, he's a useless piece-of-shit politician. Now get me my fucking chopper."

"How about we get him out of here first?" asked the American.

"Not a fucking chance," screamed Stratton. "If I go, so does he."

"Okay, give me a sec. I'll have to radio my superiors." He motioned for Terry to step out into the corridor.

The SEAL pretended to talk over the radio loud enough for Stratton to hear. When he wasn't holding the pretend conversation, he whispered to Nolan.

"Can you take him with that?" he asked looking down at the silenced Walther. "Before he blows us the fuck up."

"Sure, but I need about half a second."

"Please," begged Kristen. "Get him whatever he wants. Just make sure he doesn't hurt Shae."

Nolan looked at the SEAL, and they both looked at Kristen and smiled.

The SEAL finished his fake conversation and stepped back into the room. "I've spoken to my superior, and as long as you are willing to let the congressman go, then he is willing to agree to your demands."

"What? You mean I'll get my helicopter and plane just like that?"

"As long as you are willing to release the congressman unharmed, yes."

"I'll release him when I get to the plane. The girl stays with me."

There was a sudden commotion in the corridor as Kristen screamed. She burst into the room shrieking and crying. Huntington grabbed her as she tried to get past him. "*Please don't hurt her!*" she screamed. "*Please let her go!*"

Stratton was distracted just enough. Nolan stepped into the master bedroom, weapon raised, just as Stratton was about to lower his thumb on the trigger. Nolan shot him twice through the throat, severing his spinal column and switching off the signals from his brain.

Stratton sank to the floor just as Kristen made another break to get to her lover.

Terry grabbed her and pushed her away. "Kristen, no, she's still wired. Get her out of here, for fuck's sake, Huntington. And get that scumbag Brennan out of here as well before I shoot the fucker myself."

One of the SEALs strode into the panic room and dragged the congressman out by his collar before fastening his wrists with PlastiCuffs.

"The rest of you, get the hell out of here as well. If this thing blows, it could take out the house."

"Sorry, sir, I'm staying," replied Huntington. "I suspect I'm better at defusing these things than you are."

Terry looked at the SAS captain. "Always said you guys were a bunch of cowboys." He smiled and shook his head. "Anyway, you're most probably right, I fucking hate bombs."

"So do I, sir, so do I."

53

MI5 HEADQUARTERS, THAMES HOUSE, LONDON,
6:00 A.M. GMT

Where the fuck are you, Nolan? K checked his watch again for the fifth time in the space of two minutes. He was seated behind the large oak desk that took up a good third of his office and was back to drinking the foul office coffee, which didn't help his mood in the slightest. Looking wistfully at his Kees van der Westen Speedster coffee maker, which had set him back over £15,000, he sighed as he took another drink of the vile office brew. *I must send out for some of my special blend before this stuff kills me.* He glanced at his watch again and came to a decision. Picking up his secure phone, he started to call his agent when his phone rang. Glancing down at the number, he saw that it was Nolan.

"About bloody time, lad. Where the hell have you been?"

"Sorry, sir," replied Terry. "We ran into a spot of bother taking the house." He went on to explain the loss of the men.

"Well, I hope it was worth it."

"Yes, sir. Stratton is dead and we have the congressman in custody. We also found Shae, and she's alive."

"Bloody good show, Nolan."

"Thank you, sir, but there's a slight problem."

"What might that be?"

"It's Shae, sir. She's in a vest."

"A vest? I suppose you'll tell me she's wearing pants too." There was a pause. "Oh, shit."

"Precisely, sir. Captain Huntington and I have taken a look and its way out of our league to try and defuse this thing."

"What do you need from me, lad?"

"Huntington has a secure iPad, and we're hoping you can patch us through to a bomb disposal expert. That way we can live stream what's happening, and they can tell us what we need to do."

"Good idea, Nolan."

"Huntington's, not mine. If this thing goes bang, I just thought I'd give credit where credit is due, sir."

"I can have one of our top people on with you in five minutes. Other than the vest, how is she holding up?"

"Surprisingly well, actually. She's been roughed up a bit and is scared to death, but other than that I'm pleased to report she still has her fingernails and her kneecaps."

"Well, that's something. Hang tight for a few minutes and I'll have our man on with you. Go and smoke a cigarette or something. Avoid drinking coffee."

"Already taken care of the smoke, sir. Understood about the coffee. Pity, really, they've got one hell of an espresso machine in the kitchen. Rivals the one in your office."

54

STRATTON HOUSE, LONG ISLAND, NEW YORK, 1:15 A.M. EDT

Terry yawned and stretched his arms above his head. Huntington was back in the panic room giving Shae a drink of ice water from a glass with a straw. All in all, thought the captain, she didn't look in too bad of a shape, only a black eye, busted lip, and some nasty bruising on her cheek.

"Don't drink too much, Shae, this may take a while."

She looked up at the officer. "Honestly, Captain, I think pissing my pants is the least of my worries right now."

Given her situation, it amazed Huntington how calm she was. He and Nolan had very carefully removed the duct tape that was holding her to the chair in the hopes that disarming the vest would have been a simple task of just cutting her free and leaving the damn thing still armed until they could get the professionals in to deal with it. Unfortunately, whoever had built the thing knew their stuff. The two main areas of concern were the mercury trembler device that was positioned across the front of the vest and the fitness band on her wrist that had wires attached running up her sleeve. God only knew what other traps were part of the damn thing, but they weren't about to screw around with it.

Terry came back into the room.

"How are you holding up?"

"Let's just say I've had better days."

Her Vicar laughed nervously. "Considering you're the one wearing the vest, you seem to be holding up a lot better than me. Listen, Shae, I really am sorry about all this."

"Don't, Terry. I got into this with my eyes wide open. Anyway, the last thing I need is for you to have a guilt trip instead of focusing on what needs to be done."

Terry tried to smile. "I should have done more to protect you. If anything goes wrong . . ."

"Bullshit, Terry. Stop getting down on yourself. Anyway, if anything goes wrong, we'll both be dead . . . right?"

Terry sighed. "You aren't wrong."

"Then shut up and focus."

Terry looked at her as if seeing her for the first time and was shocked at how composed she was. He knew of others that were trained professionals who would have been scared to death in a similar situation, but Shae seemed incredibly calm. "Okay, you got it." He smiled. "Thanks for the pep talk, I needed that."

"You're welcome. Now, if you don't mind, can you please get this fucking thing off of me?"

"Right. Listen, before we do this, are you up to answering some questions, just in case?"

"Sure, Terry," she replied. "It's not as if I've got anything planned for the next hour or so."

"Very funny. So, tell me, who put you in the vest?"

"That was Stratton, but he didn't build it. It was some old Irish guy. He was a total shit, wanted to shoot off my kneecaps and a bunch of other nasty stuff."

Terry pulled up some photographs on his phone and showed her what he thought would be the relevant one.

"That's him," she said.

Terry showed it to Huntington. "Fuck, Patrick O'Keith."

The officer nodded and left the room to call his boss and let him know they had a positive identification of the terrorist.

"Who the hell is Patrick O'Keith?" asked Shae.

"He's from the bad old days. Trained in Libya in the eighties and really knows his stuff. I know of a number of people who fell afoul of his devices. Unfortunately for us, he is very good and extremely deadly at what he does."

"Great, that's just great," replied Shae sarcastically.

"So, I have to ask. Why didn't he shoot your kneecaps?"

"There was a woman who stopped him. She said there was no point, as everything was working out nicely."

"How so?"

"I guess they were more interested in grabbing bigger fish, meaning you. I think they wanted to find out more about what you knew of the operation."

"But I didn't know anything until I found the thumb drive you stashed."

Shae shrugged and then froze when she saw the fear on Terry's face at her sudden movement. "Sorry about that," she whispered. "Force of habit. One thing I do know is that you finding Lander wasn't part of their plan. That kind of threw them for a loop. The woman, she went nuts when she found out."

Terry reached over and pushed an errant hair from her face. "I wonder how she knew? It wasn't on the news or anything."

"Not a clue."

"What about Kristen? Why go after her?"

"Leverage on me, I guess. That was the lady's compromise to O'Keith. Seems she wanted me in one piece to give you a message."

"And what might that be?"

"That she is going to destroy everything you care about. Your sister, her kids, your ex-wife, the lot. All before you fail saving your country from ruin."

"What the hell's she got against me?" he mused aloud. "I mean, I've had some bad run-ins with terrorists in my day and left a number of widows, but nothing that should lead to this. Hell, even my ex-wife doesn't hate me this much." He turned back to Shae. "Do you know where O'Keith and this woman are now?"

"They left yesterday morning. I heard one of the guards say they were flying to England."

Hmmm, they left right after I took out Lander. That must have really spooked them. "You don't happen to have a name for this woman, do you?"

She was about to shake her head no, then stopped herself. "Sorry, no. Nice enough looking but she seemed bitter as hell. Put it this way, if these bombs are the real deal, then she will take a great deal of pleasure in setting them off."

"Unfortunately, Shae, they are most certainly real. If you saw her again, you'd recognize her, right?"

"Absolutely." Shae smiled mischievously. "If you can find a police sketch artist who wouldn't mind spending an hour or so with me right now, I'm sure he can knock up a fairly good likeness."

Huntington returned to the room and stared at the explosive vest. "I think we may have a problem finding a volunteer."

"No shit," she replied.

The FaceTime feature on the iPad rang.

Huntington snatched it up and answered. A woman's face appeared on the screen—a brunette in her late thirties or early forties.

"Hello, ma'am, Captain Huntington here." He turned the iPad to face Nolan and the girl. "This is Terry, and the young lady is Shae. I hope you can help us with our situation."

The woman scowled a little at the officer. "Captain, let's dispense with the ma'am, shall we? My name is Leslie Mitchell. I'm an explosives expert with the government and an instructor for the British military and the police. If it can go bang, I'm the one you want telling you how to disarm it. Let's take a look at the device and we can figure out what we need."

"Okay, Leslie," replied Huntington. He turned the iPad around and started to slowly show her a close-up of what they were dealing with. As he moved the iPad around the vest, he could hear her say "Aha, hold it there" or "move it closer." She seemed to take a particular interest in the fitness band. When he was done, he turned the screen around to face him.

"Thank you, Captain. Luckily, there doesn't seem to be a timer on this thing, so there are no worries about that. If there was, I suspect we wouldn't be having this conversation. This is going to sound like a silly question, but were you two planning on defusing this thing yourselves?"

"Yes," they answered in unison.

"Well, I'm very glad your boss reached out to me, Terry, because we have just avoided you two having a very unhealthy Forrest Gump moment."

"A Forrest Gump moment?" asked Terry.

"Yes," replied Leslie. "Stupid is as stupid does, gentlemen. You would have blown yourselves and the lady into the next life. I have a colleague with the New York Police Department who runs their bomb disposal unit. All I want you both to do is sit tight and smoke cigarettes or do whatever it is you do. Now all I have to find is a Doppel."

55

STRATTON HOUSE, LONG ISLAND, NEW YORK, 2:50 A.M. EDT

It took about an hour and a half for the professionals to arrive. Terry had stepped outside of the house for a cigarette and to see how the others were doing when the NYPD helicopter came in to land, shattering the quiet of the night. By now, all the bodies of the guards and Stratton had been bagged and tagged by the East Hampton Town Police Department, and an FBI medical examiner was on the way to haul them off. The SAS men and the Navy SEALs sat off to one side, avoiding the stares of the police officers, enjoying some beers liberated from the Stratton refrigerator. Terry didn't care how much they drank; they'd all had a rough night. As long as they didn't start raising hell, no one would complain. There was something about the comradery between members of the special forces community that he'd always found refreshing. Kristen was curled up on the back seat of the Lexus, sound asleep, having been given a sedative by the SEAL doctor. He picked up the blanket that had been covering her and draped it over her as gently as possible, then stroked away the hair from her face. He stood looking down at her for a few minutes, touched his fingertips to his lips and then touched her on the forehead before gently closing the door. The East Hampton Town chief of police was walking over to talk to him as the welcoming lights of the helicopter appeared to distract him.

Terry took one last long draw on his smoke before pitching it aside and heading toward the landing area. As soon as the skids touched the ground, a door slid open, and an NYPD bomb tech stepped out. He started to haul out a number of large duffel bags and was then joined by another tech. Terry intercepted the chief of police and waved him aside. The last thing they needed was a pissing match with the locals, but he was damned if he'd let this guy insert himself into what was happening. The chief scowled at Terry, but did as he was told and started walking back toward his own men, no doubt to bitch and moan and say how he would deal with this later. Which, of course, he wouldn't. This was way above his pay grade. It wasn't like providing security for a celebrity party given by the likes of Billy Joel or Jerry Seinfeld.

The MI5 agent ran under the rapidly slowing main rotor blades, shook hands with the two men and picked up one of the heavy bags before heading back toward the house. They stopped in front of the stone steps leading up to the front patio area.

"Are you Terry or Huntington?" asked one of the men.

"I'm Terry. Huntington is inside looking after the girl."

"My name is Max," said one of the men. "This is Antonio. Leslie called and said you have a bit of a problem."

"You could say that," he replied. "Did you manage to get your hands on a Doppel?"

Max handed him something that resembled a wristwatch and was designed to simulate a heartbeat. Leslie had told him that it was supposed to help calm people who were stressed, and that it also had other uses.

"Where on earth did you get it?" Terry asked. "Leslie said it was only available through the manufacturer's website."

"She called the owner of the company and explained that the British government needed some help. She got a list of names of the people in New York who had purchased one. After that it was as simple as driving out to friggin' Long Island City and knocking on this guy's door and requesting his help. We would have been here sooner but the first place we tried, in Sea Gate, nobody was home."

"How exactly is that going to help again?"

"The fitness tracker on the girl's wrist is measuring her heartbeat. That signal is transmitted to the detonator. So as long as it registers a heartbeat, it won't go off. The only way to remove the fitness tracker is to connect it to the Doppel. It's the last thing I'll do before taking the vest off her."

"Damn. Nice one, gents. Come on in and see what you are dealing with."

Terry led them to the master bedroom.

After being introduced to Huntington and Shae, the bomb techs went to work looking over the vest before walking back outside the house with Terry. They both opened bags and pulled out the different components to an advanced explosive ordnance disposal suit. Max started to get dressed in the cumbersome gear with Antonio's help.

"This bomb suit is eighty pounds of Kevlar and foam," Max said as he placed one leg and then the other into the lower half of the suit. "Leslie was telling me you guys were going to try and defuse this thing yourself."

Terry nodded.

"Today's your lucky day, pal. I'd've put two bucks down that you'd have blown yourselves up in thirty seconds. That suicide vest is a bitch to defuse, but don't worry, we'll take care of it."

"You're sure?"

"Piece of cake."

Antonio handed Max a small tool bag and a metal canister.

"What's in there?" asked Terry, pointing to the canister.

"Liquid nitrogen."

"What's that for?"

"We're gonna use it to freeze the mercury in the trembler device in case I can't disconnect it. Problem is, buddy, there are six wires leading to the damn thing. Typically, your friendly neighborhood bomb maker only uses two. So what are the other four connected to, huh? Most of the time, you burn away the plastic on the wires and connect them with another wire using crocodile clips. The issue with this sucker is that if you connect two of the wrong wires together . . . BABOOM!"

"Shit."

"That's one way of putting it."

Antonio lowered the helmet over Max's head and connected him to the battery powered air conditioning pack, so he didn't overheat in his protective cocoon. Now all suited up, Max gave Terry a thumbs up and started walking back into the house. Terry followed. Antonio stopped him.

"Where do you think you're going?"

"In there with you guys, to help."

"That's not how this works. I'll have a radio channel open so you can listen in, but as far as being in the room, no way. The last thing we need is you causing a distraction. We'll send out your friend after we get her out of that thing." Antonio looked Terry in the eye. "Trust me, she'll be okay." He smiled. "Max's life depends on it."

Terry turned away and sat down on the steps before lighting another cigarette and saying a quick Hail Mary as he remembered it from his childhood.

56

STRATTON PROPERTY, LONG ISLAND, NEW YORK,
3:00 A.M. EDT

Huntington had come out of the house and was pacing back and forth. Nolan was surprised to see the SAS captain so on edge, but it had been a long night and the waiting was even getting to him. Ten minutes later, he couldn't stand sitting on his hands anymore, so he decided to do something about it.

"Hey, Huntington, how about we have a little chat with our illustrious congressman?"

"I'd love to, but we can't. If I heard correctly, FBI agents are on their way to whisk him off to God knows where."

"Oh, come on, mate. I'm sure they won't mind as long as they get him in relatively one piece."

Huntington cracked his knuckles. "Fine. He's in one of the East Hampton police cars, and I don't think their boss likes us very much."

Terry looked over at the group of Navy SEALs. "I'm sure they'll help us liberate him for a little chat."

Huntington tilted his head. "I guess we'll find out, sir."

It took under three minutes before two of the burly SEALs returned with Brennan in tow and uncuffed. One of them smiled at Terry. "Where do you want him, sir?"

Terry gestured to the side of the house, away from prying eyes. The congressman looked at the MI5 agent and tears began to roll down his cheeks. "You can't do this, I'm a sitting United States congressman," he whined. "I have rights."

"Not from where I'm fucking standing you don't," hissed Terry an inch from his face, "Let's go, lads."

Brennan continued to whine as the now-laughing SEALs dragged him around the side of the house.

"Thanks, lads. You may want to join your friends now, as I wouldn't want you to get in any trouble."

The SEALs threw the man roughly to the ground and walked back around the front of the house.

Terry squatted down in front of the congressman and patted him on the cheek. "Now listen up, you little shit." The man's eyes darted around like those of a cornered animal; fear was emanating from him like some primal ooze. "I don't know what you know about me, so let me give you a heads-up. I'm a complete bastard, and I don't give a shit how much fucking pain I cause you. But know this—you will talk, and you will tell me the truth, otherwise I will fucking cripple you so badly they'll be spoon feeding you in prison for the rest of your miserable life." Terry patted him on the cheek again, only this time harder. The man winced and began to bawl like a baby. A large wet stain appeared around his crotch.

"Jesus, Captain, I don't think this wanker would last five minutes in your mob."

"I don't think he'd make it off the bus, sir," said Huntington, referring to the buses that brought potential recruits from the train station to the SAS training facility.

Terry took the silenced Walther from the holster under his arm. "Now, how about we set the ground rules." He grabbed the congressman by the wrist and pressed his splayed hand against the ground, pushing the barrel of the gun against the back of it. He looked over at

Harrington. "You may not want to be here for this, lad. You boys play by a different set of rules than I do."

"If it's all right with you, sir, I'll stick around. Most of my family lives in London, including the wife and kids during the school year, and it's not like I can call and warn them to get out of there, can I?"

Terry shook his head. "No, son, you can't."

"Right then, let's get on with this."

Terry pressed the tip of the barrel even harder against Brennan's hand.

"What do you want to know? I'll tell you anything," he begged. His eyes looked into Terry's pleadingly.

Terry looked right back at him, and not an ounce of mercy could be seen. "Nothing yet." He pulled the trigger.

The man began to scream as the bullet shattered the bones.

The MI5 agent spat on the congressman. "That's just a little something to remember me by. The next one is going to be an ankle, and we'll work our way up from there. How does that sound?"

"Fine by me," said the officer, reaching down and grabbing Brennan's leg and pushing it against the ground.

Terry pressed the barrel against Brennan's ankle. "What's the name of the woman?" he demanded.

Brennan began to wail, now knowing what was coming. "I don't know!" he screamed. All I know is she's from Belfast!"

"Fucking bullshit," replied Terry. "Do you think he's bullshitting me, Captain?"

"I think he's bullshitting you, sir," replied the officer.

Brennan watched in horror as the agent began to slowly pull the trigger. "Wait, wait, *wait!*" he screamed. "The only name I ever heard anyone call her was An Dailtín."

"An Dailtín?" asked Huntington. "What the fuck does that mean?"

"It means 'The Terror' in Gaelic," replied Terry, easing off the trigger.

"Sounds like my mother-in-law," replied the captain.

"Why is she called that, Congressman? What's so bad about her?"

"She rules with an iron fist. You screw with her, even in the slightest, you're done, gone, no mercy, just gone."

"Oooh, she's got me scared, Captain. How about you?"

"Shaking in my boots, sir," Huntington replied with a smile.

"How did you get hooked up with this mob?"

"The woman's loaded. Got more money than God and the connections to match. She helped me get elected."

"Why? I mean you're a US congressman. How does that help her?"

"Being a congressman from New York means I have a lot of pull and can help grease the skids, get things done in the city, if you know what I mean."

"You mean you're her little errand boy," piped in Huntington.

"I guess that's one way of looking at it."

"Where in England did she fly into, Congressman?" asked Terry.

The man looked terrified. "If I tell you that, I'm a dead man. She'll have me killed."

Terry began to pull back the trigger again. The man struggled to pull his leg out of the way, but Huntington forced it against the ground; his grip was like a vice. "Don't you get it yet, Brennan, you're a fucking dead man no matter what you say. The only way you have a chance is to cooperate, and the only question you should be asking yourself is 'Do I cooperate with a limp . . . or without one.'"

"*Okay, okay!*" he wailed. "*Biggin Hill, they flew into Biggin Hill! That's all I know.*"

"Good boy," replied Nolan. "And one last thing. Where are the bombs going to be set off?"

"They never told me. Like you said, I'm just the errand boy."

"Ah, but you have ears, don't you, you sneaky little bastard? So I know you heard something."

"I didn't hear anything. I really don't know."

Terry squeezed the trigger all the way this time, but instead of shooting Brennan in the ankle, he shot him in the foot. Brennan started screaming again.

"Shit, I'm losing my touch, I seem to have missed his ankle." Terry ignored the screaming and returned the tip of the barrel to the congressman's right ankle. "Don't worry, I'll fix that right now," he laughed. He started to squeeze the trigger again.

"You're a fucking bastard!" screamed Brennan.

"And here I was, thinking I was being nice," said Terry to Huntington. He got in the congressman's face. "You have no fucking idea, mate," he spat. "You think you're scared of her? I make her look like Mother Fucking Theresa. Now tell me where the fucking bombs are going to be set off in Manchester and London, you fucking maggot."

Brennan could have sworn he saw Terry's eyes grow red—he knew his death would be very slow and incredibly painful. He moaned, followed by a deep breath. "All I know is that I heard them talking about vans and boats."

"Boats?" said Huntington. He shot a glance at Terry.

"Yes, boats," he replied. "Please, that's it, that's all I know." Brennan looked at Terry, pleading.

"Get this piece of shit out of my sight," Terry said to Huntington.

57

STRATTON PROPERTY, LONG ISLAND, NEW YORK,
3:20 A.M. EDT

What was taking so long? Terry was tempted to call K but decided to wait until he had news about Shae. He was tired now. The adrenalin surge had passed, and he could feel his energy level dropping. *Feeling his age*, his father would have said. What he needed was about a gallon of coffee or a comfy bed, but neither would be happening for hours. As he walked back toward the front of the house, he lit a cigarette and inhaled deeply. *A nice cold glass of vodka wouldn't go amiss either. Maybe I can hitch a ride on that nice NYPD helicopter and have it drop me at the Plaza.*

Looking over at the area where the East Hampton Town police cars were gathered, he could see that the Navy SEAL medic was patching up the congressman. Across the other side of the wide driveway, SAS soldiers were brewing tea. *Now that is exactly what the doctor ordered.* As he was walking over toward the men, out of the corner of his eye he noticed a pissed off chief of police walking toward him. *Here we go*, he thought with an exaggerated eye roll. He knew what was coming.

"What can I do for you, Chief?" he asked with a smile.

"What can *you* do for *me*? You have got to be joking!" he yelled. He got about two inches from Terry's face and waved his hand back toward the congressman. "Who the fuck do you think you are? You're going to fucking jail for this, and I swear to God, I am personally going to see you prosecuted to the fullest extent of the law."

Terry saw a couple of the SAS men get to their feet and walk toward them. He waved them off. The last thing he needed was a dead chief of police and a half dozen of his men in PlastiCuffs.

"I suggest you calm down, Chief, or you're going to give yourself a coronary."

"Fuck you," he replied. "Now turn the fuck around, I'm taking you in."

The MI5 agent noticed the chief unclipping his holster. "I really wouldn't do that," he said. The smile was gone now, replaced by the expression of a man who could badly hurt people. He nodded toward the two SAS men, who now had their weapons in their hands, ready to go.

The chief looked over his shoulder and scowled. "Do you think I really give a shit about those two? My men . . ."

Nolan had taken out his phone. It was time to shut this down before it got out of hand. He dialed K.

"What's your cell phone number?" he asked the officer.

K answered the phone. "Nolan, what's going on?"

"What?" asked the police chief. "Why do you want my number?"

"One second, K," replied Terry. He put the phone on speaker. "If you want to keep your job, you'll give me your full name and phone number."

"I, I . . ."

"Now."

The chief seemed utterly confused and deflated. He spoke the information into the phone.

"You get that?" Terry asked K.

"Yes. What's the matter? Trouble in paradise?"

"You could say that. The gentleman seems to think he can arrest me for asking Congressman Brennan a few questions."

"Oh, he does, does he? I'll take care of this. Let me give the prime minister a call, and she will call the relevant parties over there. Hang tight, lad."

"Yes, sir." Terry hung up. "It will just be a few minutes," he said to the chief. They stood there, looking at each other, not speaking. The chief's attitude went from belligerent to puzzled to curious to apprehensive, an impressive display of nonverbal communication. Terry's face remained placid, inscrutable.

It took seven minutes for the chief's phone to ring. He looked at the number and saw that it was blocked. He looked at Terry as he answered; all the agent did was smile benignly and light a cigarette. A woman's voice came on the line.

"Chief Senters?"

"Yes."

"This is the White House. Please hold for the president." There was a click on the line.

"Chief Senters?"

Terry could have cried laughing as the chief's eyes widened. "Yes, Mr. President?"

"What's this about you wanting to arrest one of our British friends?"

"Well, yes, sir. It appears he shot Congressman Brennan, once in the hand and once in the foot during an interrogation."

"Hmm, really?"

"Yes, Mr. President."

"I'm sure you're wrong about that, Chief. It is my understanding the congressman was wounded during the assault on the house."

"I believe you're mistaken, Mr. Pres . . ."

"I don't think I am, Chief. Do you understand?"

"Uhhh . . . yes, sir. I understand."

"Good man, Senters. Now about the drugs you found."

"Drugs, sir? But there weren't any—"

"Oh, but I think you will find there were, Senters. You, with your men and the FBI, after a prolonged raid where your lives were very much in jeopardy, brought down one of the largest methamphetamine labs ever discovered on the Eastern Seaboard, seizing over a ton of the finished product. Unfortunately, the FBI helicopter that was helping with the raid suffered an engine problem and crashed. Thankfully, there was no loss of life. It also appears that United States Congressman Nathan Brennan and businessman Kevin Stratton from New Jersey were an integral part of the production and distribution of the drugs. Congressman Brennan, who suffered non-life-threatening wounds in the assault on the property, will be brought up on charges as soon as he is able to appear in court. Does that sound about right, Chief Senters?"

The chief had just been given his morning press release by the president of the United States. "Yes, that is precisely what happened, sir."

"Good, good. Now you see that our British friends and my Navy boys are looked after. Is that okay with you, Chief Senters?"

"Absolutely, Mr. President."

"And let's keep any mention of them out of the press, shall we?"

"Totally, sir. As far as I'm concerned, they just happened to be in the area."

"You are a good man, Senters. Have a good rest of your night, Chief. Please put our British friend on the line."

"Yes, Mr. President, and thank you sir." He handed the phone to Terry. "He wants to talk to you."

"Yes, sir," said Nolan.

"Hello. Just what can I call you?"

"Terry's fine, sir."

"Terry, okay. How are you holding up? I hear you've been through the wringer."

"You could say that, sir, but I'll live."

"Good. Where are you off to next?"

"It seems the trail goes cold here now, sir. So I will be going back home to see this through."

"Good. I was beginning to wonder if anyone would be left alive on the East Coast by the time you were finished."

Terry laughed. "I was beginning to wonder along those lines myself, sir."

"Now make sure, when this is all over, you and your boss come over and give me a private briefing on all this, okay?"

"Yes, sir. If you could just run it by the prime minister, we should be good to go."

"Great. I'll look forward to it. Now if you don't mind, Terry, I'm going to get a little more sleep. Thanks again for all you've done. Good night."

"Good night, sir." The line went dead, and he handed the phone back to Senters.

"So, are we good, Chief?"

"It appears we are. I hope you got what you needed out of Brennan."

Terry smiled. "We'll see, Chief. He's still alive, so that says something. You may never know the half of it. As for the congressman, I suggest you offer him a deal of, say, fifteen to twenty years, as long as he keeps quiet about what he and his group were really up to. I'm sure the Feds will want a piece of his ass as well, so we should be good as far as keeping this under wraps."

"If you don't mind my asking, how bad is it?"

"It's about as bad as it gets, Chief. Let's just say, if we don't stop this, I wouldn't plan any vacations to my country for a very long time."

"How long might that be?"

"Thirty years. Maybe a little more, maybe less."

"Jesus," replied the Chief.

"Unfortunately, Chief, I think the Son of God is on vacation right now. So, it's down to me with a little help from my friends."

58

MI5 HEADQUARTERS, THAMES HOUSE, LONDON,
8:45 A.M. GMT

K was in his office trying to catch up with the mundane paperwork that seemed to constantly gather on his desk. He wasn't really accomplishing much, but it helped keep his mind off the dire situation the country was in. What he really needed was an update from Nolan, as that would give him an idea for what their next steps should be. He signed his name at the bottom of a requisition for a country estate in West Sussex that was part of the National Trust; it would become MI5's new home if they failed to prevent the upcoming attack on the capital. He sighed heavily as he placed it in his out tray; this was something all the government department heads were doing, although most would never know why unless the unthinkable were to happen.

The government's main concern was the civilian population and the support services needed for a mass exposure of radiation. At a cabinet meeting the day before, which had been attended by all the major commissioners of the regional police forces, the head of the National Health Service, and himself; the discussion had focused on what to do with the people. There were plans in place on what to do in case of a nuclear or biological attack, but the writers of those plans had assumed a large death rate and therefore a much more manageable number of survivors. The problem with a dirty bomb going off in a major city was that the initial casualty count would be fairly low, but the area affected by the radiation could be vast depending on the strength of the wind and its direction.

At first, they had discussed decontamination and hospital care for the very sick. It was decided that all current patients in NHS facilities who couldn't be sent home would start being moved to outlying hospitals. Excuses such as an E. coli breakout or a flu epidemic were floated round as an explanation for the moves, as the press would be all over the government within twenty-four hours. This plan would free up doctors and nurses to be moved to field hospitals and clearing stations that were already being set up to the north and south of London and Manchester.

Then the topic of evacuation had been raised. Some of the cabinet members had insisted they warn the public and that they should self-evacuate as soon as possible. K told them that was insane, and the room exploded. After a few minutes of outrage, K calmly explained that it was highly likely that both of the bombs were already in the designated target cities and could be moved at a moment's notice into position for detonation. If any public warning was given, the terrorists would certainly detonate the bombs, or even worse, move them to cities that weren't being evacuated.

"Then what do you suggest?" asked the prime minister.

"Have the population shelter in place and then evacuate them in stages. The most affected areas first, then moving outward into other areas. We can even bring in enough CBRN suits to protect them from further exposure," replied K.

"And the sick and injured?" she asked.

"We can funnel people through decontamination stations around the city at a manageable rate and treat those with severe radiation poisoning at our field hospitals," replied the head of the NHS, who had discussed this with K and the police commissioners before the meeting. "Those needing less care can be shipped off to other regional hospitals."

"And how do we get millions of people to shelter in place, might I ask?" said the deputy prime minister.

"Use the emergency broadcast system. After all, that's what it's there for," replied K.

"But that will still alert the terrorists," said the secretary of state.

"Yes, it will," replied K. "But we wouldn't do that until the day we think they are going to launch the attack anyway. That will give us time to prepare. We need to open every mothballed military base and set up tent cities for the evacuees. We can also have the police and Army cordon off every road out of both the cities the day before the announcement. Every vehicle will be searched, just to make sure that they haven't got wind of anything."

"But the death toll will still be high given the amount of radioactive material," replied the deputy prime minister.

"Yes, but small in comparison to what you'd have if millions of people were out on the streets trying to get out of London and Manchester on congested roadways. Plus, can you even comprehend the difficulties for our emergency services trying to rescue people during a mass evacuation fueled by full-scale panic? It really would be disastrous."

"Right," said the prime minister. "You've given us a lot of information to discuss. We will get back to you by the morning with our decision on how to proceed. I pray none of this will prove necessary."

"Me too, Prime Minister."

A day after meeting with the prime minister, he was even more exhausted and frustrated with the way things were progressing. He yawned and looked at his watch yet again. Five past nine, and still nothing from the prime minister. Or Nolan. K pushed the intercom button for his secretary to make him another coffee when his phone rang. It was Nolan.

"Jesus, lad, you had me worried there. I thought you might be in a cell by now."

"Thank you, sir, but no. The call the president made did the trick."

"So what's going on, Nolan?"

"Like I said earlier, sir, I had a little word with our congressman."

K could imagine what a little word from Nolan, given the

circumstances of the mission, could entail, and he had to admit, he was surprised the man was still with the living.

"The problem is the woman—her nickname is 'The Terror,' by the way."

"Oh, that's just icing on the cake, isn't it?"

"She and Patrick O'Keith flew out yesterday by private jet for Biggin Hill. Unfortunately, sir, I don't know if they flew into another EU country first to clear immigration. I really wouldn't be shocked to find out they landed in Shannon first, then flew on to Biggin Hill."

"Great, that's just bloody great."

"I know, sir, sorry, sir. And one other thing—the congressman overheard them talking about vans and boats. My guess, sir, is the terrorists may load the bombs onto one or more boats and use the waterways and canals to get them into position."

K heard cheering in the background. "What the hell is going on there, Nolan?"

Terry started to laugh and let out a loud cheer. "It's Shae, sir. She just walked out of the front door of the house."

"Bloody marvelous, Nolan. Bloody marvelous. What do you need from me next?"

"I need passports for Shae and Kristen as soon as possible and a private plane to get us and our SAS lads back to the UK."

"Why do Shae and Kristen both need passports?"

"Because Shae is the only one who can recognize this woman, and gauging by the reaction of her and Kristen right now, there is no way in hell we'll be able to separate these two."

59

NOLAN'S APARTMENT, LONDON, 10:30 A.M. GMT

Getting out of the States had been easier said than done. The delay was in procuring British passports for Shae and Kristen, as they weren't from the United Kingdom. Terry was tempted to shoot the consulate's pencil-pushing twit, who was gumming up the works, but then a letter had been faxed over from the PM herself telling them to process the damn passports, which had finally gotten the ball rolling. Then there had been an issue with the paper. It had gotten damp somehow and was unusable. A new batch of passport paper had to be brought up by courier from the embassy in Washington, D.C. It had taken a total of eleven hours from the time they walked into the British consulate on forty-eighth Street and Second Avenue to even begin the journey home. After a brief helicopter ride out to Teterboro Airport in New Jersey, the flight time by private jet to Heathrow was six hours.

The one positive thing about being constantly out of the country on the government's dime was that Nolan's bank account was doing very well, as he wasn't spending any of his paychecks. He'd made a bundle from the sale of the apartment after the divorce and had invested wisely, eventually buying a high-rise apartment in the Isle of Dogs area of London with cash.

When Terry arrived at his apartment, he looked in the bathroom mirror and was not too impressed by the image that stared back at him. His ribs hurt like hell. A third of a bottle of Grey Goose and half a pack of cigarettes, plus one of the SAS doc's happy pills, took care of that. It always felt strange to him when he got to lie on his own bed. Welcoming, but strange, as it was such a rare occurrence. He woke at ten thirty after only five and a half hours of sleep. It would have to do. He was paying the price for the Grey Goose with a nasty headache and a mouth that tasted like an invisible magic gorilla had taken a shit in it during the night. *Got to stop writing checks my body can't cash.*

After a prolonged hot and cold shower and a decent shave, apart from the two pieces of bog roll sticking to his face to staunch the flow of blood from a couple of nicks, he finally felt human. He made himself a triple espresso with the one possession he couldn't live without, a La Marzocco GS3 expresso maker. It had cost him an arm and a leg—over £6,000 including VAT—but he didn't care; he loved the damn thing. His naked feet slapped across the light pine floor as he made his way out onto the balcony for his first smoke of the day. He had to admit, the one thing he missed most of all when away from his home was the view of the Thames River from his lofty perch. He played with his wedding ring, turning it around on his finger. Despite his divorce, he'd never taken it off.

His phone started to ring, and he stubbed out the cigarette in the ashtray before answering.

"Yes?"

"Hi, boss, it's Huntington. I just heard from K. Myself and the SAS lads, the ladies too, are to meet him at the Crimea, his private club, for lunch before heading over to MI5. You're to come as well, of course."

Terry smiled at Huntington's use of the word "boss" instead of "sir." In SAS circles, it was the ultimate sign of respect. "Okay, Captain. What time do you need me there?"

"Noon. Just out of curiosity, how's the food at the Crimea Club?"

"Stick to the fish, lamb, or roast beef. The rest of it tastes like shit."

Huntington started laughing. "Will do, boss. I'll give the lads a heads-up."

Nolan looked at his watch and made a beeline for the master bedroom. He'd have to get a move on if he was going to be at K's club by twelve. After dressing in a dark suit and slate-gray shirt, he slipped on a black pair of oxfords over his black socks and headed for the noise of the city. He hailed a black cab to take him to his destination. Rather, halfway to his destination. After switching cabs at Piccadilly Circus, he arrived at 139 Piccadilly Square at twelve on the dot.

Huntington and what remained of his team were already waiting in the impressive reception area. All the men were watching over Shae and Kristen as securely as they would protect their own daughters. It made Terry grin to see how nervous they looked. After all, waiting to meet the head of MI5 at his club was a pretty big deal. To the SAS men, having lunch with him was unheard of. The NCOs were all wearing navy blue blazers with regimental ties, the unofficial dress code of the British military when attending something of importance. They also all sported the telltale bulge under their armpits of men who were armed, as did Nolan. The ladies wore dresses, he surmised there had been a hastily arranged shopping trip earlier in the day.

On arriving in the country, a decent hotel had been arranged in the city. The SAS men had three rooms, on each side of Shae and Kristen's room. Huntington's room even had a connecting door that was to be kept unlocked. The room one floor below Shae was rented and occupied by a member of the security team as well. It may have seemed overcautious, but they weren't about to take any chances with the one person that could describe An Dailtín.

Terry walked over to Huntington. "Nice to see you, Captain, I must admit you guys clean up pretty well."

The officer laughed. "We try, boss. We try."

Next he went to shake Shae's hand, but she ignored it and gave him a big hug. He smiled and hugged her back, a little too hard, as his ribs started to loudly protest. He gasped a little and she backed away.

"Sorry, Terry," she mumbled. "I forgot."

Terry put his hand under her chin and lifted her face slightly and smiled. "You can crush my ribs any day, Shae. I'm just grateful that you're still with us." Looking at her face, he was amazed at how a little makeup applied correctly could cover up almost anything. There still was a slight swelling on her lower lip, but otherwise there were no signs of bruising. No one looking at her would ever imagine that she had just been rescued from a violent terrorist organization.

Next, he approached Kristen, who didn't even give him the opportunity to offer his hand. She threw her arms around his neck and kissed him on the cheek. She looked at him deeply in the eyes, tears welling up in hers and then looked over at Shae before turning back to him.

"Thank you, Terry. Thanks for everything."

He grinned. "It was my pleasure, Kristen, and thank you. I couldn't have done any of it without your help. Anyway, it's not quite over yet, so save the thanks for later. If there is a later."

He stood looking at her, her arms still wrapped around his neck, and he was suddenly overwhelmed by a sense of sadness. *What the hell is this, some sort of premonition?* He sighed heavily and released himself from her grasp.

He was about to shake hands with the rest of the men when he saw K walking through the heavy revolving door at the entrance to the club. He walked over and shook K's hand.

"Good afternoon, sir. It's a pleasure to be back. Assuming we're not about to all become radioactive anytime soon."

"Nice to see you in one piece, son. My apologies for being late, but I had to see the PM this morning." He smiled tightly. "As you can imagine, not exactly my favorite way to begin the day."

60

MI5 HEADQUARTERS, THAMES HOUSE, LONDON,
2:00 P.M. GMT

Nolan had been mistaken about the shoulder of lamb with rosemary sauce. Although it was cooked perfectly, it seemed the Crimea Club chef had some aversion to seasonings; it was totally bland—the kind of meal that gave British food its international reputation. The SAS team had all ordered the filet of beef with Béarnaise sauce—cooked to a perfect medium rare and looking delicious. Shae and K had gone for the grilled Dover sole with lemon and herb butter. When Kristen began ordering the salmon fish cakes and K had coughed to attract her attention and subtly shook his head no, Terry had to suppress a laugh. After that warning, Kristen had also ordered the sole. As the waiter walked away, K made a comment comparing the fish cakes unfavorably to axle grease, which he claimed was not only more tender but more flavorful. The entire table burst out laughing, bringing looks of consternation from the elderly club members in mid soup-slurp. No wine had been ordered with the meal. Apart from the ladies ordering Diet Cokes, the rest of the table had ordered coffee with instructions to the waiter to keep it flowing. The only interruption to the meal was when a waiter entering the kitchen dropped a plate. Instantly, guns were drawn, and the men were on their feet forming a protective cordon around K and the two ladies. The other diners were shocked, of course, and the men returned to their seats, but the maître d' expertly smoothed things over, and the meal was finished without further incident.

After lunch, K told his four-man permanent security team to have two more cars brought over to drive them back to Thames House. At last, Terry was coming home to roost. K had Nolan and Huntington ride with him and during the drive gave them a heads-up on the prime minister's decision to follow his plan to have the residents of the city shelter in place.

"Has Her Majesty signed Queen's Order Two?" asked Huntington.

"She did so this morning," replied K.

"So, the entire British military is being deployed?"

K nodded. "As of yesterday, all leave was cancelled, and troops currently away from their units were ordered back to base. Reserve and territorial units are being called up, and all police officers and civil defense personnel are on a two-hour notice to report for duty. That will most probably change by morning. Soldiers are being deployed as discreetly as possible to Northern Ireland to try and prevent any follow-up attacks. Also, troops are to be deployed to every major city. Food rationing is going to be implemented to prevent hoarding."

"Bloody hell," said Nolan. "This is not going to end well."

"No, I'm afraid it's not," replied K. "That's why we have to stop this."

"What's next?" asked Huntington.

"Today we're going to have Shae work with one of our people to put together a photofit of the woman and also look over our mugshot database. We've already put the word out to the local constabularies, ports, and airports to be on the lookout for Patrick O'Keith. If we can grab him then he'll tell us where the woman is once our inquisitors get their hands on him."

"That's if she's here," said Huntington.

"Oh, she's here," replied K. "My people have been looking at CCTV footage from Biggin Hill, and they were both spotted going through the small terminal building there. Unfortunately, she knew she'd be surveilled and was wearing a hat *and* kept her head down. We do, however, have a clear shot of O'Keith. They were picked up by private car, a white Range Rover, which we tracked almost to the city but lost when it exited the A23 near Streatham Common. The car was found abandoned near the North Dulwich train station an hour ago. What vehicle they used after that we have no idea. We have over a hundred officers from the Metropolitan Police reviewing CCTV footage of every vehicle on the surrounding roads, checking the four-hour period when they would have ditched the car, but it's like looking for a needle in all the haystacks in Great Britain combined. We don't know where our two main players switched cars—it could have been miles away from where the car was left."

"So we're screwed," replied Nolan.

"There is one thing," said K. "It's the reason I wanted to talk to you two away from the others. We need to offer some bait to get An Dailtín to make a move."

"I don't particularly like the sound of that," replied Nolan.

The car came to a halt, and K looked out the window. "We're here. We shall discuss this further—later."

Terry was more than a little surprised that the vehicles had stopped outside the main entrance to the building instead of going straight down to the underground carpark, but he shook it off as paranoia.

It had been a number of years since he had been in the building, and he was quietly surprised at how much had changed. Gone were the desks that had lined the room with their antiquated computers, replaced by modular cubicles and the latest high-end computer systems. Banks of monitors dotted the room, forming large screens when needed. He also noticed a kitchen in one corner that had a stock of various pastries and snacks. *I guess the war on terror has significantly increased MI5's budget.*

Shae spent an hour working on the photofit, and after it was completed, they ran the sketch through the facial recognition database. One of the people handling the identification process told Nolan that Shae was handling herself like a boss, which surprised everyone, given her recent ordeal. They got a couple of hits, but these were quickly dismissed. Then it was on to the mugshots. After an hour, Shae requested a break, as the images were beginning to blur into each other. The group headed to a coffee shop a couple of blocks away and sat outside in the crisp London day enjoying the fresh cool air. Then it was back for another marathon session. Before they left for dinner, K called Nolan and Huntington into his office.

"So, no luck?" he asked.

"Sorry, sir, nothing so far," said Terry. "We are planning to come back tomorrow to look through the Interpol and FBI mugshots, but to be honest, I'm not holding out for her having much luck."

"I guess that brings us to the other matter we discussed earlier."

"The other matter?" inquired Huntington.

"He means the bait thing," replied Terry.

K sat back in his chair and ran through the idea he'd come up with to draw out their female adversary. When he finished, there was an uncomfortable silence between the three men.

"Well?" he asked. "What do you think?"

Huntington remained silent and looked over at the MI5 operative.

"Please excuse my language, sir," Terry said, "but are you out of your fucking mind?"

61

MAZE GRILL, CENTRAL LONDON, 7:00 P.M. GMT

K booked a private dining room for them at Gordon Ramsey's Maze Grill Mayfair at Grosvenor Square. Apparently, he had heard Kristen talk about how she wanted to eat at the celebrity chef's flagship restaurant, Restaurant Gordon Ramsey, but they didn't have private dining for a group of nine—two new SAS men had joined the group earlier in the day to bring the team up to a full strength of six, so K had suggested the Maze Grill instead. Kristen was speechless and settled for giving K a peck on the cheek.

They set out in three armored Jaguar XJ saloons with three SAS men each in the lead and trail cars providing security, Nolan and the two ladies in the middle car. Each vehicle also had a driver who doubled as additional security. Nolan, in the front passenger seat, had been unusually quiet as they made their way to the restaurant, still mulling over the conversation he and Huntington had with K before leaving, but Shae and Kristen, in the back, made up for it by talking incessantly as they drove past the sights of London. Shae, having lived there, was happy to point out all the places she remembered, and Kristen, whose international experience had been a trip to the Canadian side of Niagara Falls, soaked it up like a sponge. Nolan sat in the front enjoying hearing the two ladies' excitement as they drove through the city. He had taken Shae to one side earlier in the day, asked how she was holding up, and had been rewarded with a huge smile. He had expected bouts of crying or even the odd anxiety attack, but she appeared to be doing well. *Christ only knows how she isn't a basket case.*

When they arrived at the restaurant, instead of pulling up to the front door, they stopped at the delivery entrance. Nolan and the two women were hustled out of the car by the SAS men and led through the kitchen to a butcher block table overlooking the kitchen. The SAS men agreed that two of them would remain outside the entrance to the kitchen at all times and would switch out periodically so they could all have the opportunity to enjoy the outstanding cuisine. Kristen and Shae were both hoping to have Chef Ramsey curse at them in person, but they were informed by their waiter that unfortunately he was out of the country taping a new reality show. Initially, they were a little disappointed, but the food more than made up for it.

The SAS men and Nolan opted for coffee or Coke, but the ladies ordered a bottle of 2016 Châteauneuf-du-Pape, Signature Domaine la Barroche. The spicy red cost £140—not too pricey by the wine list's offerings. Shae offered Nolan a glass, but he opted to abstain. He was armed and wouldn't be of much use if his reactions were slowed. He pushed aside all thoughts of K's decoy suggestion and decided to enjoy the evening. He would, however, make a point of talking to Huntington about it later.

For dinner, the group ordered three appetizers each of the chili and garlic prawns and the grilled octopus. Both were spectacular and were polished off rather quickly. As for the entrees, they all settled for the beef Wellington with seasonal vegetables, a specialty of Gordon Ramsey, so how could they not order it? When the food arrived, the table became silent as each diner's focus was on the delicious meal—they wanted to savor every morsel. For dessert, the men decided to go with the sticky toffee pudding; as Huntington pointed out to the ladies, "It's an English thing." Kristen and Shae both went with the vanilla crème brûlée on the understanding that they would be offered the opportunity to try the pudding. None of them were disappointed with their selection, and both ladies agreed that if they had the opportunity to return to the restaurant, they would order the sticky toffee pudding.

As they were finishing, Kristen and Shae waylaid Nolan as he was returning to the table from the bathroom.

"Why are we all just sitting around doing nothing? It's driving us both nuts," said Shae.

Nolan smiled. "Unfortunately, ladies, at present it is kind of out of our hands. We have every police department in the country out beating the bushes as well as MI5 and MI6."

"But there must be something we can do?" pleaded Kristen. "Can't they release something on the television and the newspapers so that people can help?"

"If we did that, there would be mass panic. Every road, train, bus would be packed with people trying to get out of the cities. So much so that no one would get out. Also, we would show our hand to the people responsible, and they would either just go ahead and set off the devices now or go underground and wait till everything died down and then set them off. Either way it's a lose-lose for us."

"I guess you guys know what you are doing," said Shae.

"I hope so, or we're all screwed," replied Nolan.

After dinner, the trio of Jags took Huntington's men and the ladies back to their hotel and Huntington and the MI5 agent back to his place on the Isle of Dogs. By the time they arrived, Terry was ready for a large vodka on the rocks. He asked Huntington if he wanted anything, and he settled for a Coke.

"Getting sick of waiting around and kicking your heels yet?" asked Nolan.

"Unfortunately, it comes with the job. Anymore thoughts on K's idea?"

"I should have known he was up to something," said Terry, taking another large gulp of the double vodka in his glass. "That was why K had the cars park outside the main entrance instead of heading for the underground carpark. He wanted anyone keeping an eye on the building to get a good look at us."

"He does have a point," replied Huntington.

"You have got to be kidding."

"No, actually, I'm not. The fates of millions of people are at stake. Tens of millions. It means we have to take risks."

"Fine, then *I'll* do it. The woman seems to have it in for me anyway, so why not?"

"Sorry, boss, I don't think that would fly. She'd immediately smell a rat. You know it, I know it, and so does K."

"Then what about a female agent? Someone who has training."

"She'd be dead within a minute. It has to be either Shae or Kristen. That's why K left the initial decision up to you on who to approach."

"Jesus, talk about Hobson's choice."

"No kidding." Huntington looked around Nolan's apartment. "I guess that's why you get the big bucks, boss."

Nolan rolled his eyes. "Oh, if only you knew, Captain. Hey, maybe you should think about a change in career; you've got your shit together, as our American friends say."

"Not a fucking chance. I've got a year and a half left with the regiment, then it's back to One Para. After that, I plan on doing a tour with the Special Reconnaissance Regiment. By then I should be a major. That'll do. I plan to call it a day then. Maybe run for Parliament or something."

"Somebody pinch me, I'm sitting in the presence of the future prime minister!"

Huntington burst out laughing at the thought. "Christ, Nolan. Then the country really would be fucked. So what about you, boss? Any future plans after this job?"

"You mean if the country is still around. Oh, I don't know, there are a couple of things I have to take care of before I call it a day." Nolan played with his wedding ring. "There's this island in the Caribbean I wouldn't mind kicking back on. Maybe buy a boat or something."

"Give me a break, boss, you'd die of boredom."

"You know, that might be a nice way to go."

Huntington suddenly became a little morose. "So . . . who's it going to be?"

62

MI5 HEADQUARTERS, THAMES HOUSE, LONDON,
3:00 P.M. GMT

By the afternoon of the following day, Shae had seen every mugshot in MI5's hands and had come up empty. K had arranged for her to meet with a psychologist who specialized in the questioning of witnesses to see if there was anything more to glean from her time being held captive. She was with the psychologist when K asked Terry to stop by his office. The two men sat for a few minutes enjoying a cup of K's secret stash of coffee, replenished the day before and brewed by his outrageously expensive coffee maker.

"Terry, when this current operation is over and after you take some R and R, I have a special job I want you to focus on."

"What's that, sir," asked Nolan, already figuring he knew the answer.

"I want you to put a team together and bring me the mole's head on a pike. Think you're up to that?"

"Given that we've been after the bastard for years, and I owe them for what happened back in the day, I can try, but no guarantees, sir."

"I understand that, son. This will be completely off the books, but you'll have access to everything I've amassed over the years. Hell, we may be wrong about there even being a mole, but I don't think so. It's just that there have been too many blown operations. Not all, mind you, but enough."

"I'll do my best, sir."

"That's all I can ask. Now, have you thought any more about what I suggested?"

"Unfortunately, sir, it's about all I've been able to think about."

"And?"

"It's got to be Kristen. The only question is, will she do it?"

"I think you already know the answer to that."

Terry let out a long sigh. "Yes, sir, she'll do it."

"Just out of curiosity, why her and not Shae?"

"To be honest, sir, it's the way she took out Lander. She lost it a little afterward, but when he was shooting at her she kept it together. Shae, she's tough but I just don't know. It's as if there's a little voice in my head saying no for some reason. Maybe it's her lack of emotion after being captured and beaten that's bothering me. If I'm honest, I can't put my finger on it, but something is bothering me. Either she is going to continue the way she is, or she is going to crash and burn, and we can't risk asking her to do something that might push her over the edge."

"Well, we better get her in here while Shae is otherwise occupied. I wonder how her acting skills are."

Five minutes later, Kristen was shown into K's inner sanctum. K offered her coffee, but she settled for bottled water.

Before K or Nolan could speak, Kristen cut them off. "What do you need, sir?" she asked.

"Why would you think we need anything?" asked K.

"Because I'm sitting here, that's why."

K tilted his head. "I think you made the right decision, Nolan." He looked at Kristen. "You're absolutely right, young lady, we do need something."

"Figures," she replied. "And I'm sure it's going to be dangerous, right?"

"Right," replied Terry. "But if you don't want to do what we are about to ask, it would be completely understandable. We only managed to get Shae back by the skin of our teeth and if this goes wrong, we may not be able to do that again."

"I understand that," replied Kristen. "But there are still two bombs out there that could hurt a lot of people, and it's time to step up and do what's right."

"This isn't technically your fight, you know," replied K.

"After what they did to Shae, it is. What the hell, I'm in."

"But you don't know what we need yet," replied K.

"Okay, run it by me, but the answer is still going to be yes."

K sighed. "Right, then. What we need is someone to act as bait. We are fairly sure that these terrorists have eyes on this building and most probably your hotel by now."

"How can you know that?"

"Because they aren't stupid and it's exactly what we would do," replied Nolan. "The thing is, we still have two dirty bombs out there, and as of now, we've had no luck in finding them. We were hoping that Shae may have been able to give us a lead with the description of the lady who held her captive. Even better would have been for Shae to pick out her mugshot, but that hasn't happened. She's not in our system and has managed to fly below our radar. Somehow, we have to find another way of getting her location."

"How will using me as bait get you that?"

K was about to answer when his number two burst into his office.

"What the hell is it? I'm in the middle of an important meeting. Haven't you ever heard of knocking before entering?"

"We think we've found one of the bombs, sir."

"You what?" said Terry, jumping to his feet.

"We think we've found one of the bombs. The one targeting Manchester."

"What? How?" said K. "Show me. Where is it?"

"The River Irwell, sir."

"And where, might I ask, is the River Irwell?"

"Of course," said Terry. "The River Irwell separates Manchester and Salford. It nearly runs right into the center of Manchester."

"And just how do you know that?"

"You forget, sir, that's where I was born. It used to be polluted as hell, but now they actually run sightseeing tours on the bloody thing."

K turned to his number two. "Tell Huntington and his team to get their gear together. No offense to our boys in blue, but I want him on this."

"Yes sir."

"Wait a minute, sir. The last thing we need is for these guys to go in guns blazing. Remember what we're dealing with. What we need is someone who can assess the situation. Someone who can maybe get on the inside."

K smiled. "Well, I guess you just volunteered for the job."

Terry's put his hands on his knees. "I guess I did."

"Good, tell me what you need."

"First of all, I think I need my head checked, sir."

K squinted fiercely at Nolan. "Why do you think we get along so well? I've known that since we first met."

63

GREATER MANCHESTER POLICE HEADQUARTERS, MANCHESTER, 11:00 P.M. GMT

Nolan had forgotten that his hometown was known as the Rainy City, but by God, the weather was reminding him. He and the SAS men had landed late the night before at Manchester International and were taken to the Greater Manchester Police headquarters for a briefing by the Counter-Terrorism Unit and Tactical Firearms Unit. Before they had left, K had informed them that the locals were not exactly happy with them being brought in to take the lead in the operation. Their anger showed on the faces of the men in the room when Nolan and the SAS team walked in.

There were twenty-eight people in the room, most being from the Counter-Terrorism Unit. A detective chief inspector who was the senior investigating officer had just begun a briefing in front of three white boards holding various photographs of a house and a narrow boat tied up to a small wooden dock. On the far-right whiteboard were slightly grainy photographs of two men, presumably occupants of either the boat or the house. The DCI started talking about conducting a breach of the house in the early hours of the morning in coordination with a smaller team tackling the men on the boat.

Terry gave Huntington a nudge and motioned for him to follow to the front of the room next to the DCI. The man kept talking until it was obvious Nolan wanted to speak.

"And you are?" he asked.

"You can call me Terry. I'm with British intelligence and this," he said pointing to Huntington, "is Captain Fred. It's not his real name, but that's all most of the people in this room are getting. He's an SAS officer. You may have noticed his men at the back of the room. They'll be conducting any assault that's necessary. Please feel free to buy them as many pints as they can handle when we're done, but in the meantime, leave them alone as much as possible, as they are here to do a job and do it well."

There was some disgruntled mumbling in the room, and even the DCI looked a little perturbed.

Terry continued. "Before we carry on with this briefing, I have to ask: has everyone here signed the Official Secrets Act? If not, raise your hand." There were a number of nods from individuals, but no one raised their hand. "Good," said Nolan. "You're not going to like what I'm about to say. I need everyone to turn in their mobile phones and to know that, for the next forty-eight hours, no one can leave this building unless you're part of the team that will be surveilling the property. You're also to have no contact with any other officers or your family, unless it is an unavoidable emergency, in which case you will be accompanied by two other officers at all times. If you don't like it, you're free to leave right now."

The groans and mumbling grew even louder, but nobody got up to leave.

Huntington tapped Nolan on the back. "What gives, boss? Why the lockdown?" he whispered.

"I don't think any of these guys really know the extent of what we're dealing with, and if you found out about what could happen, and you were a regular copper, what would you do?"

Huntington thought for a minute, then it clicked. "Call my family and tell them to get as far away from the city as they could."

"Right! And what's the first thing that family would do?"

"Call other family members, friends, and neighbors."

"Then they, of course would do the same, and you have panic, and someone is sure to call the press."

"And then, bang. They set the thing off. Or both of them."

"Right!"

The room slowly, with much cajoling of the DCI, settled down.

"Okay, folks. Call your families now and let them know you will be on a job for the next few days and not to worry. If they do need to contact you in an emergency, tell them to contact the operator here and a message will be passed along. Do not tell them the nature of the job. Understand?"

It took ten minutes for all the calls to be made and then, reluctantly, all the phones were handed in.

"Right," said Nolan. "I'll be working directly with DCI . . . ?"

"Philips," he replied.

"Philips, good. I'll also be meeting with all detective sergeants and other team leaders after the briefing. All members of the Counter-Terrorism Unit and the Tactical Firearms Unit will meet with Captain Fred." Terry smiled. "Sorry, Fred, it was the best I could come up with at the time."

That brought some nervous laughter from the room.

"And the rest of the SAS team," continued Nolan. "Now, as to the reason for the lockdown and what we are dealing with."

The door opened, and a woman, along with two of her colleagues, entered the room. Nolan waved her up to the front of the room and shook her hand. "Hello, Leslie, it's a pleasure to finally meet you in the flesh. You remember Captain Fred?" He gave her a wink as Huntington shook her hand. He turned back to the room.

"Now everyone, I would like to introduce someone whose job it will be to save our combined rear ends. This is Leslie. I'm told she has the rank of colonel. She is here to stop bad things exploding. If you see her running away, may I suggest you all follow as quickly as possible."

That brought even more of a laugh from the room.

"Also, don't call her ma'am, she doesn't like it."

More laughter.

"Let's get down to the nitty-gritty. It's my understanding that we are dealing with a four-man terrorist cell. Correct, Philips?"

"That's correct, sir," replied the DCI.

"Okay, that fits with what we've dealt with in the past. Now for the million-pound question you're all wondering about. What we have here, people, is a four-man NIRA unit that is guarding a radioactive dirty bomb."

The room was suddenly very loud with people shouting questions. Terry held up his hands, and the room began to settle down.

"The problem with these particular devices is the amount of radioactive material. We estimate it to be around two hundred pounds with a hundred pounds of C-4 to aid in its dispersal. I've also been informed that this is a particularly nasty form of radioactive material called Tc-99, which has a half-life of over two hundred thousand years. If this does go off, it's going to ruin a lot of people's lives. Maybe ten thousand generations' worth." There were murmurs around the room as the officers present looked at each other, comprehending the gravity of the situation.

One of the younger officers raised a hand. Nolan nodded in his direction to speak.

"What is it, lad?"

"If someone wants to pull out now, can they?"

"Only if they are willing to spend the next few days in one of the cells," replied Nolan. "Sorry, mate, if that seems harsh, but we really can't risk this information getting out and winding up on the ten o'clock news. Does that answer your question?"

The young man didn't look particularly happy but nodded yes.

"Now, if there is nothing else, I'll leave it to Leslie to go into the details of the construction of the bomb and why there's little chance of radioactive contamination in its current form. To be honest, those details are way above my pay grade. I'll then have Captain Fred go over the initial plan for the assault on the property and the narrow boat. If you could hold off any questions until they are finished, that would be helpful. Finally, if someone could direct me to the nearest mug of coffee, I would very much appreciate it."

The DCI took him to his office and his own personal coffee maker—an elderly Russell Hobbs drip machine—while the others continued the briefing.

"So, what are the chances of pulling this off?" DCI Philips asked.

Terry shrugged. "To be honest, I'd say fifty-fifty. The problem, as I see it, is getting aboard the boat before whoever is on it decides to set it off. That's where I come in."

"You really think these people are that insane that they would blow themselves up?"

"Unfortunately, sir, they seem to have learned a great deal from our Jihadi friends and are more than willing to die for the cause."

"Fuck me," replied the DCI.

"Precisely," replied Nolan taking a sip of his absolutely God-awful cop shop coffee. Damn, it was good.

64

RIVER IRWELL, NORTH OF MANCHESTER, 1:00 A.M. GMT

Rain was coming down in buckets, which pissed off Terry to no end. Not because he was soaking wet lying in a hedgerow with a night-vision scope trained on the house and which he periodically turned to the narrow boat, but because it was playing havoc with their listening gear. He found his mind considering what they were up against and how insane it was that this faction of the NIRA were willing to potentially kill hundreds of thousands of civilians to achieve their goal. It was really pissing him off that, after so many years of relative peace, they were still hell-bent on reigniting the Troubles all over again. It had been over thirty years since he had first been sent to Northern Ireland in the bad old days, and here he was still fighting the same old fanatics, except this time they had the money and expertise to bring his country to its knees, and that made him mad as hell. What they hadn't counted on was that when he got mad, he was especially dangerous.

The sound of the heavy rain was making it difficult for the parabolic microphones aimed at the narrow boat to pick up the conversation between the two men on board. This was extremely frustrating for Terry, as he needed to hear not so much what the men were saying, but the way they were saying it. The laser mics were not having an easier time of it, either. These worked by firing a laser beam at the windows and turning the minute vibrations in the glass caused by a conversation into actual sound. On single-pane windows, they worked a dream, but on double-pane insulated windows, not so much. Also, if someone was playing loud music in the room or had the TV volume up, it caused the system to be next to useless. In this case, the heavy slanting rain beating on the glass was causing enough of a vibration to make any electronic intelligence gathering intermittent at best.

Terry thought about sticking small microphones directly on the windows, as they were small enough that the chances of one of the occupants spotting them close to nonexistent. But the house had motion detector lights all around it, so the second anyone got close, the entire property lit up like a Christmas tree.

The men on the boat were switching out with the two men in the house every four hours. In the house, the men's time seemed to be spent eating, drinking a few beers, or sleeping. This was great news for their watchers as, depending how long they had been maintaining this rotation, it could only mean one thing; they were tired. As for the two men on the boat, there was usually one on the deck at all times and one down below, babysitting the package. And this was the tricky part. They would have to take out the terrorist on the deck as silently as possible, so as not to alert the man below. This ruled out shooting him—a body falling on the deck would most certainly cause concern. The man on deck would have to be removed up close and personal with a knife. Easy enough, but then the issue became how to get below. The men on the boat exchanged positions once every hour, and the change always occurred below deck. That was where Nolan hearing the men speak to each other came into play. All he needed was thirty minutes of clear conversation and he was good, but at present it just wasn't happening.

He sighed with frustration and slowly backed out from under the hedge and headed back to the dark blue Ford Transit van that was parked down the street. Once he cleared view of the house, he lit a cigarette. He walked slowly, aware of the twenty or so pairs of eyes on him belonging to the Counter-Terrorist Unit and the Tactical Weapons team. He had to give them credit—they were doing a marvelous job of staying out of sight from the next-door neighbors, as well as civilians driving past. That would change in daylight when most of the local population left for school or work. But Terry's plan was for it to all be over by then. Earlier in the day, they had actually had a close call when someone walked their dog, an enormous Newfoundland, oblivious to the police presence, and the shaggy black beast had cocked its leg on a bush concealing a tactical officer wearing a ghillie suit. The man walking the dog had been none the wiser, but the officer in question had sworn, to the laughter of those present, that the Newfie knew exactly what he was doing and where he was aiming.

Terry threw the cigarette away and knocked on the back door of the van. It opened immediately and he climbed in the back.

"Any better luck with the sound gear?" he asked the four men present.

"Sorry, boss," replied Huntington. "Not a bloody thing."

"Shit!" he replied. He helped himself to a Nescafé instant coffee—*Beggars can't be choosers*—and lit yet another cigarette as he settled into the most uncomfortable plastic chair designed by man. He looked at the four men hunched over the mass of equipment that lined either side of the vehicle. Besides the sound equipment they were using to monitor their targets, there were also TV monitors that were hooked up via Wi-Fi to various cameras they had placed around the property. They were also connected remotely to all the CCTV cameras in the area and could follow the path of their subjects pretty much anywhere they went in the UK. This would have been great if any of them had left to go to the grocery store or even stopped by a local takeaway, but so far, they hadn't left the property. They could even get a direct link to a drone, but in this weather all it would have shown was an aerial view of more rain, so that monitor was blank.

Terry looked over at Huntington, who was desperately trying to decipher the intermittent conversations about football and girls that seemed to be an ongoing thing between the men on the boat. Obviously, they were as bored as the men in the van.

"How long before the next shift change?" Terry asked.

"Fifty minutes," replied Huntington.

"Are your lads ready to go?"

Huntington smiled and nodded. "Whenever you are, boss. You're the one who'll be freezing his balls off in that bloody river."

"Yeah, well, slight change of plan there, mate. You're coming with me."

"Wait, what?"

"I've been thinking about it. If something goes wrong, you're going to have to try and take out the other bastard down below."

"Hang on a second, boss. I thought the whole point of you doing this was because you can pull off a Northern Irish accent. That would give you just enough of an edge to get down below far enough to shoot this fucker."

"That's true," he replied dropping into a perfect Belfast accent. "But one should always plan for the shit hitting the fan."

Huntington sighed. "Right. When are we going?"

"Twenty minutes. Should give us enough time to swim upstream and climb onto the front of the narrow boat." He turned to one of the men talking into a radio. "Are the tactical officers ready to take out the lights and also cut the power to the house?"

The man on the radio gave him a thumbs up.

"Listen, this is bloody important. I need someone to activate the security lights right before I take out the guy on the deck. That will keep him distracted long enough for me to take him down, okay?"

"No problem, sir."

"The second you see his head turn toward the house, cut the power and shoot out the battery powered emergency security lights. As soon as you see me go belowdecks, the SAS boys are to move in."

"No problem, boss," replied Huntington.

Terry smiled grimly. "At that point, it won't matter if I fail because we'll all be fucked anyway."

Terry took off his combat jacket and the sweater underneath. He'd remove the rest of his clothes when he got to the riverbank; no point in freaking out a civilian who saw a couple of guys walking down the street in their underwear and T-shirts. Huntington followed suit. Terry put his silenced Walther in his shoulder holster and shoved a couple of Fairbairn-Sykes fighting knives in the webbing belt he was wearing. One could never be too careful, so he brought a spare in case he lost one during the swim. He also picked up a set of night-vision headgear. Huntington followed suit, but he carried a silenced 9mm SIG. He also put a couple of tubes of camouflage cream in his pocket. Lastly, both men inserted earpieces and then a small piece of cotton wool to keep them dry. They were now connected to the communications net.

"Radio check," said Nolan. Whispered voices of those taking part in the op filled his ear.

"Leslie, are you ready to go in case we need you?" he asked.

"Just say the word, Terry," she replied.

"Ready, boss?" asked Huntington.

"Never more so," he replied.

65

RIVER IRWELL, NORTH OF MANCHESTER, 1:43 A.M. GMT

The water was bloody freezing, cold enough that each man gasped involuntarily as they slowly slipped into its darkness, using the low boughs of a weeping willow tree for cover. They swam slowly toward the bow of the seventy-foot narrow boat. Now the rain was a godsend, and Nolan silently prayed that it continue. When they finally reached the painted wood of the bow, both men took a position on either side and slowly, silently slipped aboard. Now to get to the rear without being seen.

There was a six-inch-wide walkway that ran either side of the raised cabin toward the back of the boat. Each of them moved forward at a crouch, their bare feet silent on the deck. Nolan was hardly breathing as he got within two feet of the rear deck. The night was pitch black, the only light coming from the terrorist's cigarette, which bloomed every time he inhaled. *Thank fuck for night-vision goggles.* Terry shuffled one step closer and took a slow deep breath.

"Now," he whispered.

It seemed to go beautifully. The exterior security lights sprang to life ,and as predicted, the man stood up and turned in that direction. Nolan made his move and stepped out onto the deck about two feet from the back of the terrorist. As he took his next step, about to end the man's existence, Terry failed to see the dark brown beer bottle sitting on the deck. His foot kicked it just as the lights of the house were extinguished. The terrorist took a step away from the sound and turned, drawing his weapon. Nolan was screwed.

"Who the fu—"

The question was cut short as Huntington stepped forward, clasped his hand over the man's mouth from behind, pulling his head back in the process. He drove his combat knife up through the man's lower jaw and into his brain. Nolan took a quick step forward and grabbed the terrorist's gun just as it fell from his hand. As Huntington slowly lowered the body to the deck, Terry nodded his thanks. Through the night-vision goggles, he saw the officer give him a thumbs up. Now he had to get a move on.

He crouched down, pulled off the man's shoes, and then undid his pants.

"Give me a hand," he hissed to the SAS officer as he tried to pull them off.

Huntington looked a little confused for a second, then seemed to realize what the MI5 agent was doing. He grabbed one of the pant legs and pulled as Nolan pulled the other. Once the pants were off, Nolan slipped them on. But the shoes were at least a size too small, so Terry just jammed his feet in them, his heels standing on the backs. At least now the man below wouldn't see a naked pair of legs walking down to the steps into the main cabin.

"Ready," he whispered to Huntington.

The officer nodded.

Nolan removed the night-vision goggles and was plunged into darkness. He was about to open the cabin door when his radio crackled to life.

"Alarm clock going off, boss," said one of the SAS men.

"Take them now," whispered Huntington.

They both watched as there was a slight flash of light in one of the downstairs windows from a weapon being fired. Less than thirty seconds later the same happened in an upstairs bedroom.

"All clear," hissed the radios in their ears.

Huntington gave Nolan another thumbs up and drew his weapon, ready to back up the MI5 agent. Nolan opened one of the twin doors that led below. He yelled at the man in his best Irish accent.

"You ready to get some sleep?"

A voice from below answered. "Bleeding right, Jimmy. I'll just put on my coat."

Nolan answered. "Good, because I'm knackered."

Walther at the ready, he took two steps down into the cabin and quickly ducked down so that he could see what was going on. He was shocked when he saw the man standing by the device pointing a gun at him.

"You seem to have lost your stutter, you British bastard." He fired as Nolan dived into the cabin.

The bullet missed his ear by an inch. He rolled as another round slammed into the deck next to him. Nolan fired twice just as the terrorist flipped a switch on the bomb. The man flew backward from the impact of both rounds into his chest. Nolan was on his feet and running toward the device when the man moved his arm trying to aim his gun at him. Terry shot him in the face.

He stopped in front of the control panel, wondering why he was still alive. Then he saw the digital counter clicking down from five minutes.

"Shit!"

Huntington appeared in the cabin next to him. "Oh fuck," he mumbled looking at the timer.

Terry was on the radio. "Leslie, the fucker activated the bomb. You've got four minutes and thirty-seven seconds to deactivate this son of a bitch."

"On my way," replied the bomb disposal expert.

He had to give Leslie her due; the lady sure could run. She was on the boat and below deck with two technicians before the timer hit four minutes.

"Terry, you and the captain get the hell out of here, now," she yelled.

"And go where?" he replied. Walking calmly back up on deck, he dug in the dead man's pockets and smiled when he found a pack of Lambert & Butler cigarettes and a lighter.

Huntington, who had been looking over the small control panel on the back of the boat, flicked a switch, and they were suddenly bathed in light. "That's better," he said. Terry sat down next to the tiller and lit one up as the SAS captain sat on the other side.

"Want one?" he asked Huntington.

"I don't smoke, sir," he replied.

Nolan shook the pack so one of the cigarettes protruded. "Well, I can't think of a better time to start."

66

RIVER IRWELL, NORTH OF MANCHESTER, 1:49 A.M. GMT

They watched as the lights in bedrooms sprang to life in houses up and down the river. Terry smiled grimly at the futility of the police officers' efforts to try and save some of the local residents from the upcoming devastation. He had to give them kudos—none of them tried to save their own skins.

"How long now?" he asked Huntington.

Huntington checked his wristwatch. "About three minutes, by my reckoning."

Nolan flicked the cigarette off the back of the narrowboat and watched in satisfaction as it was extinguished in the river. "Well, Captain, if Leslie can't deactivate this thing, it was a pleasure knowing you." He reached out his hand. The officer shook it firmly.

"Pleasure's all mine."

Nolan heard a voice on his earpiece. "Sir, we have your boss on the line, I'm patching him through now."

"Nolan, where are you?"

"Oh, just relaxing on the back of this narrow boat enjoying the night air. You'll be glad to hear it's finally stopped raining, sir."

"Jesus, son, can't you get out of there?"

Nolan sighed. "And go where, sir?"

"Listen, Nolan. I managed to get Amanda on the line. She wants to talk to you, okay?"

"I'd like that, sir." Her voice suddenly filled his ear.

"Terry, honey. Robert told me what's happening. Is there nothing you can do?"

"One minute," said Huntington.

"I'm sorry, Amanda, but there's no point running. Listen, I need to be quick." He sighed heavily and tears welled up in his eyes. "I'm so sorry, sorry for everything." The words began to choke up in his throat, but he had to get them out. "I'm sorry for how I treated you when Miranda died. I'm sorry for not being there when you needed me."

"It's okay, Terry. I forgive you. I always have."

He sighed. *What a bloody fool I've been and now it's too late.*

"Twenty-five seconds, sir," said Huntington.

"I love you, honey. I'll say hello to Miranda for you."

She was crying now. "Terry, pleas—"

He hung up the phone and looked up into the dark sky . . . and nothing. He looked over at Huntington. "How come we're still breathing?"

"No idea, boss," he replied, getting to his feet and walking down below. Nolan followed.

Leslie was sitting back against one of the galley cabinets holding a small pair of wire cutters. Her two techs were smiling ear to ear and shaking hands. Nolan walked over to the bomb . . . The timer said three seconds.

He laughed. "Bloody hell, Leslie, cutting it a little close, weren't you?"

Leslie looked up at him. "No shit, Terry, I think I need to get out of this business. I could do with a beer."

Huntington walked over to the fridge and opened the door. Inside there were five bottles of Smithwick's Irish red ale. He realized that the Irish were becoming as Americanized as the Brits. Beer in the refrigerator? To heck with it. "This will do nicely," he said passing Leslie a bottle.

She twisted off the top and took a long drink. "Thanks, Captain, that really hit the spot."

Terry got on the radio. "It's all clear, Leslie disarmed it." He heard laughing in reply and a number of people yelling. He opened one of the bottles. "Cheers. Here's to not getting blown up today." He promptly drained half the bottle and let out a burp. The others on the boat let out a burst of nervous laughter.

"Is it safe?" Huntington asked Leslie.

"For now. All I did was disconnect the timer. We still need all the cell phone towers shut down while I dismantle the rest of it, but as long as I don't do anything stupid, we should be fine."

"Best you keep evacuating the local residents, sir. At least for tonight," said one of the techs.

"Okay," replied Huntington. "I'll let the locals know. We'll put it down to a gas main leak or something. Anything else?"

"Yeah. Whoever designed this bloody thing really does know their stuff. I had to get past two traps just to stop the timer," said Leslie. "I was lucky, Nolan. Anyone else trying to disarm this thing, I don't think they would have made it."

"Got it," replied Nolan. "Just remember that we have another one out there somewhere." He finished his beer. "Come on, Captain, I think there are a few people in London waiting to talk to us."

67

GREATER MANCHESTER POLICE HEADQUARTERS, MANCHESTER, 7:30 A.M. GMT

They were back in the briefing room. All the officers who had taken part in the operation were there, including some of the top brass. A full British fry-up breakfast had been laid on by the canteen, complemented by urns of tea and coffee. Terry had arranged for a local off-license to open early and had supplied everyone with enough beer and liquor to sink a battleship. It was all going on MI5's account, and K had been happy to approve it.

K had been ecstatic when Terry had called him on a secure line from the communications van. His response when Terry had informed him about their close call had been direct and, in the circumstances, quite fitting. "You lucky bastard."

Terry had even had the chance to talk to Amanda; he had cleared out the van for that. She had agreed to lunch with him when this current assignment was complete, and they had even discussed his retirement from MI5.

"You've done enough," she said.

"I can't disagree with that," he replied. "After this is over, there's one more thing I need to take care of, and then I'm done."

She sighed. "Terry, isn't there always going to be one more thing?"

"No," he replied. "Anyway, this one is personal."

"What is it? What can be that important?"

"I'll tell you when we meet, okay? It involves what happened to your father. Well, partly."

"Fine, we'll discuss it later. You take care of yourself."

"I will," he replied. Then she was gone.

Leslie and her two techs walked into the room and a huge cheer went up. She looked drained but happy and was immediately surrounded by a number of officers who wanted to shake her hand and pat her on the back. Finally, she was able to break herself free from the crowd and get some breakfast as well as a flowerpot-sized mug of coffee. She joined Terry and Huntington at a table.

"That's that, then," she said. "All safe."

"What's next?" asked Huntington.

"Well, we have a shitload of nuclear waste to dispose of, but that doesn't involve me. As for the C-4, that will go to a range and be detonated. Meanwhile, I have to detail the steps I took to disarm the bomb just in case anything happens to me and someone else has to take care of the next one."

"You did a hell of a thing today, Leslie. I hope you know that," said Terry. He held up his coffee and clinked mugs with her.

"Thanks, Terry," she replied. "What's next with you?"

"Back to London with these guys," he replied, slapping Huntington on the back. "We still have one more of these things to find. If K is right, we haven't much time to do it."

"Jesus, good luck with that. Just out of curiosity, how did they find this one?"

"We had some equipment flown in from the States that detects gamma rays and neutrons. Then we put the detectors into helicopters. Apparently, the Yanks kindly sent us six of them, which allowed us to cover a much wider area. Luckily, the Manchester bomb wasn't shielded well, and once we started to focus on waterways, that made life a little easier."

"Thank Christ for the Yanks," said Huntington, raising a cup of tea.

"Can't disagree with that," replied Leslie as her and Nolan raised their drinks.

"I meant to ask," said Huntington. "Do you have kids?"

"Why? Are you asking me out, young man?" replied the bomb disposal expert cheekily.

Huntington blushed. "No, not at all. Not that I wouldn't be honored or anything . . ." His voice trailed off as he tried to think of what to say next.

"Be careful, mate," said Terry. "You're digging that hole deeper."

Leslie smiled broadly. "Just kidding, Captain. Actually, I have three. Two boys and a girl. They are currently tucked up in bed safely at home in East Sussex with their dad. Here, I'll show you some photos." As she reached into her pocket, Terry's satellite phone rang. It was K. Terry got up from the table and found himself a quiet corner of the room.

"What's up, sir?" he said, waving at a group of officers as they raised some beers in his direction.

"You need to get back here right away and bring Huntington and his team with you. And Leslie and her people."

The smile left his face. "Why, what's happened?"

"It's the girls, Nolan. They're gone."

Terry was already striding toward Leslie and Huntington. The SAS officer looked up at the MI5 agent and frowned. Nolan tapped himself repeatedly on his head with the flat of his hand, the universal signal in the military for "on me." This meant "stop what you are doing immediately and come to where I am." Huntington jumped to his feet and ran over to Nolan.

"What's up?" he asked.

K was speaking but Terry interrupted him. "One second, sir. Captain, get your guys together with Leslie and her people. We have to get back to London right now. Now, sir, you were saying?"

"As our security team was bringing them to Thames House in the armored Jags about ten minutes ago, they were ambushed on a side street. The lead vehicle was taken out with an RPG, and the terrorists shot the two security officers that were in the car with the ladies. The Jags can take small arms fire, but they're no match for a rocket propelled grenade."

"Jesus Christ!"

"The only reason we got a heads-up so quickly was one of the men in the vehicle with the women managed to get off a brief radio message before he was killed."

"Fuck! Any demands or anything yet?"

"Sorry, no."

"Please tell me you had that tracker implanted in Kristen's arm?"

"Sorry, son. That's what they were heading over here to get done. Kristen had wanted to talk it over with Shae first."

"Damn, damn, damn."

"Cars are waiting outside," interrupted Huntington. "Ready to go when you are, boss."

Terry started running for the main doors to the building.

"How soon can you get back here?" asked K.

"That all depends on how fast that bloody jet can fly."

68

MI5 HEADQUARTERS, THAMES HOUSE, LONDON, 9:15 A.M. GMT

The Global 5000 made the trip in under fifty minutes and landed at London City Airport. A small fleet of Land Rovers were already waiting for them and whisked the group to Thames House in record time, as K had arranged for a police escort to clear their way through the morning rush-hour traffic. Upon arrival, they were whisked into the underground garage away from prying eyes and led straight to a conference room next to K's office.

"Any news?" asked Terry. "How in the hell did this happen?"

"Nothing so far," replied K. "It's as if they had insider information."

"You mean the fucking mole. I swear to God, I am going to take a great deal of pleasure killing that bastard. So what are we doing to try and find them, sir?"

"We have all the helicopter assets up that we can muster and every police officer in the Greater London area is out looking for them. The helicopters containing the American radiation detection units are en route. The people at the Met found the Jaguars on CCTV and have been reviewing footage as quickly as possible, so maybe we'll get something from that."

"I wouldn't hold my breath, sir. These guys aren't stupid—they would have switched vehicles as quickly as possible and then most certainly changed them again. I think the best thing to do is keep looking for the bomb. The thing that I don't understand is why they would make a play for them in broad daylight? The risk must have been incredible. There's more to this than meets the eye, I just can't figure out what."

"I don't know, and I completely agree it's pretty irrational." K turned to Huntington. "I'm sure you and your men are wiped out, but are you up for another job? I have a feeling you may be needed before the day is out."

"Absolutely, sir. We wouldn't have it any other way." He walked outside the conference room and ordered his men to gear up. They scattered for their equipment.

"Good man, that," said K. "Maybe he'd be interested in joining our mob."

"I wouldn't bet on it, sir, but I wouldn't be surprised if he became prime minister one day."

K raised an eyebrow. "Well, perhaps he could be an improvement."

That brought a snigger from the other MI5 personnel in the room which was immediately silenced with a stern look from the head of MI5. Just then, C walked in the room.

"I heard what happened. Anything I can do?"

"We're good for now, old man," said K. Both men had served in the Guards Division and were firm friends but still jealously guarded their fiefdoms, but given the current situation, all competitiveness between them had been pushed aside.. "I think it would be helpful if you could put as many people on the street as possible. Also, if you wouldn't mind getting back on with GCHQ and make sure they are doing what we talked about yesterday. If you have to get the prime minister to make the call, then do it."

"That is going to get a lot of people's knickers in a twist, old chap," replied C.

"If we don't do it, I'm sure they're going to be even more upset."

"Good point. You think today is the day?"

"Either today or tomorrow. I think the terrorists know we're closing in on them. I wouldn't be surprised if they grabbed the girls partly in retaliation for taking out their Manchester operation. Maybe as a way to force us to expend resources. I'm beginning to think Nolan was right. We need to forget about the two women and focus on the bomb."

"So, the royals?" asked C.

"It's time for them to go," interjected Terry. "And the government. Get the lot of them either into shelters, or better yet, completely out of the city. The same goes for you lot. It's time to start thinking about getting out of here."

K nodded. "The lad has a point, at least as far as the government and the royal family are concerned. As for me, I'm way too old to be hiding in dusty old shelters. If you don't mind, Terry, I'll just stay exactly where I am."

"But sir—"

"No buts. What sort of message would that send if I ran away like a damn coward? Sorry, but I'm staying."

"Well put," said C. "If you don't mind, I'll hang around as well." He looked at Terry and shrugged. "He has a better single malt collection than I do."

Terry was about to say something when Huntington returned with his team. They were all wearing black balaclavas and were armed to the teeth. Huntington was carrying a fifty-caliber AW50 festooned with an electronics package and a sight Nolan had never seen before.

"What the hell is that?" he asked.

"This," replied Huntington, "is an AW50 fitted with a new sight we've been developing. You know how in movies you see them using a thermal sight to look inside buildings?"

"Yeah, and it's complete crap," replied Nolan.

"Well, my friend," Huntington said with a smile, "this turns the make-believe into reality. It combines thermal with an ultrasound pulse technology to generate a picture of the inside of a building. I tried to get the prototype before the Manchester op, but they were working out a couple of kinks. Anyway, when I found out about the girls, I had them rush it over from BAE Systems. They managed to iron out nearly everything, but it still takes about three minutes to build up a solid image on the sight."

"Three minutes? I'll take it," said Terry.

"My feelings exactly, boss."

Terry's satellite phone rang. The number was blocked. He looked at K and shrugged his shoulders as to who it could be. He answered and was greeted by a robotic female voice, obviously someone using a voice manipulation device.

"How's your day going, Nolan? Sweating it over the ladies, I should imagine, yeah?"

"Who is this?" he asked. He snapped his fingers for a pen and paper. One of each was slid across the conference table in his direction. I THINK IT'S HER, he scribbled.

"Oh, come on, Nolan, you can't be that stupid."

"Just thought I'd check," he replied. "What's your name? What should I call you?"

"How about we save the introductions for later, yeah? Now, are you up for a little exercise, Nolan?"

GET THAT TRACKING DEVICE, NOW, he scrawled. One of K's assistants ran from the room.

"It depends how much, I'm a little out of shape."

The woman laughed. "That's not what I've heard. Shame about the ribs."

"Comes with the territory," he replied coldly. "Why take the girls? They can't mean anything to you."

"All in good time, Nolan. Now, are you ready to go for a little jog?"

"To be honest, I don't see the point. Seems to me you're going to set this damn dirty bomb off whether I show up or not."

The woman really started laughing now. "Oh, Nolan. How wrong you are. I've saved the best for last. This one isn't a dirty bomb. It's a nuke. An honest-to-goodness nuke."

Nolan was writing frantically now. In large letters he wrote, NOT DIRTY BOMB, FUCKING NUKE!!!

"Shit," said C, and he ran out the door looking for a secure landline.

"I tell you what, Nolan. If you don't follow my instructions, I'll blow the thing right now. If you do, I'll give your masters forty-eight hours to get as many people out of the city as they can. Your choice, Nolan. What will it be?"

"I need a minute to think about this. What about Kristen and Shae, do you promise to let them go if I do what you ask?"

The assistant returned with the tracking device and was about to shove the needle into his upper arm to inject it under the skin when Nolan stopped him. He lifted up his shirt and ripped off the dressing covering the bullet wound over his ribs and pointed to the stitches.

"I give you my word that no harm will come to them if you follow my instructions. You deviate from them in any way—they are both dead. Now what are you going to do? Ten seconds, Nolan." The voice started to count down from ten.

The man hesitated and grabbed the pen. THIS WILL HURT, he wrote. Nolan looked at him angrily and pointed at the wound again. Then he thought about it and wrote PASSIVE? The assistant wrote back, NO, WE TURN ON AND OFF REMOTELY. Nolan nodded and gritted his teeth as the assistant slowly pushed the needle between the stitches.

"I guess I'm going for a jog," he replied. He looked at Huntington and wrote CHOPPER NOW on the pad. NOT HERE, BUILDING WATCHED.

Huntington nodded and pulled K to one side.

"Good decision, Nolan. The first thing you are going to do before you leave that building is ditch that phone, understand? If one of my people see you using it, then all bets are off."

"Okay, I can do that." He wrote: GET ME REALLY SMALL EARPIECE.

"Good. Now you have ten minutes to get to Cannon Street Station. There is a newspaper kiosk there. Look under the stack of the *Financial Times*, you'll find a burner phone. Answer it when it rings. Got that, Nolan?"

Another assistant appeared with a small earpiece and handed it to him. He shoved it in his ear as far as possible.

"Yes," he answered. "Cannon Street Station. Newspaper kiosk. *FT* stack. Burner phone. Got it. But what happens if I don't make it?"

"I think you already know the answer to that." She hung up.

Nolan checked his Walther and made sure there was a round in the chamber. He turned to K. "I need a really small .22 handgun. Have someone meet me downstairs with it. I have ten minutes to get to Cannon Street Station." He started running for the stairs.

"What do we do in the meantime?" yelled K after him as he left.

"Pray that I'm not out of shape!"

69

GUILDFORD, THIRTY-THREE MILES SOUTHWEST OF LONDON, 11:09 A.M. GMT

Nolan had been glad to take a break from running after he picked up the burner phone. The female terrorist had immediately called and directed him to board the train at Wimbledon on the Guildford train line heading southwest out of London. He was instructed to get on the third carriage from the front, in the third seat from the front on the left-hand side. She warned him not to talk to anyone. If he did, she would know. He had been sitting, minding his own business thinking how this was like some plot from an eighties action movie, when he heard a phone ringing under his seat. He retrieved it and answered.

"Enjoying your little rest, Nolan?" Again, the robotic sounding female voice.

"Yes, thank you," he replied.

"That's good, I'm glad. Unfortunately, you are going to have to do a little more running. When the train stops at London Road Station in Guildford, you are to get off the train, run down to York Road, take a right and then run down to Denmark Road. Take a left. A car will pick you up there. You have five minutes, Nolan, so don't be late." The line went dead.

He looked around the carriage but couldn't see anyone on a cell phone, and no one seemed to be keeping watch on him. He had to admit that An Dailtín sure as hell had a network of people working for her. It could also be some unsuspecting private detective who had been told she was his wife and that she wanted to make sure he wasn't cheating on her. Either way, he had to play it straight. He saw the sign for the London Road station and got up, heading for the door.

"You get that?" he whispered.

"Got it," answered Huntington. The helicopter containing the SAS team was flying about a thousand feet overhead and about a third of a mile to one side. Any further and they would have been out of range of his communication device and the tracking device in his side. It was a risky move, but they had little choice in the matter.

"Shut down the tracker and the earpiece before I get in the car, then turn them back on after five minutes," he whispered.

"Roger that," came the reply.

The train came to a slow grinding stop, and he was out of the door and running. Luckily it wasn't rush hour, as he would have hated to try and negotiate his way through the mass of commuters that normally would have been gathered on the platform. He hit the main door to the station at a run and nearly went flying over a baby stroller.

"Sorry!" he called out over his shoulder as he regained his footing and continued his sprint down the street. He didn't quite make out her reply, but he was sure it wasn't complimentary.

Nolan was a little pleased with himself, after the full sprint down York Road to Denmark Road, that he wasn't more out of breath. He stopped and looked down the street for his ride. A blue Ford Focus pulled out of a parking spot and drove toward him. In the driver's side and passenger seat sat two angry looking men. *Yep, this is definitely for me.* He smiled and gave them a little wave; they didn't seem to appreciate the gesture. They pulled up next to him and the back passenger-side door swung open.

"Get in," said one of the men through his open window. "And no funny stuff, Nolan."

He climbed into the cramped back seat and smiled. "Top of the morning to you," he said in his best Dublin accent.

"Shut the fuck up," replied the driver. "Paddy, pat the fucker down and scan the bastard."

Nolan held up his arms as the passenger turned around so he was kneeling on the seat. First, he pulled a scanning device from his pocket and swept it all over Nolan's body.

"He's clean," he said to the driver.

Nolan went to lower his arms; Paddy frowned and motioned for him to raise them again. He started to frisk him and stopped when he felt the Walther under his coat. He reached in and removed the weapon.

"Oops, how on earth did that get there?" said Nolan with a smile. Without a word, the terrorist punched him hard in the mouth. Nolan felt his lip immediately begin to swell as he tasted blood.

"Now then, Paddy, what sort of a welcome is that on this fine morning?" he said as he dabbed at his bloody lip with his sleeve.

Paddy drew back to punch him again, but the driver yelled at him. "Enough! You know what she said. As it is she won't be pleased you hit him."

"Fuck her," replied Paddy. "This fucker killed my cousin."

"If you want to keep breathing, you'll keep your comments about her to yourself and do what she says," warned the driver.

Paddy crossed his arms and sat staring out of the window. Nolan wanted to push him a little more but thought it wise to keep his mouth shut until they arrived at their destination. Fifteen minutes of backtracking later, obviously to make sure they weren't being followed, and the car pulled into an industrial estate on the west side of the city. Near the back of the cluster of ugly, stucco-clad, gray buildings, they stopped in front of a pile of broken and disused pallets at the entrance to what looked like an abandoned warehouse, complete with newspaper stuck over the windows to keep out prying eyes.

The driver looked over his shoulder. "Get out, Nolan, and don't try anything heroic."

"Wouldn't dream of it," he replied with a smile.

The two men followed him to the main door and Paddy stopped by the entrance.

"If you don't mind, I'll give you a nice tip for the ride when you drop me back off at the station," said the MI5 agent, a big grin spread over his face.

"Fuck you."

The driver shoved him through the door and into the warehouse. There was a large metal desk with two men holding MAC 10s on either side of it. Sitting behind it was a woman with her back to him. He walked slowly across the concrete floor, his running shoes making little noise as he approached the desk. The driver made Nolan stop about ten feet in front of it, then he went around to the back and whispered something in the woman's ear before putting the Walther on the desk.

"Go and wait outside, all of you. I'll let you know if I need you," she told the men and then sat silently until she heard the door shut behind him.

"Good morning, Terry," she said starting to turn around. "Nice of you to join us."

"Good morning, Ciaran," he replied even before he had a chance to see her face. "Long time, no see."

70

WAREHOUSE, WEST OF GUILDFORD, 11:30 A.M. GMT

He gasped noticeably at how the years had changed her. Gone was the welcoming smile, replaced by a thin line of bitterness. Her light olive skin, once so warm to the touch, was now taut and pale. She wore the hate in her for all to see. The only thing about her that seemed to remain from her youth were the dark deep pools of her brown eyes. He looked in them now and felt a sadness for what she had become.

"You look well," she said. "I'd say you haven't changed a bit, but I'd be lying."

He wanted to tell her to go to hell, but he had to give Huntington and his team time to get into position.

"I could say the same about you," he replied.

She laughed at that, but it was hollow and soulless. "You always were a good bullshitter, Terry. Look at me—I fell for it hook, line, and sinker."

Nolan shrugged his shoulders. What else could he do? It wasn't like she was lying.

"I have to ask—when did you figure out it was me?"

"Honestly, not until the car ride over here. It's been bugging me this whole time who could have that much hate for me from my past and who would need to hide their real voice over the phone. I kept thinking it might be the widow of someone we removed—"

"Murdered, Terry. You mean murdered."

"How about we split the difference and say killed, for the sake of argument? Anyway, the driver finally sealed the deal when he told dear old Paddy to stop hitting me because you'd be mad. Then it came to me. What was it Sherlock Holmes said? 'When you have eliminated all which is impossible, then whatever remains, however improbable, must be the truth.' All that was left was you."

Ciaran started to clap. "Good for you, Terry, and you remembered the quote perfectly."

He bowed slightly. "All down to a good Catholic education. So, what happened to you, Ciaran, or do you go by An Dailtín these days?"

"You have to admit, 'The Terror' does have a nice ring to it, but you, Terry? You can call me Ciaran."

"So, what gives, Ciaran? You were never part of this shit. It was all your father and his thugs."

"They murdered him, your SAS buddies. Near the border, they shot the car he was driving to shit. Apparently, they never even gave him the opportunity to surrender, they just murdered him."

"Oh, come on, Ciaran. He was a terrorist and would have gladly done the same to them given half a chance."

"He was outnumbered, and they killed him without a second thought. They acted as judge, jury, and executioners."

"So, you decided to step right into his shoes?"

"Something like that, but I'll tell you more in a minute. What about you, Terry, why did you just leave?"

He saw a tear well up in her eye and she angrily wiped it away.

"You know why, or at least you must have guessed." He raised his voice slightly in anger. "My job was to get that scumbag, Martin, and get the hell out."

"But what about me? What about us?"

"What do you mean?"

"I was in love with you, I would have come with you no questions asked. You know I would have."

Nolan sighed. "It actually crossed my mind. I was going to hang around after we eliminated him, against orders, I might add, and make an excuse to come back to Manchester and bring you with me. You most probably don't believe me, but I was seriously considering it. Then, the night of the shooting, everything changed."

"You mean when you were wounded?"

"No. Before that, when you came out of the bar and saw Martin and his two cronies dead."

She looked at him quizzically.

"You cried, Ciaran. You actually cried over their deaths."

"But they had just been murdered, Terry. What would you expect me to do?"

"Bullshit, Ciaran." He was trying to hide his anger, but it started to show its ugly head. "That fucker had blown up a bunch of children, for fuck's sake. You knew it, everyone knew it, and the lot of you treated him like a goddamn hero."

"I didn't know," she said sadly.

"Like hell you didn't. There was no way you couldn't have known."

"Honestly, Terry, I didn't." There was a sadness in her voice for what might have been. "My father kept all that away from me."

"Yet here you are willing to cut down thousands, possibly millions, of men, women, and children and for what, some crazy notion of revenge or an idea that Northern Ireland will be free from the United Kingdom. Jesus, talk about madness. You have become so twisted by hate and revenge you can't even comprehend how insane this is."

His earpiece crackled to life. "Four down at the front of the building. Keep her talking, Nolan."

I guess Paddy isn't going to get that tip.

"Well, you may have been a late bloomer to your cause, but you sure as hell made up for it. Where are Shae and Kristen? You said they were here, unharmed."

The coldness was back in her face as she smiled. "That's right, we mustn't forget about the ladies. Come out, come out, wherever you are," she shouted.

71

WAREHOUSE, WEST OF GUILDFORD, 11:40 A.M. GMT

A door swung open at the back of the warehouse, obviously leading to the offices. Kristen was roughly pushed out into the bright light, her wrists bound with zip ties, her mouth duct-taped shut. There was panic in her tear-stained eyes, and Terry was afraid she might start running. He made an up and down sign with his hand for her to take it easy and she nodded. Slowly she started walking toward him.

"Where's Sha—" He was stopped short as she walked out of the same office, smiling and carrying a gun, which was trained on Kristen. He looked back at Ciaran and saw the vengeful joy in her face. He was about to ask what was going on, but he didn't have to because he already knew the answer.

"Hello, Dad," said Shae. She started to laugh at the look of shock on his face.

He looked at Ciaran. He wanted to scream, to ask what the hell was going on, but all he managed was, "*Dad?*"

Ciaran started laughing now, great gales of insane laughter that reverberated around the walls of the empty building. Then she stopped as quickly as she had started. "Yes, 'Dad,' Terry. Say hello to your daughter."

"But how?" he stammered.

"How the hell do you think? Didn't anyone ever teach you about the birds and the bees, Terry?"

He rubbed the stubble on his chin. "Why didn't you tell me?" he asked. "I would have done something, anything."

"And just how was I going to do that?" she asked. "I found out the day we went out that night, and I was going to tell you later in the evening, but then you disappeared. They said you had been wounded by fucking Protestants and then they said you had died. I even went to your fucking funeral!"

"I had no idea," he whispered.

"Can you imagine the shame? I was pregnant by a fucking Brit in Belfast," she hissed. "And I wasn't married. After my father stopped kicking the shit out of me, he sent me to America, supposedly for my education. They made me give her up to a good family who were supporters of the struggle. They had just lost a baby girl and raised her as their own. She even had to take the name of the girl they lost, Shae Cochran, which is how she got past your security checks."

"But there must have been a death certificate?"

"Sure, but when you have enough money, things can be made to disappear. They moved shortly after I handed her over so as not to raise suspicions."

"What about their family, someone who would figure it out?"

"Sorry, no. They were older and both had no immediate family members left alive. Thing is, I still got to see her, and she knew I was her real mother, so I taught her all about the struggles." For some reason, this brought a smile to Ciaran's face.

He wanted to leap over the table and smack the shit out of her, but he closed his eyes and took a deep breath. "So, being the loving mother that you undoubtedly are"—he could barely contain the sarcasm—"You brainwashed her into becoming a terrorist. You must be proud."

"It was shortly after I returned from America when my father told me you had been responsible for the ambush outside the bar. At first, I didn't believe him, but he showed me proof. He had a picture of your

MI5 identification card, and clear as day, I knew he was telling the truth. That's when I started working for the IRA."

"Jesus," he muttered. *There really is a fucking mole, and she just gave me the proof.*

"Want to know how we found out you were still alive?" Shae was smirking as she asked the question.

His earpiece came to life again. "Three minutes," said Huntington.

"Let me guess . . . when I first met you in the restaurant."

Shae giggled. "Ding, ding, ding, you win a prize. I couldn't believe it. Mum had showed me your photo over the years. Not the ID but a photo she had of you taken in some bar. She never even told me you were a fucking spy. But then, when I saw you in the restaurant and that MI5 bitch friend of yours introduced me, I knew."

"But you were engaged to her."

"I know, and it was great listening to her go on and on about her job and why she couldn't say anything about us. It was even better when she told me about them tracking that arms shipment and how she would have to go away for a while."

"It was you. You set her up?"

Shae laughed again. "Totally! And you know what the best part was?"

He silently shook his head.

"The best part was when you came and told me that bullshit about her death and the fact that you felt so bad for me that you kept in touch. It was fucking priceless."

Nolan shook his head and looked down at the floor. "I don't know who's more crazy, you or your fucking mother."

"What an awful thing to say about your little girl," said Ciaran.

"Anyway," continued Shae, "Mom heard MI5 was sniffing around her company."

"NY&E is yours?" he asked.

Ciaran smiled. "And all funded by donations that had been meant for the IRA and my dad siphoned off."

"So, I started working for her, and guess who came along like a little puppy dog?" continued Shae.

"Me," he answered. He felt sick to his stomach; she had been playing him the whole time.

"Yes," giggled Shae.

"So why did you try and grab Kristen at your flat? She had nothing to do with any of this."

"Because we couldn't be sure if she was working for you, and we had just shipped the packages, so we figured it was time to find out what you knew."

"What about the information on the thumb drive? If you hadn't left that for me to find, we would have had nothing to go on."

"Shae sent the text just in case anything went wrong with our people grabbing you on your boat," replied Ciaran. "We needed a way to get you in a position to catch you. The information we left was enough to keep you involved as you always have. To save the day, right, Terry? Those idiot security guards at NY&E were supposed to do the job but failed miserably and then we got word you and the bitch were heading for my brother's house. Unfortunately, that failed as well."

"There has to be more to it than that?" said Nolan.

"I also wanted you here with me when I destroyed your capital city. Just to see the look on your face knowing that you failed is going to be priceless."

"Jesus," he whispered. "But when we found Shae, she was wearing an explosive vest. That was a crazy risk to take, wasn't it?"

"Oh, that. That was a mistake that should never have happened."

"A mistake?" he asked.

"I didn't know O'Keith had told Stratton to do that. You see, he had no idea who Shae really was."

A voice in his earpiece said, "One minute."

"So where is O'Keith now?" he asked, already knowing the answer.

"I should imagine by now his body has been swept out to sea down your lovely River Thames," replied Ciaran with a smile.

He looked at Kristen. "Why don't you just let her go? You know she hasn't got anything to do with this."

Shae kicked Kristen in the back of the knee, and she fell forward onto the concrete floor. Kristen tried to lift herself up, but his daughter planted her foot directly in the small of her back, holding her down.

"Let her go? Let her go!" screamed Ciaran. "She killed my baby brother!"

"What are you talking about? The only person she killed was Lander . . ." Then he realized why the man had seemed a little familiar. He'd met the mouthy sixteen-year-old only once, by chance, when he had been out with his big sister. He had wanted some money and she'd warned Nolan not to say a word, as the kid would have told her father about the Brit seeing his sister.

"One more thing, Nolan," said Ciaran. Reaching into her pocket, she pulled out a phone. "I lied about not setting off my little present, and after I do that, I'm going to shoot this bitch. Then, after you've watched her die, nice and slowly, I'm going to have Shae blow your fucking head off."

"Twenty seconds," whispered Huntington.

Ciaran pressed the send button on the phone. Nothing happened. She looked at the face and saw that it said the call had failed. She screamed, "But it's a satellite phone. Nothing can block a satellite phone!" She tried again. Still nothing.

Nolan laughed, partly with relief that his plan had worked and partly because of the look of confusion on Ciaran's face. "You surely can't be that stupid. You don't think GCHQ can't shut down every cell tower and communications satellite with the flick of a switch?"

She screamed again and picked up his Walther. He started to move as she aimed it at him and pulled the trigger. Nothing happened. She tried pulling back the slide, but it was locked tight.

It wasn't the first time the chip planted in his hand, that allowed only him to fire his weapon, had saved his life. He was running toward Kristen, frantically digging the small .22 from his waistband behind his belt buckle.

"Shoot hi—" Ciaran never got to finish the sentence as an enormous fifty-caliber round tore through the side of the building and ripped through her insides.

Shae looked confused. She watched the blood spray from her mother as she fell to the floor. "You fucking bastard!" she screamed as she raised the gun to shoot him, but Nolan was faster and shot her twice in the chest. She looked at him for a second, confused as to how her own father could have shot her, not seeing the irony that she was about to shoot her father with the intent to kill him. Shae fell to the floor, blood splattering out of her mouth every time she took a breath.

Terry knelt down next to Kristen and gingerly pulled the tape from her mouth. She was sobbing hysterically, and he held her close. "It's okay," he whispered in her ear. "It's going to be okay." He looked over at Shae and saw the hate in her eyes as she was struggling to breathe. He got up and walked over to the body of Ciaran and retrieved his Walther. Turning back, he walked over and stood over Shae. Slowly he raised the gun.

"You can't, Terry. She's your daughter."

Terry looked at Kristen, and what she saw scared her. There was nothing. His eyes were empty. It was like seeing death himself. Then he looked down at Shae.

Kristen jumped slightly as he pulled the trigger once, shooting Shae through the heart.

"Orders. Anyway, I only ever had one daughter, and she died eighteen years ago." It was then that Kristen saw the pain for what might have been on his face. The terrible sadness showed in his eyes for a brief moment and then was gone. Swallowed back down to the place where men like him hid their grief.

The SAS men burst through the door and ran over to check the bodies. While four of them continued through the door to the offices to clear the rest of the building, one of them helped Kristen to her feet and cut the zip ties.

Huntington walked over to the MI5 agent. "All good?" he asked.

Nolan sighed. "All good. Nice shot, by the way."

"Thanks, boss." They walked over to check on Kristen. "Any idea where the bomb is, by the way?"

"Back in central London somewhere, no doubt," replied Nolan.

Terry returned the Walther to the holster under his arm and reached behind his neck, releasing the chain that had hung there for so many years. He had an odd feeling, as if a weight had finally been lifted from his shoulders. The guilt and grief that had plagued him for so many years over his daughter's death seemed finally to have been washed away. He couldn't explain why, but it had, and he felt it was okay to live, really live, again. He looked up, gave the Saint Christopher medal a final kiss and whispered. "I'll always love and miss you, my little girl."

Kneeling in front of Kristen he stroked away an errant hair that clung to her cheek. Gently opening her hand, he placed the Saint Christopher medal in it before closing her fingers over his most precious possession. He leaned forward and kissed her on the cheek.

"Miranda would have wanted you to have this," he whispered in her ear.

She looked at him with tear-stained eyes. "Terry, I can't, it's all . . ."

His eyes welled up as he smiled at his friend and delicately touched her bruised lips with his finger. "It's okay."

Rising to his feet, he started to walk out of the building. He lit a cigarette, stopped, looked at it in disgust, and flicked it away across the warehouse. He continued heading toward the door.

"Where are you going?" said Kristen. "You can't just leave, for God's sake. You just saved the country."

Nolan stopped again, looked over his shoulder and smiled. "I have a lunch date I don't want to miss."

ACKNOWLEDGMENTS

I would like to thank my parents, who both sadly passed when I was a teenager. When I was a child, they were great believers in the written word, so I was encouraged to read from an early age. For my tenth birthday, they bought me *The Complete Works of Sherlock Holmes* by Sir Arthur Conan Doyle, and my love of crime fiction and crime thrillers was born. From that point on, I read everything I could find at the library, especially Agatha Christie.

A few years later I watched John le Carré's *Tinker Tailor Soldier Spy* and *Smiley's People* starring Alec Guinness on the BBC and was so enthralled by his portrayal of the spymaster Smiley that I saved up my pocket money to buy the books. I was hooked on the spy/thriller genre. I would go to the library on a Saturday and bring home books by such authors as Graham Greene, Alistair MacLean, Gerald Seymour, Frederick Forsyth, and James Grady as well as many more. In short, I would like to thank all those thriller writers for how they influenced a young, working class, English teenager into one day pursuing a writing career.

Thank you to all those who have been willing to act as beta readers for this manuscript, especially fellow chef and writer Will Pieratt who, over many a glass of bourbon, has offered advice and encouragement.

Many thanks to Doctors Meek and Barko for their input regarding any medical questions and all those with the local medical examiner's office who were gracious with their time and extremely helpful.

To the exceptional people at Blackstone for all their assistance in bringing *The Vicar* to fruition. Especially Josh Stanton, Josie Woodbridge, Levi Coren, Ananda Finwall, Alex Cruz, and Celia Johnson.

Lastly, to all the men and women of the British Army with whom I served. It was an honor and a privilege.